REALM
OF
WRAITHS

REALM OF WRAITHS
© 2020 by Taylor Balasavage

www.aurelialeo.com

Balasavage, Taylor.
REALM OF WRAITHS / by Taylor Balasavage 1st. ed.

ISBN-13: 978-1-946024-94-7 (ebook)
ISBN-13: 978-1-946024-96-1 (paperback)
ISBN-13: 978-1-946024-95-4 (hardcover)
Library of Congress Control Number: 2020931988

Editing by Leah T. Brown
Cover design by www.bukovero.com
Book design by Samuel Marzioli | marzioli.blogspot.com

Printed in the United States of America
First Edition:
10 9 8 7 6 5 4 3 2 1

CHAPTER ONE

The world was quiet and still, only the faint sounds of squirrels leaping from branch to branch overhead could be heard. The river kept moving onward, rushes of water lapping against each other in tiny folds as the current hurried toward the east. The river was wide enough that one might be able to swing across it if they dared; otherwise, most people, myself included, knew that the middle of the river would be too deep and the current too strong. The water was glistening underneath the warm sunlight that broke through the thick canopies of trees that nestled against each other where those squirrels scrambled playfully. Enya was a quiet continent—there would never be the bustling sounds of cities by the thousands as there were in Pushka, or the harsh break of raging sea against the cold coast like in Creo.

Yes, Enya was quiet. My brothers and I had raged through the thick woods like beasts kicking up dirt, grass, leaves, snow, anything that Enya would provide to us. We frightened the black squirrels often and kept the horned coyotes away from our home. Our home: built from wood and stone by the hands of our father and mother, isolated deep in the forest where we sustained ourselves and only made trips into the villages when it was necessary.

Now, a plume of smoke rose in the distance from the house behind me while I danced in-between the long, thick blades of grass that separated our fields from the wild backyard. Some of the grass had been pressed down, a makeshift path that signaled my brothers had been to the river and back. A small quirk of satisfaction fell on my lips when I thought about Emeric and Vale. I pictured their brown-haired heads bobbing as they tried to beat each other to the water, diving in to escape the sweat and heat that they accumulated while they helped my father tend to the hens.

As I stepped closer to the water and then plopped my feet into the cool current, I let out a sigh of relief. My ankles and wrists were sore from tugging on weeds and freshening up the garden; dirt was caked into the creases of my palms. It didn't take long for me to wash it away and freshen my face, hiking the breathable slip gown that I wore to my waist in order to clean the length of my legs while I shuffled deeper into the river. As soon as the dirt and mud was scrubbed from me, I took a fistful of my dress and the sudden urge to leap closer to the embankment took control of me.

I could only inhale sharply as my feet landed on rock and then, with the force of my weight, slipped completely. The rock's hardness was replaced by a thick grime from the water and I toppled over, too late to break my fall before my head smacked against the surface of the river and then against one of the ragged, pointed rocks sticking out from beneath the current. Pain shot through the back of my skull and leaked downward into my neck, gripping me tightly. My world went dark.

Death is not like sleeping.

The words were like a whisper inside of my mind when I lifted my cheek, eager to pull myself back up. Warm, fast-paced water filled my nose and my throat. Even as I lifted my gaze and found the world very much the same, blinking quickly, I knew something was changed.

I was a body sprawled near to the riverbank, caressed by the warm sunlight and the rustle of branches in the canopies. I tripped and caught myself many times as a child, but this time...this time was different. The sensation that pulled me down felt as though it was going to be more permanent, like hands of destiny pulling me until I was broken flat against the rocks. And it had been quick. So quick that I felt as though I blinked in one world and was now waking in the next.

My eyes traveled to the riverbank where the long grass swayed gently, catching the small breeze that carried over the water. I was about to pull myself up out of the water and into that grass when I froze, a black mass demanding my attention. I could sense its attention turned toward me like a small touch down my spine. It—whatever *it* was—was perched between the reeds like a predator watching its prey. My breathing hitched and I stood, every inch of me feeling like it was coated in thick black oil. *Run! Get away!* My feet scrambled along the slippery rocks, each of them coated in slime that made it hard to find any traction.

The creature watching me was a black, shivering little thing before it stood to its full height, taller than a man. Its arms extended so long that they began to drag on the ground, and its eyeless face twisted, turning so that it became an overcrowded concoction of needle-like teeth. Blackness radiated off of it in waves, reaching toward me like instilling fear was some kind of power it had. The mouth extended and twitched, a dark pool of smoky liquid oozing from the depth of its throat. The creature tilted back, releasing a terrible shriek into the atmosphere like a warrior king of its domain.

I turned and screamed, launching myself further into the river with a desperate lunge. *I cannot let it get me. I cannot let it get me.*

I had heard once that we are all born with instinct, the same kind of instinct present in wild animals. Particularly, instincts that we cannot avoid no matter how hard we wish to. Our hearts will always quicken at a sudden exclamation of action or noise. We will raise against terror or flee for our lives. In that moment, I understood. I was nothing more than a bundle of instinctual desire to flee far, far away. The creature— the monster, I knew—started after me. I cast a horrified glance behind to see it give chase, its horribly long limbs snatching and slapping the grass, then the rocks, then the water, which splashed up high into the air around us.

I simply was not fast enough.

Its claws snaked out to greet me, wrapping around my waist and pulling me tight. I gasped, screaming in gut-wrenching terror as the monster forced me beneath the water in the middle of the river. My feet kicked out, looking for any sort of ground, but there was none.

I was able to scarcely surface, but my hands were now touching the monster, which was, in truth, revolting. It did not feel like skin or any other fleshy creature, but like clutching at slippery shadows with no solidity to them, just emptiness that made me feel like I was choking. Despite myself, I opened my eyes beneath the water in order to stare up at my assaulter; my short nails unable to wound, and my feeble strength nothing more than an annoyance for it.

Vale and Emeric had asked me many times what it was like to die and be dead. Usually they would ask before I helped tuck them to sleep, the white hue of the moon breaking through our windows. How foolish I was then, telling them it was something too far off for us to really know or wonder about.

Staring up through the blur of water, the monster looked like nothing more than a shadow blocking my view of the blue sky past its head. Its strong grip held me beneath the current, the cream fabric of my gown cast against my body was not a comfort. Even in my fit of resistance, I knew I could not drown. Something curled into my chest, reminding me that the damage had already been done. I squeezed my eyes shut and felt myself fall into the last moments of my life that I could readily remember among the chaos. My *real* life—the life where I had my brothers, my father, my breath, my heart, my lungs, my future.

Bare feet on warm, wet rocks. Songbirds chirping in soft, high-pitched symphonies above me. The sun's warmth on my skin, radiating like a warm blanket thanks to the thinness of my dress and the cloudless sky.

A twist of foot against slippery rock. A cracking sound. Then, I had lifted my cheek.

Beneath the water, I allowed myself to go limp in sorrow and shame. I should have told my brothers that I knew nothing of death. That I was just as terrified as they were. I should have offered to kiss them goodbye before I wandered into the woods toward the river to bathe. I should have known death would be nothing like sleeping, that instead it was a realm where everything remained and kept you on the outside, like an intruder peeking into a cozy home. Where monsters destroyed you, binding you underwater for eternity.

How could this have happened to me? The question felt like a bee sting to my very essence. It wasn't fair—not that I had ever been in the position to determine what was fair and what wasn't. But how could this have happened to *me*? I thought that death was only something you heard about in stories or in passing. It required a simple moment of appreciation and recognition before time kept moving onward and life kept being lived.

The warm current vibrated around me, ears blocked from the rushing sound that was nearly deafening. The monster's long arms curled around me and lifted me from the river painfully slow. I could feel the strength in its body go slack against me. Would it eat my heart? Would it gorge itself on my memories? Would it hold me captive?

The slowness of it all was nearly maddening. I wondered whether my mother was able to actually see me from the beyond, to guide me as I did my best to take care of my brothers in her absence. What a tragedy that I would not be able to see her again. Never be able to smell her, touch her, or lean against her with all of my wishes and woes simply because a monster had found me and taken control of me, shoving me down beneath the river, likely now pleased that I had given up. But what was left to fight for? I was about to lose it all. My brothers, my father, and even my mother. It was a cruel twist of fate that had been bestowed on me. I wanted to curse, to shout, to scream with all of my might. This was *wrong*. This wasn't how it was supposed to be. I never planned to die.

My face broke the surface, but I did not allow myself to gasp or even let out a whisper of fear as water trailed down the sides of my temples. My bushy hair peeled back and away from my face. The slip of my dress dangled behind me as the monster held me in his arms. I felt one of its hands tuck some of my curls behind my ear. It was a delicate gesture, one that made me wonder whether or not this was the type of monster that tried to seduce before it struck with its evilness.

Strangely, I had never been touched so intimately before. It was like the monster knew exactly what I was craving, what kind of movement would demand my attention.

A long moment passed before I got the courage to look it in its teeth-ridden face. When my eyelids lifted, I expected horrors beyond comprehension. To peer into the face of a monstrous creature about to devour my very soul and take away all joy and happiness that existed inside of me.

Instead, I found the face of a young man peering down, cradling me against his chest amid the cold current of the river we waded in.

CHAPTER TWO

As a child I often wondered how monsters came into existence as fuel for horror stories.

My father would often put me on his knee and describe in great detail the types of monsters in the world. Ghosts were one thing, but monsters with the ability to possess your soul and make you their puppet were another. I had heard of dark magic and curses enough to not doubt that it was something I should take care to avoid. I never believed in the afterlife, so monsters and saviors were just entertainment indulgences from my father's lips to my own ears.

But I could never help looking over my shoulder as I crept from my room in the pitch blackness. I could not deny that once or twice I prayed that a monster would not crawl out from under my bed and start cutting me to pieces. I feared long tongues, sharp claws, and pointed teeth. When my mother grew ill and died, I even prayed to the creator of the universe that it would come down and save her. People from Enya believed that the entire universe was created by one entity, so why couldn't it help me when I needed it? When my mother was not returned to me, I was all but certain that nothing beyond death was available to me. Not monsters, and certainly not saviors.

As I caught the eye of the young man holding me against his chest, I could not help but feel cheated. My fantasies were filled with monsters like the very one that had just been chasing me. The tales my father told me never mentioned that monsters could, or would, disguise themselves as something quite beautiful.

Not that the something holding me was beautiful. He was perhaps average at best, with brown hair that took blond highlights in the direct path of the sun. It was cropped short yet cut messily, as though it was in style socially to cut it in pieces and then carefully style it to the side. His nose was straight, and his jaw was angular with a pointed chin. His skin was fairer than my own, like he had not ever sat in the sun other than the occasion to terrorize young girls who slipped on rocks. His eyes, framed by thick lashes, were a pale blue color that reminded me of a bluebird. I heard once that those kinds of birds were notoriously cruel.

Human-looking or not, this monster could not trick me. A heartbeat passed between us while we watched each other, taking in the moment. Then I remembered what it was that was holding me and what it wanted.

Struggling, I could feel the screams bubble inside of my throat. "Get off me!"

The monster's jaw clenched, and he started to drag me through the water. This time my feet tripped over themselves as we waded back toward the bank, catching parts of the rough and slimy texture of the jagged rocks. When I began to kick in violent protest, he lifted me effortlessly into his arms and threw me completely. My body landed with a hard thud against the grass, yet I scrambled to gain my footing once more, rounding on the monster and preparing to fight.

I wish I had a weapon. My father had often taught the boys how to throw punches, but never me. More shame and regret flooded my veins. I would have been better prepared to fight if I had learned how. Maybe if I had known that I would *need* to. Enya was not a place that saw intruders or strangers, ever.

I took in the monster's appearance, clothed as a young man would be. He was wearing a royal blue that matched his eyes—and reinforced my bluebird comparison— with dark slacks. A brown, well-fitted leather jacket clung to his torso. The clothing was standard to me yet had an edge to it that I could not quite put my finger on. Nonetheless, I recognized that the monster was not as tall in this form. He had shrunk to a normal height, as normal as anyone who had ever lived.

"Stay away from me," I warned. "I will not let you take me. I will not let you eat me."

"It's alright," the monster said smoothly, voice as even and steady as any other boy ever met. "I'm not here to hurt you. And...I'm not here to eat you, either." Amusement shone in his eyes, kicking up water while he approached the bank and stepped out of the river.

"I'm dead," I blurted out suddenly, perhaps stupidly. A question and statement all at once. My hands began to quiver, pulling my focus away. Did death not protect against the parts of me which I loathed in life? The shaking hands, the hitch of a breath, the rapid beat of a heart?

"Yes," he said. "Look. Your body is right there."

I followed his gaze, but a whisper told me it would hurt to do so. Sure enough, near the edge of all this commotion, a girl lay. Something inside of my chest tugged, willing me to draw closer for a look. My bare feet slid into the mud as I slowly approached her, taking in the way her bushy, curled hair covered her face so as to conceal it. Her hair flowed to the top of her shoulders but arched outward, giving her a fuller look. The thin, cream-colored dress was plain and long enough to cover her ankles if not for the fact that the current tried to sweep it away.

She was small for a young woman, nearly looking like a child herself. Her skin was beginning to turn red from the sunlight shining down on her, but even so it kept a light tan complexion that complimented the coloring of her hair. Hair that was beginning to become soaked in blood with each second that passed. Blood from the kind of wound that you expected someone to never recover from.

What was most disturbing was that as I looked upon her, I knew what I would find. I knew that if I pushed aside her hair, I would see a round face. That I would find the front of her dress was tied in a lazy bow of drawstrings. That her cheek would be planted firmly against the warm, gray rocks. I knew that this girl was not just a girl.

She was me.

I gritted my teeth in response. I could not cry, not now. Not in front of a monster that would prey on my weakness and my sadness. I could not afford to lose the best parts of me, the memories of my upbringing and my family and my last moments. My sadness would not be used for his pleasure.

A dangerous stillness passed over me. How could I be laying *there* and existing *here*? I didn't want to be just a soul. I wanted to be whole again. I wanted to be alive again. Even though the world seemed the same, I could sense something *different* about it. Every instinct inside of me whispered that I should still be with that body and that, from this moment, there was no such thing as moving on. There was now only disconnection and disassociation. My body had turned into a shell, one that was going to start to decay without me to occupy it.

I turned to the monster and did my best to hide the devastation on my face. "Yes, that's me. And I'll be damned if I give you what you want."

"And what do you think I want?" he asked darkly, placing his hands inside his pockets. The nonchalance that it showed made me pause.

I studied the frankness of its face, the straight curve of the nose that twitched slightly. "You want to capture me...eat me...take my soul. Right?"

He scoffed. "I don't eat souls. We have something in common. I wasn't expecting it—when I saw you fall, I was certain you were going to lay there forever. When you looked up, I thought 'Wow, this could get interesting.'"

Anger coursed through my veins, bubbling and hot. I could not help myself from staggering forward through the tall grass and stepping closer. His appearance was an upgrade from the teeth and swirling blackness that made it easier to approach him, but still my body trembled at the thought of what I was speaking to. Even in death it seemed that moments of anger and rashness outweighed terror and cautiousness.

We were close enough so that, if I desired, I could physically push the monster-boy back into the water. Yet the thought of putting my hands on it was revolting.

"Interesting?" my voice echoed, sharp as a razor. "My death to you was interesting? How dare you. You filthy, disgusting monster. You chased me! You tried to drown me! I am *dead*!"

He did not flinch from my hysterics. Those blue eyes looked down at me, his lips pressed into a hard line of both amusement and boredom. "I think we've established that you are dead. First of all, I'm not a monster. Stop calling me that. I'm a—well, I'm something. Second, I did not try to *drown* you. You were already dead. You can't drown a dead person."

His tone was so matter-of-fact, so flippant, that I could not help but gape in shock. What sort of afterlife was this? Were monsters not only disguised as young men—were they also as infuriating as them?

"Then tell me what you want and what you are doing here," I snarled.

He laughed, low and throaty. "Trying to give you your chance at peace. I was waiting for you while I was on the riverbank, but you turned and ran off after you saw me. Souls usually don't have that reaction, you know." He paused. Then he added, "Actually, I guess you wouldn't know."

"Please, I cannot take any riddles. If you are not a monster, why did you look so…" I struggled to find the words, choking on the memory of what had chased after me.

He tilted his head, preoccupied with something in the water. "I can explain that later. Come with me. I know others who will want to meet you. And we can teach you about what to do next."

My hysteria and anger suddenly receded, leaving me cold blooded. Fighting back the urge to cry, I willed the terror in my chest to hide itself between my ribs. I was struck with several horrible realizations. First, that this creature wanted me to go with it. Second, there were others just like him. *More* of him. More terrible, disgusting monsters that would try to trick me into trusting them.

"I'm not going anywhere with you," I decided at once. "I'm not leaving my home."

The monster turned back to look at me. His face was even, somewhat soft, and something like regret flashed in its blue eyes. "I told you, I am not a monster. I am a person just like you. My name is Warren."

"Warren?" I repeated suspiciously. This monster had a name? "You expect me to believe you are not a monster? I saw you. I saw what you were. So don't lie to me."

His lean body shifted, hands pulling his leather jacket tighter in a nervous gesture. "My job is to wait for dead people to cross over and then help them leave so they don't get stuck here. I help them cross over to wherever it is they go. If you don't come with me now, what else are you going to do?"

I kept my eyes on him, desperate to not look over at the body that lay in the water. But he seemed to see the thoughts inside of my brain, shaking his head in disbelief.

"You're going to stay here and watch your body rot?" he shot, voice cold. "Watch your family come find you or maybe not at all? What happens if the animals start to eat you? You really think you can witness that? I heard the animals here in Enya are quite ravenous. Ever wonder what your flesh tastes like?"

I stepped back, my face scrunched. "You're disgusting."

"No, I'm realistic. That's what happens to bodies. And you're not a body anymore. So come with me or sit here and watch yourself turn into food."

Trust was a fragile, feeble thing. I was not the type a girl, and never had been, who could thrust it easily into the hands of others. Once I trusted my father to catch me as I fell backwards. Arms spread wide, eyes closed, I rolled back onto my feet into his safe arms. But his arms were not there at all, and instead my skull cracked against the floor of our house. It had taken three days to rid myself of the goose bump that formed on the back of my head. It took me even longer to rid myself of the idea that I could not trust my own father.

A moment passed and finally I spoke, studying the harsh blue of his collared shirt, afraid to look into his eyes. "I don't know if I can trust you," I admitted weakly. "How could I be so sure you're not tricking me to take me somewhere terrible? And what do you mean 'cross over'? Isn't this where everyone who dies ends up?"

Warren stepped closer to me, so near that I could feel warmth from his body. *Warmth! Were we not dead?* His hand reached out to take my own and I felt myself tense, afraid he might turn into that preying creature of swirling darkness. But he remained the same, long fingers curling around my wrist.

"I was once flesh like you were. I was once a body, and then a soul. You can trust me. We are...the same. Different, but the same. There are others too. We can stay together."

I dragged my eyes up to meet his, dark green clashing wildly with pale blue. A battle between trust and mistrust, known and unknown. Slowly, I turned my gaze toward the girl who had been laying so near to us. She had not moved at all.

"Where else could I go?" I whispered to her. Hoping she'd sit up and answer. Hoping that she would look at me, smile, and then start wandering back toward the makeshift path that her brothers had carved toward the house.

Warren, still clutching my wrist, began to pull us away from the scene. My feet slid across mud and then soft, warm grass as he began to lead us deeper into Enya's forest. We were not, to my disappointment, going toward my home.

"What's your name?" he wondered.

I swallowed the urge to apologize for not giving my name at the time he gave his. What were formalities and apologies even worth now?

"Sonnet." My voice was raw.

"Like a poem? Interesting. Pleasure to meet you. I'm known as the Traveler, one of the soul stealers," he chuckled.

"A soul stealer?" My eyes widened in alarm. "You steal souls?"

Sensing the panic in my tone, he let go of my wrist and gave me a crooked grin. "Not particularly. I've only stolen *one* soul. Just as you have."

I paused. "I've never stolen a soul."

He did not respond at first. We walked only a brief distance before he pulled me to a hard stop. His hand reached outward, and at first I believed him to be pointing toward someone or something. Instead, his hand slipped through the air and tore it completely, peeling away from the scene like unwrapping a gift.

I simply could not comprehend what I was witnessing.

The rip he tore was like looking through a frosted window. Possible, yet a strain on the eyes to truly decipher what was beyond it. It had to be some sort of ancient magic bestowed upon him by the universe, I decided. This kind of magic or ability did not exist. It could not exist, not as far as I was concerned. Then, like a thief who stole that magic away from something else, he stepped into the hole he unwrapped, pausing to look back at me with a raised eyebrow.

Warren reached his left hand, the only one visible as the other was gone through the gateway, toward me to take. "Of course you have. The same as the rest of us. You've stolen your own."

I glanced backward toward the river. My body, the only body I ever had, was laying there, waiting for someone to find it and waiting for someone to bury it. With a jolt, I realized that the only person who could do such things would be my father. No doubt he would come searching for me when he started to feel as though I were missing. Tears burned my eyes and I blinked them away rapidly, hoping that Warren would not notice.

Did I want to stick around and see my father's reaction? What was worse— seeing your own dead body or seeing a family member identify your dead body? Both were heartbreaking. I could not bear to look into my father's eyes and expect him to understand that I was still present. That I could still feel the wind and the spray of the water, even the dirt beneath my bare feet. All he would know is that my body was there, and my soul had departed from it.

I swallowed the lump that formed inside of my throat and took Warren's hand, flinching as he pulled me through the little magic portal that he had made.

My brothers once had a dog. She was a large thing with round paws and a rolling tongue. She made them feel safe. Once, when I was ready to give her a taste of hen, she jumped onto me and placed her paws squarely on my hips. I toppled to the side abnormally fast and was able to catch myself on our dining table, but stood again with a vibrating sensation inside my brain. The force and weight of such a gentle creature motivated by primal desire momentarily blurred my vision. It had felt like I narrowly avoided terminal collision, like taking an abrupt path fate did not expect.

Such was stepping through the torn gateway made by Warren. He never let go of my hand as he guided me, partially because I clung to it desperately like a small child. There were no sensations other than frigid coldness and held breath when I stepped through the frosted window.

Death, it seemed, was truly like slipping from one room to the next. Unnoticeable if not watched carefully. So quick that a single blink could miss it entirely. Though my phantom body and thoughts were still intact, I could sense that the universe looked upon our act with contempt. Fear struck my heart, and I knew we had cheated fate somehow.

The river which Warren had nearly drowned me in had glistened under a bright blue sky and harsh sunlight. It was a territory known for its lush, wild forests and bustling rivers. It was home, nestled away in the rural thicket of our homeland, Enya. Most people on the small continent lived simple lives and stayed to themselves. My family included. But here the sky was light gray, and the clouds were thin, which allowed a golden sunset to peek through onto the landscape. The ground we stepped onto was flat and moist, where damp moss blossomed, and a dirt path led to the only structure I could see. A quaint, pointed cottage constructed with stark white bricks stood alone on the horizon. Its shutters were solid black, and it could not be more than two stories in height. Beyond it, there was no backyard or property. It merely sat so close to the cliff side that it threatened to topple over completely.

Indeed, the air was saltier here than I was used to. We were on top of a grand coast, where miles of plains were vacant and haunting. I expected to see animals—perhaps double-wool sheep happily grazing, or even milk cows—but there was nothing on the plains except tall, unkempt grass that looked like it was rippling every time the wind blew. It tore at my body and my dress, even pulling my hair back for me as I stared out toward the water. The ocean was dark and violent, clashing against the bottom of the ragged cliffs. We were so high up that if anyone were to fall, they certainly would lose their life.

A strange thought occurred to me that I no longer had any life to lose—what would it be like, then, to take advantage of such an opportunity?

I turned away to examine the rip we had stepped through. It was gone, mended like a wound. And like a wound that had been stitched, there was scarring; the air looked the same, but my eyes could not quite decipher what exactly was misconstrued. It was as though I knew there was a scar, but it was so faint I could not see the beginning and end of it. I shivered.

"Impressed?" Warren inquired. His face was honest and interested, but his eyes betrayed hints of unspoken arrogance. I immediately took back my hand and folded my arms over myself, an act partially because I was feeling cold in my slip of a dress and partially because I was feeling disturbed by what had just happened.

"More confused, honestly," I admitted.

"I'll explain. Let's go inside."

I followed him as he walked the dirt path, my bare feet a true nuisance. Was I condemned in this afterlife to always have my feet stuck, poked, and pinched by rocks and sticks? Not to mention my dress was quite thin and I wore nothing beneath it. The only true value of it was that it was not quite see through. If such were the case, could I die of embarrassment while already being dead?

How lovely it would have been to die in a coat like Warren's, just thick enough to shield from cool winds. I considered asking him whether he was particularly fond of it, or if he would let me have it for my sanity. But then again, wearing clothing that belonged to a monster far beyond the horrors of my mind felt like an open invitation to becoming friendlier. I would do anything I could to prove to Warren that I did not trust him. I did not believe him when he said he was like me, even if his hands had been delicate when they tucked hair behind my ear.

As we neared the cottage I could hear the sounds of the sea, of waves crashing against hard rock and birds screeching. It was quite noisy but comforting, and it was nothing like where I suspected monsters like Warren might reside. I could not completely disregard the idea that he would never turn back into a swirling mass of black air without eyes and with long, white teeth.

I stared at the back of his head, searching for any sign he might be quivering in anticipation for luring me into his domain so he could finally eat my heart. But I found none.

Surprise struck me when I stepped into the cottage. It was like a real home. The room we stepped into invited me to feel its plush, intricately designed carpet that lay over wooden floorboards. Reds and whites stitched with golden florals caressed my feet. Maybe being barefoot wasn't a bad thing after all.

The walls were painted stark white, the exact same brick that adorned the outside. Unfamiliar paintings were hung, as well as an astrological map illustration. There was also a fireplace and a dark brown mantel that held candles and several different books with their spines pointing out. In the center of the room, a velvety sofa in a bright gold color and a wooden table completed the furnishing. Glass-paned windows faced the ocean, a beautiful and inviting view to admire its gloominess.

I hated to admit it, but it was charming. My own home had been made of stone and wood. We didn't have carpets or any illustrations hanging on our walls. They were just nuances and pleasures that couldn't be afforded when things like food and clothing were more important. We were not poor, though, just merely average among a continent that made a living through exporting food and livestock. The other two continents, Pushka and Creo, were far more advanced. My father used to tell me that there were great cities where thousands of people lived at a time. Beneath the canopies of the trees in southern Enya, I always found that hard to believe. We did not have a neighbor for miles.

"This is your home?" I asked Warren, who stepped in before me and was already looking quite comfortable. He promptly threw himself across the golden sofa and placed his arms behind his head as though he were ready to take a nap.

"I live here. But I do not own it."

My eyes caught the mantle of the fireplace where the books beckoned me. One of the spines declared that the book was about different species of bugs. Whoever owned it likely was someone interested in all the workings of all the creatures of the world.

"So you...haunt it, then?" I suggested, forcing myself to look away from the mantel. Behind me he barked a throaty laugh. I turned, not feeling friendly toward him at all for laughing at me. In fact, I felt like hitting him. How *dare* he bring me to his home and then treat me like I was something to be laughed at.

"Is that what you think of me? A ghost?" he wondered, lips quirking.

"You're either a ghost or a monster. I don't know what to think of you. But you are dead, aren't you? Like I am?"

Warren's smile turned into a frown. "Yes, like you. You're taking it well. I expected you to panic. I think I did, once upon a time."

"Dead is dead. I knew it would happen eventually."

Perhaps he could detect something in my voice, because his frown twitched and his eyes flashed. I averted my own before I could truly decipher what were in his. "And yet here you are, soul stealer."

My eyes narrowed. "Yes, about that. What did you mean by that earlier? I *stole* my own soul?"

"You would not be standing here with me now if you didn't," he offered, as though it were an obvious fact. Studying my features, no doubt etched with impatience, he let out a sigh. "Most people die and pass through us to wherever else they go. They know we are here to help them find peace. Usually by touching them. It's like they're half asleep, unaware of themselves in limbo. It was why I was so...forceful with you in the water. I was hoping you were just a little more awake than most. But it turns out you're a stealer."

"I was not half asleep," I protested stiffly with a shake of my head.

"Maybe when you first woke you may have felt disoriented or off. But you lifted your head, and I could see that your eyes were clearer than what I'm used to seeing. When you ran from me, I knew you had just stolen yourself away."

Stolen my own soul from peace? Great. I should have reached for him and passed on. Instead, I stupidly ran and condemned myself as some sort of ghoul, likely for the rest of eternity.

"There are others like you?" I wondered suddenly, not bothering to hide my caution.

His confirmation was clear in a nod. "Like you too. I told you, we're the same. Different, but the same."

I was nothing like him. Nothing like the creature he was pretending not to be. "And you've witnessed them all die?"

Warren sat forward and rested his elbows on his knees. He lifted his chin slightly. I wasn't sure what he was looking for, so I stared back at him with a look that I thought conveyed my seriousness. If he was going to bait and tease me like a mystery, then I was going to drill him like I was someone who lived to solve them.

"No," he murmured at last. "You're the first I've witnessed die and become a stealer. The others have been here longer than me, with the exception of one."

"So you just wander around and try to help souls cross over?" I mused, hoping I was following this all correctly. It seemed strange to me, perhaps even crazy. The only hope I had was that he was telling the truth. There had never been any book that would explain exactly what I was up against when I died. Just musings and faith, like believing that our souls watched over each other in the afterlife and that there was no more suffering.

"And that thing you did earlier...that magic? Was that some sort of...portal? Can I do that as well?" I continued.

"Interesting way of describing it," he noted, but closed his eyes as though it was not very interesting at all. His blue shirt looked strange against the gold of the sofa. "No, and I would be surprised if you could. We each have our own...talents. Mine happens to be traveling. The others have their specialties too. I'm sure *you* even have a specialty."

Traveling? I would hardly call it travel. It was more like a thief's way of slipping through a crowd unnoticed. Or the way a child would creep unheard through the darkness instead of sleeping, hoping not to wake their mother.

"I don't think so. I've never been able to do anything special," I muttered.

"Neither did I when I was alive. But you'd be surprised what waits you in death," he said gravely.

"And where are these others?" I sighed, wandering over to the sofa. I kept a careful distance away from him, still afraid that this was some sort of trap laid out for me to bring my guard down. Or maybe even a sick, twisted game.

Warren smiled. "On their way to meet you as we speak, Miss Sonnet."

CHAPTER THREE

The rest of the cottage was just as minimally furnished as the first room. My own home had been built and constructed to house a small family, but here I had the suspicion that whoever owned the cottage was not a permanent resident. For one, I could tell that despite apparent squatters like Warren and the others, the house was dirty.

Few items had been moved properly, such as the chairs, tables, and books. The kitchen delighted me, and was a brilliant display of white and black tile, gray walls, and wooden cabinets. Near me, pots and pans hung from a rack beside one of the few windows, but their insides were coated with small dust bunnies that sent a shiver down my spine. My feet were cold on the kitchen tiles and I sighed, once again damning the thin dress I had unwittingly chose to die in.

I decided to slowly walk around the cottage to investigate and leave Warren on the golden sofa. However, my investigating did not get me far, as I soon heard the front door creak open and a series of steps falling onto the plush carpet. The sound of the opening door was foreign to me, scratching my eardrums enough to make me wince. Small murmurs traveled to my ears, then I heard Warren call out my name.

There was no issue in meeting new faces. I was quite friendly toward any strangers I had ever known in my life, simply because where I lived we did not have many. But trust and friendliness are not mutually exclusive—at least not to me—so I was typically able to make new acquaintances while keeping them outside the reach of my trust.

Ghosts, ghouls, monsters, saviors, or not—these creatures would not have my fear to strengthen them.

I swallowed down the lump in the back of my throat and tightened my arms over my body. It was poor body language, but the dead were beyond caring about those things, weren't they? I stepped out from the kitchen and crossed into the front room, my eyes cast on the gold-embellished carpet that felt like a blanket on my feet. Very carefully I lifted my gaze to meet the new figures standing to greet me.

And suddenly I felt better about being in the dress that I was in after all. My eyes found a girl first, perhaps my age of seventeen. She had fair skin like Warren; her face a petite narrowness that made her look dainty and fragile. Her hair was a beautiful copper color, pulled back loosely into a knot at the back of her head. Few pieces of hair stood out, just enough to catch the slight wave of its texture. Where mine was fluffy and hard to manage, hers would no doubt have gone obediently into its confines. What most stood out to me was the dress she wore. It was an odd looking piece, something I had never seen women wear before. At least in Enya no woman would wear such a thing, not when it was poorly designed for working in fields or tending to the house. It was a deep violet color and made of soft velvet. It tightened at her core and then flared out to her waist. I imagined it was uncomfortable to sit or stand or do anything in, but the girl smiled pleasantly like such a thing did not bother her at all. The dress was puffy around the shoulders, making her thin arms look even more delicate and the dress itself rather ridiculous. At least to me, anyway.

How did she even die in that? As much as I was frustrated by my thin slip of a gown, hers was far too thick and formal for me to ever be comfortable in.

The other stranger was a girl too. Her skin was rich black, much darker than my own, and her similar dark hair fell to her waist in braids. It framed her round face and eyes to match. As my own gaze moved across her, I found that she had died in something she must have chosen rather carefully. She wore a silky and long-sleeved shirt that buttoned around her elbows in a shimmering silver color that complimented her skin tone. The shirt was paired with tight black pants and tied leather boots—expensive by the look of them. It was a very urban style I supposed, and a bit unique to my eyes. Nobody would wear such a thing unless they lived in a city.

What I knew to be fact was that she was the most beautiful in the room and had obviously won in the areas of afterlife wardrobe. There was an attractive quality to her that radiated confidence and certainty, her gaze curious as she studied me just as closely. The first girl was thin and petite—the second was her counterpart, all curves and warm demeanor, even with her confident attitude. Both girls regarded me with surprise and interest.

"And who is this?" the first wondered, voice passive and curious. Her eyes flickered to Warren for answers, but he seemed unable to get off the couch to explain my situation.

"Sonnet," I introduced myself weakly.

"Ah...I write a sonnet here or there, if I can find time," the girl acknowledged with a smile. I briefly wondered how a dead person couldn't have enough time, especially a ghost. Didn't we have all the time in the world? Then she stepped forward and gave her best curtsy, much to my own shock. *To think I thought they would not care about formalities!*

Warren stood from his sofa and fixed his jacket, inviting me further into the room.

"Edythe likes to show off," he explained quickly. "I never could get into poetry myself, though."

Edythe, in her violet dress, gave a small blush, resting her hands together in front of her mildly. "I'm sorry if I offended you, Sonnet."

"No...no, of course not," I said, then turned toward the other girl expectantly. She did not get closer, but dipped her head in acknowledgement.

"I'm Naya," she declared, folding her arms to mirror my own. "I don't write sonnets, but you can bet I'll ask some questions. How did you die?"

The question did not offend me, but I could see both Warren and Edythe shift uncomfortably. I stole a glance at the former, whose eyes caught my own, his expression unreadable.

"I fell," I said simply. "I was walking in the river and slipped on a rock." Naya seemed pleased with my answer, her eyebrows raising in interest; however, it was Edythe who cried out after my admission.

"Oh, you poor dear." She sniffed, sauntering close so she could reach for me. I jumped slightly at the sudden contact as she unfolded my arms and held my right hand in her two tiny ones. Up close I could see that her eyes were a dark brown, like two hungry shadows searching my face for troubles to feed them. "Don't fret. It is so common you would not believe it. It was sudden, was it not? Much easier than, say, choking to death?"

Her words surprised me. I had considered her dainty and feminine, which she was, yet there was a bluntness to her that I did not expect right away. The mask of feminine daintiness hid a sharpened edge.

It occurred to me that her comparison must not be random. I absorbed the look in her eyes, the dress that she wore, and the slight formality in her voice that gave her away as someone who valued pleasantries. In Enya we would have called her the daughter of wealth, someone who had been exposed to a lavish lifestyle and likely never worked in any sort of labor in her life.

"Is that how you died?" I guessed.

"Yes! At a formal dinner with my parents too. I have been dead quite some time now, though. But I can tell you that you will start to feel like yourself again soon. So do not worry, we will be here for you."

Her words were meant to be reassuring, however I knew that they gave no comfort to me, as comfort was not something I lacked. I feared the absence of time running out and being among monsters, but most things about me still felt the same. The only thing that had changed was that I was, apparently, dead.

Naya began to play with her braids, shrugging indifferently. "Or you'll never start to feel like yourself again. That's an option too. But I don't mean to be cynical." She tossed her hair over her shoulder and smiled, lips pressed tightly. Her eyes flickered to Edythe. "Would you get the door, please?"

Edythe let go of my hands and fluttered toward the door, reaching for it quickly and slamming it shut. Again the sound made me wince, but I merely turned toward Warren for further explanation. Before either of us could speak, Edythe addressed me once more.

"Would you like me to open the window?"

All the dust and dirt in the cottage did make it quite stuffy, yet I found her question to be unusual and off putting. Not wanting to be rude, I agreed, and she happily made her way toward the window. A few seconds later, she lifted the glass panels. Cool breeze flew into the room and I wished I would have declined her request, goosebumps beginning to rise on my arms and legs. Unable to help myself, I let out a shiver.

"So," I began rather awkwardly, watching Naya and Edythe lean against the wall and Warren move toward the fireplace mantel. I felt it would be easier to sit on the velvet couch where they all could see me more clearly, so I did. "Where is this, exactly?"

"It's called Foxcoast," Warren replied. "Perhaps you've heard of it?"

"No, I haven't. How far are we from my home?"

"Quite far. This is on the other side of the world, in Creo."

My eyes widened with shock. I had never left southern Enya, let alone the continent. "The *world*? You can't mean that your little trick took us from one side of the world to the next?"

To my right, Naya laughed. "You're dead, and this is what you concern yourself with?" Beside her, Edythe smiled, her castaway hairs catching the breeze from the window.

"But how is this possible? There is no magic, no powers...how can you do such a thing? Who gave that power to you?"

Warren looked at me squarely, nearly challenging me to ask even more daring questions. "How do we even have souls in the first place? Who made this world and put souls on it? It's just another question we'll never have an answer to."

I jumped up from the couch. Panic rose through me, sharp and icy. "You're telling me I died but I get no answers? Dying is supposed to be an answer itself. I was hoping for eternal rest, not an eternity of questioning!"

"You and me both," Warren muttered at the same time that Edythe spoke from across the room.

"That is because you're a stealer," she supplied. "Most people do find answers. We...don't."

"It's a price to pay," Naya agreed.

I found it hard to believe that these three individuals were once living and breathing. That they had hopes and dreams, a wonderment that kept them fearing death and questioning what came next. They were all young, like me—did they not grieve over their lost life? We could have been old with grandchildren and memories. Instead, we were something like ghosts. And they seemed not to mind at all.

I could handle dying and being dead. It was afterlife that began to terrify me.

"Price for what? Being a ghost? Will I never sleep again? Will I never dream? And my family...?" My phantom heart suddenly ached, words flowing from my mouth in a rush. I hurriedly stood to my feet, making way for the door. "I have to go back home. If I can't be with my family anymore, at least I can watch over them."

"No, you can't," Warren said sternly, pushing off of the mantel to stalk closer. His jaw clenched and his eyes narrowed as he reached for my wrist, clasping his warm fingers around the small bit of flesh he found there. His hold was like steel and I began to tug away, horrified. "Trust me, you won't like what you find there."

"Get off me!" I commanded. Warren did not budge.

"He's right, Sonnet," Edythe whispered evenly, her expression grave. She shook her head, eyes catching mine. "The living can feel the dead. It makes them colder and meaner."

"But I have little brothers," I cried. Tears filled my eyes but I kept them from spilling over, still not entirely sure that these people wouldn't feed on my sadness. Still not convinced that they had ever even been alive like I was.

This could *not* be happening. How many times had I wished my mother was somewhere in the universe looking down on me? How many times had I waded the river and not slipped because of her gentle, guiding touch of protection? Or so I had thought. To think that it was all lies now. My mother had never been with me at all, only inside my thoughts and my longing. Her spirit had gone elsewhere, and I had an inkling that where I was now was not where she was. Stealing my soul away not only jeopardized my chance of living in peace, but I would never be reunited with the ones I loved most.

Warren, likely unable to handle my crying, released his grip on me. His stern voice was considerably more empathetic. "Nothing has changed, Sonnet. You are dead, but that does not mean you have to be gone. You must have realized that somehow. When you ran away from me, you had to know that nothingness was not what you wanted."

I turned to look up at him. He was considerably taller than me, but I would never shrink from intimidation. No matter how blue his eyes or soft his face, I knew I could not forget the swirling blackness and oozing mouth. I knew a monster was hidden there somewhere. Why was he trying to feign compassion toward me?

"Don't pretend," I whispered harshly. "Don't pretend I had any choice in this. You know why I ran! It was because of *you*."

"What do you mean it was because of me?" His features hardened, eying me suddenly like I was covered in filth. "I didn't do anything to you."

"Yes, you did." I pointed, reaching out to push him. I barely made a slip to his stance, and he pulled his jacket closer from where I had muffled it, annoyed. I could see dark blue veins bulging from the back of his hands like he still had blood to pulse through them. Like his heart was quickening from my words.

"All I did was bring you here to the meet the rest of us. We're all we have here, you know. There's nobody else. What, would you have rather I left you in that river?"

I gaped at him, my voice rising with each word I spoke. How dare he stand there and act like he was some sort of hero in this story. "Left me at my *house*? With my *family*? Yes, I would have preferred that. Instead you swept me away to the other side of the world!"

"Because *this* is where we live," he snarled. I remembered the darkness that lurked inside of him and forced myself to bring my voice down a level. Despite it all, I was still terrified of the creature that had pushed me under the water. There was no denying that, should I see it again, it would render me unable to speak.

"I bet. How do I know you didn't steal them away too? We could all be prisoners here. *Prisoners* because you're some kind of monster who enjoys stealing souls!"

Naya let out a sharp scoff and Edythe opened her mouth to speak, but her voice was drowned out from the sound of Warren scuffing the bottom of his shoes along the carpet and his outburst of disbelief. "So I'm your villain, then."

"Considering you chased me looking like some kind of creature that crawled out of my nightmares, yes. Now is that so hard to *understand*? You're disgusting."

Warren's soft gaze hardened and pain etched his features. He stepped backward and ran his eyes from the top of my head to my lips. With a shake of his head, he turned away and cut me off with a wave of his hand. My eyes narrowed on his back.

He stormed from the cottage, disappearing right through the wall where the illustrations hung completely. It was so ghostly that I felt nausea bubble in my stomach. I had never seen someone do the things he did. It was starting to feel unnatural or impossible, like I really *was* living a nightmare that I forgot to wake up from. The reality that I now faced was hard to accept, to come to terms with. No matter how easy it was to accept that I was now dead, the strangeness of what came after was beginning to become too much for me to reasonably handle.

CHAPTER FOUR

Children are notorious for their questions. Vale and Emric were like any other boys discovering their world, once dipping their hands in mud puddles and pulling away only to wonder how that mud came to be. After they found out, they questioned what they could do with that mud. Could they build a horse? Could they build a castle? We were children raised in the countryside who wondered what life was like in large cities. Questioning and pretending became a source of enjoyment and hope for the three of us. It was never a torment.

Yet I was tormented. And I was like a child in the room, asking questions that I should have realized the others may have gone out of their way to avoid. The closer I looked past my panic, the more I began to see. Edythe's small face wrecked in sorrow. Naya's desire to remove herself completely from the conversation. Warren's shock and flush of anger when I blamed him for my own misfortune.

Slowly, I sat back down on the golden sofa and felt Edythe sit beside me. Naya still stood against the wall where she avoided my gaze. I don't know why I suddenly felt embarrassed, but even in death I could not shake the shameful feeling that came with raising my voice and allowing my temper to control my words. As embarrassed as I was, though, I was not capable of apologizing to them. Not when I was still uncertain I could truly trust all that they were telling me.

"I'm not sorry," I warned Edythe as she smiled softly.

"I don't think you should be. Just as I don't think Warren should be angry with you for asking questions or for being afraid. He asked a lot too."

"He did?"

"Oh, yes. He died before you and Naya joined us, but he still has questions. Even I do, and I've been here the longest." She threw a comforting arm around me and I flinched. Warren had been warm, but Edythe was slightly colder. Was skin just another phantom organ?

"How did he die?" I wondered quietly.

"It's impolite to say. You should ask him yourself. But in the meantime, I can answer some questions if you'd like."

Her generosity and politeness was so strange. Even the way she sat, legs curled to the side and tucked beneath her dress, seemed too formal. Her speech was laced with an elegance I knew I could never imitate. The fabric of her violet dress brushed up against me, thicker and softer than my plain gown. And much more expensive. I imagined that if I knew her in life it would be because I was selling her fresh eggs.

"How can I...feel?" I started, hoping it was not too broad of a question. If it was, neither Naya nor Edythe revealed such a thing. In fact, it was Naya who answered me.

"The same reason you're able to sit on that couch. Or the reason you don't fall through the floor, or even this cliff side right down into the water. It's just some sort of illusion," she grinned, finding it humorous. Her braids swayed as she turned to look out the window, catching the cold breeze on her face and savoring it. "The breeze isn't actually passing over me. I just know it will be cold and refreshing. So it is."

"So I'm not actually sitting on this couch?" I asked, shifting slightly.

Edythe laughed. "Not really. The couch is here for sure, but we...well, what did you call us before? Ghosts? We are like ghosts with the ability to assume our own reality. We expect this couch to be able to be sat on, because that's what we know couches are for. And so it is."

I could not help but stare at her in concern. *Assume* a reality? The afterlife could not be so magical, could it? But then again, I had seen Warren reach into time and space to transport me across the world. I watched him walk through a wall. Perhaps it truly was possible that we were conjuring the obvious into a twisted form of our own reality.

Naya pushed away from the wall and stood in front of us both, arms crossing over her midsection tightly. "You can probably feel your heart beating. Or feel yourself blush sometimes. That's what you think is happening, or what should happen. For your whole life your heart was beating so why should it stop in the afterlife? It's very hard to not be human."

I *had* seen Edythe blush earlier, I realized. I supposed that if she thought she was blushing it would create an illusion for everyone else. I had been calling them phantom feelings, and they really were. Just ghostly sensations that I expected to happen. Like sitting on the sofa, how a dress would feel, or how flesh would feel.

Suddenly, I thought about my father. How many times had he told me all my anxieties and worries were just in my head and they were not to dwell on? I knew thoughts and expectations were powerful enough to influence my reality physically. It seemed even in the afterlife I had been right.

"And my clothing?" I asked, and could not help but eye Naya's outfit with envy. She was stylish and practical in her shirt and pants. Why couldn't I have taken a kick to the head by a horse during a ride, clothed in long pants and a thick shirt? Instead I was doomed to wander the world without shoes, thankful that my thin slip was not see through to humiliate me forever.

"It's unfortunate, of course. We can't take the clothes off," the dark-eyed girl responded with a knowing smile, lips pressed tight. Very rarely did she smile with her teeth. "I'd love to be barefoot like you, though."

"Like me?" I recoiled in surprise. Edythe pulled her arm back to her side from my sudden jerk of moment.

"Of course. I would die again just to feel the grass under my feet. Or even dip my toes in water. Do you know how lucky you are?" She stomped one of her dark leather boots into the carpet to prove her point.

The path to the cottage had been rocky and dirty, but her words sank through me. I was able to feel the water of the stream when Warren chased me. I had stepped into the tall grass and it had tickled my ankles. Even though the path later had been rocky, the pain was merely an expectation. For me, these were feelings that would be possible. But for Edythe and Naya, it would never be again.

My quietness made Edythe laugh suddenly. "I bet you will enjoy the feel of the ground beneath your feet in death even more than you did in life."

It was such a positive way of thinking that I had to merely look away in faux misery. "Why can't we just...imagine ourselves in different clothes or something?" I mused.

Naya and Edythe looked at each other to deliberate my question. Then Edythe gave a small gesture of uncertainty. "It would be like trying to change your hair color or your eye color. It just isn't right."

I snuck a glance at Naya, not bearing to ask sweet Edythe the question that crept to the tip of my tongue. "So...why did Warren look..."

"Like a nightmare?" she cocked an eyebrow, voice hardening. I swallowed thickly, suddenly afraid that the confidence I had admired in her could easily turn into hostile bluntness. "Who knows. It probably has something to do with the fact that everything else in our afterlives is just an illusion."

"Something gets distorted in the way we look," Edythe explained gently. "We do not really know how or why. But it happens. Typically before we're ready to take a soul to their eternal rest."

"So that means you two are..."

"Yes," Naya answered. Her hands reached up to smooth out her braids nervously. "We look like Warren. But he looks the worst."

"Naya," Edythe scolded sharply. Her neck flushed and she cast a hurt glance toward her companion.

"I'm sorry to ask. I just need to know." My own hands flew up to my chest, liking the feel of my phantom heart fluttering quickly beneath it.

I was suddenly afraid for different reasons than I had ever been before. Despite having just met them, Edythe and Naya gave good first impressions. Edythe was sweet and well-mannered, capable of bluntness with sincerity. Naya was confident and casual, intimidating yet softer than I expected her to be.

Neither of them seemed like they could be monsters.

"Don't fret over such things," Edythe said hurriedly, still red. "For now, perhaps it is best to reconcile with Warren. The most important thing to know is that nothing can hurt you here except loneliness. So we must do our best to remain friends."

"Why do I have to make up with him?" I demanded. "I meant everything I said. He's horrible. I *do* blame him for what has happened to me. Who else is there to blame?"

"Yourself, maybe," Edythe pointed out. "You *did* run. You *did* die. That's hardly his fault."

I supposed she was right. I let out a loud, dramatic sigh, not capable of vocalizing my discomfort and worry. Then I stood and made my way toward the door, my feet sliding across the carpet. Before I could reach toward it, Edythe was already there, pulling it open for me with a hurry. She had said she was dead for a long time, and her actions made it clear to me that she was more different from me than I could ever imagine. But I never suspected wherever, and whenever, women wore formal gowns and kept themselves proper in speech and mannerisms would also force them to open doors and windows for other people.

I murmured a small thank you and winced as she pulled the door open for me. The breeze picked up and filled the entirety of the living room, coldness clutching me. No doubt it was making my bushy hair bounce rapidly, curls entangling on each other like fighting, horned coyotes. Salty air filled my nose, and I stepped out onto the gloomy coast, my eyes scanning the open plains for sight of where Warren had run off to.

Nestled on top of the cliff side, the cottage had the advantage of privacy. Like before, the change in scenery from what I had grown up with was surprising. Thick trees and grassy paths were now flat plains of dark, damp moss accompanied by dirt. Miles of green, flat tops spread themselves into the horizon, breaking off into the jagged ruptures of the coast. Down below, the waves crashed against the cliff side, causing mist and wetness to evaporate into the clouds.

As my eyes peered out across the plains, I spotted the bright blue of Warren's collared shirt among the dreary scenery, looking like a little bluebird caught in dark browns, greens, and grays. He was standing on the edge of the cliff, so close that I felt my breath hitch. Whether you liked someone or not did not matter when they stood so close to death.

But of course, Warren was already dead. No matter what he did, he could never die again.

Not wanting to step on rocks, I jumped into the dark grass and halted. My toes squished into the wet cluster, clear water filling beneath my toes as they sank deeper. Mud stuck to the edges of my toenails just as comfortably as they would have in life.

This was something I was imagining? Impossible. Could I truly believe that this was all within the expectations of my mind? The salty air caressing my skin, the wind catching my curls, the press of toes into the wet ground?

I began to jog to Warren, letting my white slip of a dress bounce around my body. It felt good to use my muscles no matter how phantom they might be. They're real to me, I reassured myself coyly. And perhaps I did not blame Warren after all. If afterlife was to be an eternity of questioning, no doubt it was my own stupidity which caused it.

While I ran up the coast, I felt the familiar burn in my lungs that signaled I was exerting myself. It was like running through the forest at home and showing up to dinner with twigs stuck in my hair. It was like running toward the river for water, splashing my brothers when they finally caught up to me. As I neared him, the gray clouds above started to release a drizzle of rain onto my skin, forming a foggy mist that settled on top of the landscape.

Warren heard my approach and turned, half of his foot dangling dangerously over the edge of the cliff. Briefly I wondered if he experienced the same urges I did—to see if what would kill him in life was able to be freely experienced in death.

His face was not as angry as it had been when he left, allowing some relief to flood through me. Relief that felt like strange poison, a traitor trait that revealed my inability to stay mad at someone for too long. Even if I did blame them for my own death.

"Sonnet," he acknowledged evenly, raising his eyebrows.

He was so absurd. Wind rustled the neatly styled hair on top of his head and his hands stuffed themselves into the coat of his leather jacket. I stopped a good distance away from him, fearful that he might plunge himself from the cliff just to spite me. Or maybe I could save both of us the shame and embarrassment by pushing him.

His own gaze took in my appearance, running along the bareness of my feet and ankles before snaking up to the fluff of my hair. I felt vulnerable under his critical eye but kept my face even, determined to prove that he could not win over my affection that easily. Edythe wanted us to be friends. I simply wanted to be able to speak without shouting.

"I'm not sorry," I said, echoing the words I had said earlier to Edythe. But this time

31

I was a little more breathless. "I did run from you. That was true."

"I know. I was there."

"But that was my decision," I explained further, stepping a bit closer. He froze and watched me approach carefully, surprise flickering in his eyes. Now I was the one dangling near the edge of the cliff, tiptoeing with death. *Death that I had already met.* I could feel a strange pull toward the edge, as though my mind was warning me to be careful. As if I still had something to lose.

"I never expected this would be the afterlife. Magic and illusions and...monsters," I confessed.

He turned to look out toward the ocean, searching for something. A ship, maybe? What did he expect to find? He was quiet, so much so that I wondered if I had said something that was wrong. Or something that had hurt him in some way.

"I don't think it's magic," he said quietly with a sigh. "I think it's given to us. When we steal our souls, we get something in return."

The wind tore at the two of us as we stood on the edge, the fogginess over the ocean drifting nearer with every phantom heartbeat. While my eyes remained on Warren, I let out a weak nod of agreement. We got something in return, that was for sure. But in stealing our souls away, what had we lost?

As the foggy mist crept over our bodies, both Warren and I decided to perch ourselves and take a moment to rest. He was more comfortable in letting his feet dangle, but I delicately curled my legs in a similar fashion that Edythe had displayed. It kept my dress from blowing up past my hips, though the sleeves whipped wildly against my arms in the wind.

"Naya and Edythe are nice," I commented weakly. Warren leaned back to rest on his elbows, tilting his chin toward the cloudy sky.

"I doubt they would be friends in the living world, though."

"Isn't that the point? Edythe has been dead for a long time."

He turned to look at me, frowning. "Did the dress give that away, Miss Sonnet? All the same, she's too well-mannered. If I had half the power she did, I would use it differently." My face must have betrayed my confusion, since he continued his next words with a smirk. "Ah, how polite of her not to tell you."

It fascinated me how quick I was to distrust Warren, yet quick to feel defensive of Edythe. Perhaps it was the fact that I had yet to see her ready to consume my flesh and soul, leaking darkness with an open mouth.

"She was polite enough not to tell me how you died," I shot back rudely. "So if she has secrets, I can respect that."

He was not fazed by my words. "The world is as it always has been. This cliff is here. The water is out there. The cottage and everything in it is the same as it always is. But we can never move it. We can never pull out a chair and sit down, it must be pulled first. Did they explain that to you?"

"Something like that. They said it was an illusion for us." I frowned.

"Maybe. The best way to think about it is a living person must do something in order for us to do something. We can only take advantage of the world as the living make it. In that way, I guess we *are* like ghosts. There is only one person who can truly do as they like, and she wears a purple dress."

I suddenly leaned forward, part of my ankle tipping over the edge of the cliff side. My hands clenched together in my lap. "You mean Edythe?"

Warren nodded. "She is the Taker. Like I said, it is a shame she is so well-mannered and kind. Only Edythe can open a door, toss a book, or kick up dirt in the living world. She could really give them something to scream about."

It made sense now that I had thought Edythe was acting like some sort of servant. She opened doors and windows for people willingly, as though she enjoyed to do so. It never occurred to me that she was reaching into a different world, or dimension, or whatever it was that separated life and death. We were loitering around somewhere, and Edythe was able to stick a hand out of it. The sound had been sharp and awful to my ears, perhaps because it was not *meant* for my ears.

My silence seemed to make Warren uncomfortable, and he suddenly sat up.

"And Naya?" I wondered quietly. "What do you call her?"

His blue eyes seemed unreadable to me, lips pressed tightly together. He paused for a second before answering. "Naya has no ability. At least not one that we know of."

"How can that be?" I mused to myself, turning away to peer through the fog and out toward the water. *So in this afterlife some souls are given powers and others aren't?* Edythe could make contact with living people if she wanted to and Warren could travel like some sort of magician. But Naya had none?

Worse, to think I should include myself in all of this. What sort of creature might I become? What sort of terrifying ability would be bestowed on me? I had been plain and ordinary with a life, and had an ordinary, though unfortunate, death. What was so special about me now?

"There's something else," Warren said quickly beside me. He pulled his jacket tighter, then reached down to smooth the folds in his dark slacks. He was dressed so casually and yet formally, I did start to wonder when and where he had died. "Or rather, someone."

"Someone else?" I echoed.

"His name is Marvell. It was always us four before you. He'll likely return soon."

"And what do you call him?"

Warren scoffed. "I'd tell you what he does, but I think it's more important that you see it for yourself. It may help with your little delusions that we are all monsters to be feared."

"Delusion?" I echoed again, despite myself. "That makes it seem like I have reason to make things up. My opinion of you all is perfectly rational, thank you. Where is this

Marvell?"

"Do you think we spend our time just sitting around the cottage?" he challenged. "Wasting away? Even dead people have things to do."

"You can't waste away if you're already dead. Now, stop dodging the question."

"I don't dodge anything, Miss Sonnet. I always face it head on." He sighed. "Marvell is out carrying souls." He leaned back completely to press his back against the damp grass, as well as his head. I imagined that when he stood his clothing would be soaked. Come to think of it, the bottom of my dress would likely be as well.

I pulled my knees tightly against my body and tilted my head, hair sticking up thanks to the drizzling rain. I could see pieces of it in my peripheral vision. "Not to sound insensitive, but Warren...do you know how many people die in a day? And what about animals? Four soul stealers can't possibly help every soul find peace. Not unless they're time travelers or something."

He stared up at the sky but said nothing.

"You're joking," I replied flatly. When he said nothing else, I felt my voice rise into a panic. "Truly? Please, you can't be serious. There is no way I can accept that there are time traveling powers—"

"Oh, Sonnet," he sighed dramatically, interrupting me completely. "I think your parents named you that because they knew you'd always be searching for an answer to something."

I bristled. "Don't presume to know what my parents thought."

He smiled, rolling his head to the side so that he could look at me. Tall grass brushed against his cheek, the ground beneath him looking like a dark background for his pale face. "Don't presume I know how the world works just because I've been dead longer."

I made a noise of disgust and looked away, allowing my gaze to peer through the fog. Thankfully, Warren said nothing else. We sat in silence for several long moments as I swallowed back the burning questions forming on the tip of my tongue. Heat bubbled through me in the form of annoyance, but the cold mist from the sea below us helped cool my skin.

Instead of asking any questions, I said, "Poetry is a search for meaning. Not a search for answers."

I heard his arms scrape against the ground and saw him sit up from the corner of my gaze. I could not help but turn to look at him fully, afraid of what I might find there. Our shoulders were nearly touching, and the warmth radiating from him felt wonderful, like something I had been missing but not quite noticed had been absent. Warren rested his elbows on his knees and folded his hands together, nodding slightly like he agreed with what I had just said. Blue eyes caught hold of mine and searched, just as thoroughly and deeply as they had been searching the ocean for what I thought would be a ship.

"I don't know if we'll ever find a meaning to all this. Or get all the answers. I still have questions, Sonnet," he said earnestly. I felt my forehead wrinkle in confusion and fear. "But they die. Curiosity can die too. It dies every time the sun goes down and back up again. The world moves on, but we don't."

Between blinks I could imagine a flash between his human self and his alternate appearance. The blue eyes, pale face, and boyish appearance replaced with something far more sinister. Swirling darkness, elongated limbs, and sharp teeth that crawled out of my nightmares. I felt my heart leap out in fear, remembering the monster that had ran toward me. Could I even trust what he and the other soul stealers were telling me?

Warren suddenly stood and offered his hand to help me up, but I remained where I was. I stared at it for a second, then peered at his face coyly. "I do have one question. One you better have an answer to."

His eyebrows raised, amused. "Ask away."

"Did you really have to storm right through the wall?" I swallowed down my fear, remembering how nauseous it made me feel to see him disappear through brick. Not to mention annoyed that he hadn't at least gone through the door. "You'll probably ruin the illustrations that are hanging up with your magical, monstrous presence."

Warren laughed, and I pressed my lips together to hide the twitch of a smile that tried to break through while I slid my hand into his. He clasped it tightly and lifted me to my feet, both of us standing together on the edge of the cliff side. The steep drop stretched beneath us as the waves spewed salty mist up toward our phantom bodies.

CHAPTER FIVE

In life, I was unusually adventurous. I had scraped my knees and broken my fingers so often that my father was certain that one day I was going to break and never be able to heal as perfectly as before. Neither of us ever expected that his words would haunt me, as cold as wind over my dead body at the edge of the river.

As adventurous as I was, I still could not swallow my hesitation when it came to passing through a door.

Edythe and Naya had just told me that the world as we knew it was only an illusion and reflected what we believed to be true. Warren confirmed it, implying the world was only ours as the living made it to be for us. And yet here we were with him telling me that I could walk through walls.

"This makes no sense," I whined. "I won't fall through the ground, but I can pass through solid objects?"

"You need to release any sort of expectation," Warren instructed, gesturing to the cottage door, which remained tight and closed. He was determined to instruct the proper way of getting into buildings, fearful that I would rely too much on Edythe's polite door-opening powers. "If you relax and allow yourself to detach from what you think will happen to your body when it touches the door, then you will slide through."

"And if I can't get through?"

"Well, do you know what a haunted house is? That will be you. You'll be stuck in the wall, or you'll get through and not be able to get yourself out. You'll really be a ghost, then."

My eyes turned toward his and he winked, making me flush in anger and distaste. Was he joking? "This is ridiculous. How did we get into the cottage the first time?"

"We passed through the door. And you didn't even realize," he said with a chuckle, then closed his eyes slowly. His features relaxed and I watched any sort of tension dissolve from his face like he was about to meditate. The harshness to his face lightened into a boyish, innocent structure. "This time will be different. You know what you are now. In life, you were a solid thing. Here, you are not. Let go of that expectation. Close your eyes and reach toward the door...then imagine your body going through it to get you where you want to be."

I looked at the wooden door, doubtful. Would I really get stuck in it? Become some sort of half-girl, half-door creature?

"Since when does being dead require training?" I mumbled.

"It doesn't. But being a stealer does. So, are you ready?" he asked lightly, then cheerfully placed his hands in his jacket pockets.

I took a deep breath, my feet sliding across the rocky path up to the door, feeling like I would have little cuts across the bottom of them by now. Around me, the small cottage loomed and its wooden door stayed painfully shut, no sign of anybody opening it for me graciously.

My phantom heart started to quicken, and my hand paused mid-stretch just inches away from the door. The air was still foggy and gloomy, and tiny droplets slid down my forehead onto my nose. I was beginning to think it might be sweat, if that were possible.

"I can't," I said through gritted teeth, ashamed of my hesitance.

"You can," Warren encouraged from somewhere behind me. My eyes remain fixed on the door. "You are not alive. You are no more than air. You're a soul."

A soul. I was a soul. My feet in the dirt, the droplets on my face, and my heart... these were illusions. Expectations of my own mind. I was neither here nor there, and the only part of me left in the world was a body that had been left by the riverbank. I could accept that—hadn't I already? These things felt real to me, but I could face my new reality. I had done it again and again.

I took a long, deep breath and held it. My hand reached for the wooden door and did not falter. As my fingertips inched toward the door, about to touch, I exhaled. *Slowly. Slowly.* My breath made a small wheezy noise as it passed my lips.

My fingertips disappeared into the wood. I pressed further, eyes widening as my arm, up to my elbow, disappeared beyond the door, no more bothered by me than it was by the wind and rain. It was like magic, an ability I had only ever dreamed of as a child. I smiled slightly, pushing myself through all the way, and fought to keep my eyes open as my head passed through the door and into the living room. It felt like simple nothingness.

It was so quick I began to think everything was like death—a single blink and you could miss that it happened. Now having emerged on the other side, I noticed Naya watching me. She was spread across the golden, velvet sofa with a knowing smile that spread from round cheek to round cheek.

"Don't get caught up in tricks and forget you're dead," she snorted.

Even though she spoke with lightheartedness, her words sent a chill into my bones. Could I really *forget* I was dead? Did she? Did anyone? Just as I was about to ask her what she meant, Warren stepped inside the cottage behind me. He was so near that the warmth of his figure helped chase the chilly ache Naya planted away. I stepped awkwardly to the side in order to make room for him.

"Like you've been dead for centuries. How do you feel?" he approved, stepping aside and pulling his leather coat close to his body. He moved to seat himself on the arm of the sofa, but Naya didn't seem to mind.

"I don't know...I guess I'm just surprised that anyone can get stuck, actually. It wasn't that hard," I admitted.

"It's more of a mental challenge than a physical one," Naya explained. "If *that* was easy for you, maybe you'll find out what your special talent is here in the afterlife."

"I don't know if I want one, to be honest." I nervously reached up to pull some curls that stuck to my cheeks. "Sounds like a pain. Opening portals and doors for everyone else? I don't think so."

If Naya was surprised to hear Warren had informed me of Edythe's abilities, she did not show it. Instead, she found amusement in my words and nodded. Tilting her head slightly, her thick braids began to swing where they dangled. "Edythe is upstairs making room for you, by the way. You should go check it out." Room for me? I could feel heat rise to my cheeks.

"It's okay," Warren reassured with a nod. "You're not a burden to anyone."

"I didn't realize I would be staying here..." I began softly, folding my arms over my midsection.

Naya sat up quickly and tossed her braids over her shoulder sharply. They were so long that the ends of them snapped against Warren's coat, tight coils cracking against leather. "I felt the same way you did. We all did. But there's no way for you to go back home, which is where you probably want to go most. You would just be miserable there."

Warren nodded, his dark brows furrowing together as he eyed me suspiciously. "You're a stealer now. Sooner or later you'll start to feel a pull toward others, to help them cross over. But it could be decades before one of them starts fighting you and steals themselves. Then you're stuck with them."

I turned toward the window, liking the way the setting sun promised an impending night. I always felt most comfortable beneath the stars.

"Is this some sort of..." I began quietly, struggling for what word I really wanted to call them. I was still uncertain what their intentions were. They *seemed* friendly. They *seemed* genuine. But each of them were only illusions of what they truly were—they were only half what they appeared to be. I could smile and laugh, but the sight of Warren's darkness was unsettling. To think they were all this way and yet were claiming to be able to help me—well, it made it complicated. "Horrible dream?" I settled on at last with a sigh, closing my eyes. Even the blackness behind my lids was not comforting.

Naya stood from the sofa and stepped closer. Her dark skin radiated beneath the glow of the golden sun pouring in from the window beside us. It would be easy to believe she could be an angel, with her thick lashes and smooth complexion. Even her dark hair had a brown, highlighted glow to it beneath the sunshine. Her hand settled on my forearm, pulling it away from my midsection. I hadn't realized I was gripping my hips as hard as I had been. They nearly felt bruised. Still, her touch lingered.

"I know you want to see your family," she sighed. "I would give anything to see mine again too. You never forget you're dead. Every time the sun goes down and comes back up, it gets a little easier. Not because you're used to it or even fully accepted it, but because that sun is always going to go down. It's always going to come back up. And we'll always be there to see it."

I peered up into her face. Whereas Edythe was delicate and pointed, she was strong and well-rounded. Her soft eyes found mine, and I could read the honesty in them like swirling fish at the bottom of a waterfall.

After a long moment, I swallowed thickly. My voice quivered slightly. "How can I live without them? My father and my brothers?"

"You don't." Her lips pressed together tightly. "Stealers don't live. We just exist."

Her hand dropped and she turned away, silent like a real ghost as she disappeared into the kitchen and beyond, where I knew the staircase must connect to the upstairs. Maybe she was going to seek comfort in Edythe. They seemed close.

"I prefer sunrises myself," Warren noted, falling sideways onto the sofa and allowing his body to dangle off the edges.

I sighed and moved to follow where she had disappeared, passing through the kitchen toward the entryway upstairs. The steps were made of dark wood cascading up through a narrow hallway. My shoulders just about brushed the evenly hung portraits above the stairs, similar to the ones that were sitting on top of the fireplace mantel.

The art was of children mostly, accompanied by what looked to be their parents. In each painting I passed I watched as young, freckle-faced girls grew up to be slim faced adults. Sometimes they smiled, sometimes they did not, but each portrait had its own charisma that kept my attention.

I swallowed the painful sting in my chest that reminded me Vale and Emeric would continue to grow. Their bodies would sprout and change when mine never would. I was nothing more than wrinkled skin pulled from the riverbank, dress muddy and skin sallow.

Was my body still there? The most likely person to find me was my father, no doubt with a spring in his step as he expected me to be idling in the woods after a bath. What did he do in his life to deserve that? To first lose a wife, followed by a daughter not many years later. I wondered if the body and soul were sacredly connected, if I could feel his fingertips across my skin as he dragged me from the reeds. Would my soul shiver? Would my breath exhale a sigh of melancholy as his own tears stained my skin? Would it be so quick, like everything else, that it would happen and I would fail to notice it at all?

The pain in my chest did not lighten as I reached the top of the stairs. The cottage opened to reveal two bedrooms across from each other so that anyone coming up could peer into each one with ease. In the one on the left, Edythe was properly seated on the bed with a book spread out before her. The bed frame was a beautiful wooden creation, clearly crafted by hand, with intricate floral patterns carved into it. Her violet gown looked odd against the blue and red patterned quilt that had been spread out beneath her. Pieces of her copper hair fell into her face as her eyes scanned furiously, so quickly that I wondered if she was really reading anything or just pretending.

I stepped into the room and cleared my throat. "Sorry to interrupt."

Edythe looked up from her book and smiled sweetly. "No need. I've made you some space in this room, if that's alright. We typically rotate." Her eyes flickered to a spot in the corner, cleared out from any sort of furniture. Was I supposed to have something to put there?

"Rotate?" I wondered.

The bedroom was rather plain, as plain as the rest of the cottage. Its white walls had small nicks and bumps from being old, and two windows faced away from the sea to overlook the ongoing plains. A brown dresser with a large mirror resting on top was pushed against the wall, finishing the furnishing. Whoever owned the cottage probably did not visit as often as they wanted to.

"Yes," Edythe nodded. "This room is currently mine and Naya's. The other is Warren's."

"And Marvell's," I supplied, studying her face. She revealed nothing that would suggest this Marvell was someone Warren had made up.

"His too."

Ah, so he is real. I leaned forward to rest my hands on the bed frame, liking the support. It felt solid, tangible. "You like to read, I see."

"Very much so," she laughed softly, drawing her attention back to the pages. "Books never go out of style."

"It's a good thing you're able to turn the page. I couldn't imagine what it would be like to have to find books the living leave open for you." There, I said it. Edythe smiled to herself but did not look up or take my bait.

"Quite a nuisance, dear. But my method would have been to simply stand over the shoulder of someone who was already reading. They can turn the page for you when they turn it for themselves."

My eyebrows lifted in surprise. She did not seem offended that I knew her tricks. "It's all fun and games until they read more slowly than you do."

Warren had called her the Taker, the only one among them capable of altering the real world. I suddenly realized that I had several books stacked and tightly closed around my bedroom at home. Should I have left them open for a stealer to read?

I was quiet for a moment, then pushed off of the bed to head toward the mirror. I expected to see my face peering back at me—tan, round, framed by my hair. Plump lips and almond shaped eyes. But there was no girl there. No girl because I had left her elsewhere, and I knew where.

"You look lovely," Edythe reassured from the bed.

Couldn't these soul stealers just be rude to me for once, and less understanding? It would make leaving them far easier.

"Edythe…" I began quietly, leaning forward to peer at the empty bed in the mirror where she should have been seated. Instead, there was nothing. Not even a small dip in the mattress to reveal her soul was there. As she turned a page of the book, I watched it flutter seemingly on its own before it glided softly back into place. "You all seem convinced I can never go home."

"Is this about your family again?"

"Of course it is. You said the dead make the living meaner. But in what way? I can't see you in this mirror," I pointed with a finger. "I know you're sitting on that bed. But to anyone else, anyone living, it's just empty space. How can visiting my family cause trouble? I'm empty space."

"Just because you can't see me here does not mean I am not here at all," she pointed out. I whirled to face her, tearing my gaze away from the mirror.

Edythe gave a sigh and closed her book. She stood, her formal dress falling to the floor in a rush of purple velvet, hiding her ankles and feet completely. As she neared closer, her small hands reached for mine, squeezing tightly. "There is no rule that says you cannot see your family. We are still souls, Sonnet. But even if you think we are nothing more than ghosts, our presence still has consequences on the world."

My jaw twitched, a sure indication I was going to start crying. A lump formed in the back of my throat. "What if I stop in to check on them?" I whispered roughly. "No more than ten minutes. Ten minutes, Edythe. How can that be a problem?"

The small freckles on her nose danced in deliberation, but she shook her head. "Ten minutes turns into ten years in a heartbeat. Let your family grieve. Don't haunt them."

"Grieve?" I repeated, snatching my hands away from her and stepping backward. My voice began to bounce off of the hard floors, down into the narrow hallway. Hot anger flushed through me, chasing away the lumps of sadness and pain that swirled in my chest. "You want me to let *them* grieve? I'm the one who is dead! I'm the one whose body is probably being eaten by animals, just like Warren said." I tried to imagine my body, soaked, already being torn into from the horned coyotes and boar foxes. "I left myself at the edge of a *river!*"

Flashes of the girl soaked and laying among the tall reeds, blood swelling from beneath her head and cascading onto the rocks pierced my mind. *It's you,* a voice whispered. *There you are.*

"This is why you cannot visit them," Edythe scoffed sternly, dropping her hands. "You are far too emotional."

My teeth snapped together, hands trembling. "I'm emotional because there's nobody to pick me up off of the dining room floor, Edythe. My father has to drag me out of the water, out of the grass and the mud. *Yours* only had to pick you up like a fallen napkin."

Edythe's fists clenched against the sides of her dress. "You're not a prisoner here—"

"Then why am I being treated like one?" I cried. "Why can't I just go home for ten minutes? Five minutes? Let me see them. Warren swept me away here and I was an idiot. I shouldn't have come here. I don't need to see that other side of you. I don't have to. You're a monster too. Just like him."

CHAPTER SIX

Edythe was not startled by my words. I hardly had the chance to gather her reaction before I stormed across the hall to the other room. The only shame I felt came from my attempt to slam the door behind me—my hand, in a fit of rage, slipped through the wood completely and left me stumbling to catch myself from tripping.

Dust and a dampness filled my nostrils, and I immediately went closer to the windows to look out toward the sea. Light footsteps sounded behind me, and I turned to see the quick flash of silver as my intruder tossed herself onto the bed. It was identical to the one that Edythe had been sitting on.

Naya curled up on top of the covers, unable to ever move them, and looked out toward the two glass windows. My hands reached up to rub at my face and I sat on the edge of the bed, turning away from her.

"Everything alright?" she muttered. I considered ignoring her, not sure how much she had heard. I assumed everything, since the cottage was so small.

"This just isn't fair. This isn't how it's supposed to be." I gritted my teeth.

"I understand," Naya whispered, sitting up so she could place a hand on my shoulder. I curled inward toward her, dropping my hands in defeat. "But you're safer here with the rest of us."

"Did you hear what I said to Edythe?"

Naya bit down on her bottom lip and nodded. "It was mean."

The two of us went quiet, laying side by side in comfortable silence. I was shocked at how Naya seemed to mean it when she said that she understood; she knew that I would not want to think about it, not want to talk about anything else at the moment. Like a good friend and not someone I had just met, she let me muse over my thoughts and was happy to stay beside me like a companion.

When the room began to darken considerably, Naya and I curled across the bed and Edythe came in with a lit lamp before slipping away downstairs. I steadily ignored her, focusing on the new shadows that lined the walls instead. I wondered what passing ships thought of the small cottage lit in the dark, sitting on top of a cliff. Ships that were likely sailing from Enya, filled with food and livestock in order to replenish the barren lands of Pushka.

"I'm going to guess that we cannot sleep," I stated after a moment's silence, between idle small talk that refused to go anywhere. Naya was not comfortable sharing her own story, but I had willingly elaborated small facts about my own. My life in Enya. My house and my brothers. My mother, who had died long ago. She received it all without comment.

"Nope."

"Is this what you guys normally do? Just sit around?" My bare legs ran smooth against the quilt in anxiousness. Laying around without purpose still seemed like a waste of my existence. Well, whatever existence I had left.

"No," Naya explained, turning to rest on her side and face me. "Warren has slipped in and out. Edythe too. It's my turn to watch you."

"Slipped in and out where?" I asked, surprised.

"To carry some souls, obviously," she huffed, picking at the end of one of her braids. Seeing my startled expression, she continued. "It's just a feeling. You close your eyes and allow yourself to just be. Then, you'll hear it."

"Hear what?"

"Death," she said with a shiver. "No, really. Souls sort of cry out when they need to cross over. You can hear them from anywhere in the world. If you answer the call, your own soul will take you there. It's kind of cool, until you see the reason why the soul was crying in the first place."

Madness. "So how does that differ from what Warren did before? When he brought me back, he didn't close his eyes. He ripped open a portal."

"A portal!" she snorted. "No, that's how he travels. When it comes to souls, he gets there the same way as everyone else. He had to come back with you last time, and you've never been here before. Lucky you."

"So how do you get back here, to Foxcoast?"

If she was annoyed by my questioning, she did not show it. For that I was thankful, since Warren seemed annoyed at being treated like an all-knowing figure. He had mentioned that being dead longer was not enough to know all. He simply knew what he knew, and didn't know anything else.

I was struggling to accept that as the truth. No answers could just not be. I *deserved* them.

"We get attached to places easily. Like being tethered somewhere. We know how to get back mindlessly no matter how far we wander." Naya shrugged, leaning into the pillow and closing her eyes. She could have been asleep if it wasn't for her woven hair, dark boots, and day clothes. I looked more suitable for bed with my thin gown and bare feet.

"I'm attached to my home and my family. I wish I could go there," I mumbled bitterly. Her hand reached out to grab my wrist, demanding my eyes to find hers.

"You can't go home," she said sharply. "I told you that. Weird things happen to places you think you had a connection to. Time moves differently when you're dead. It's so quick. One day you think you've been dead for a week—then you go home and realize it's been fifteen years."

I pulled my wrist back and searched her face for any indication she was talking about herself, but Naya seemed to just have strong opinions on the subject. I exhaled loudly and didn't bother to hide my annoyance. But I didn't want to fight with Naya too. Satisfied, she sat up. The orange light from the lantern should have cast a dark shadow onto the white wall behind her, but it was absent. A sure sign we were elsewhere—in this room, but not at all.

"I think Marvell is here," she whispered.

I felt my muscles stiffen, listening. Apparently you needed to be dead longer to recognize when other souls were around, because I felt nothing and heard nothing. Warren had said he didn't want to surprise me with Marvell. I wondered why—and the thought made me feel sick. Was he monstrous?

Naya hopped off the bed and signaled for me to follow. I nervously fluffed my hair and pulled my dress back down to my shins, cursing that I felt any sort of obligation in doing so when meeting a stranger. This wasn't the living world anymore—it shouldn't matter what I looked like or how I carried myself. And yet I felt like it did. If I couldn't make a first impression, what else did I have?

Downstairs, I followed Naya obediently through the kitchen and back into the living area. Someone—well, probably Edythe—had placed several candles around to help us see. It seemed, much to my disappointment, that not even ghosts or monsters could see in the dark. Just as I tore my eyes away from one that had been flickering on top of the fireplace mantel, I caught the tall, shadowy outline of a figure standing in the very center of the room.

He was the largest of us all, nearly swallowing up the room completely with his presence. His dark skin shimmered beneath the yellowish hue of the candlelight, casting angled shadows on his handsome face. His black hair was cropped so short it hardly had any length at all and helped give him a tidy appearance. The navy coat he wore was thick, falling down to his knees and framing his neck with an upturned collar. By all means, he was most fashionable and most attractive; more regal than Warren, more sophisticated than Naya, and more familiar than Edythe.

Above all, my attention was most caught by his round eyes. They mirrored the bright, welcoming smile that stretched across his face as he met my gaze.

"You must be Sonnet," he mused softly, reaching out his hand for a shake. His lips curved his words so that I could detect the faintest sound of an accent. I sauntered closer, peering up at him as my hand wrapped around his. His skin was soft and warm, as alive as any hand I had ever held in my living life. "It's a pleasure. I am Marvell."

The fear and suspicion I had in meeting him simmered in my chest. He seemed kind and normal, no sign of sharp teeth or leaking shadows anywhere. My eyes turned to Warren and Edythe, each stationed themselves behind him eagerly.

"Yes," I began with a small clear of my throat. "Nice to meet you."

"It's unfortunate we meet in circumstances like this. But I am glad to see another stealer," he laughed. "Our little cottage will be getting crowded, though."

"Oh, don't worry about that." Edythe said hurriedly, stepping forward so that she stood beside him, placing a delicate hand on his forearm. He looked down at her with a smile. "We're all so in and out anyway. Just one more person won't be a bother."

Marvell studied her face and nodded slightly. Then, he reached for the hand she had placed on him and held it gently.

"Of course," he agreed, leaning down to place a kiss against her knuckles. His dark hand in her pale one was such a contrast that I found myself thinking it was beautiful. The act was so gentle it was sure to be a demonstration of affection.

"You guys never considered moving to somewhere more...um, populated?" I stammered, feeling a bit nervous. They were so proper and so well put together I really was starting to feel like an outsider. I wondered whether it was only a matter of time before they started to boss me around like their own servant. Little did they know that I was from the land of thick trees and wilds, not meant to be stuffed up waiting on someone hand and foot. Wherever they were from, it no doubt was kept alive by Enya's resources.

"When you become attached to a place, it's hard to let it go," Marvell nodded to me.

"We're very lucky to have found Sonnet," Edythe insisted, pulling her hand away in embarrassment or shyness. Her hands moved to smooth down her velvet corset as she tilted her head toward Warren standing behind them. "Warren finally has himself a little companion."

"A companion?" I wondered aloud, stiffening. Her kind words about me were unexpected, but I supposed she didn't want to tell Marvell right away about what I had said to her. My eyes flickered to Warren, who kept his gaze averted. His jaw clenched as he stepped closer into the candlelight beside Marvell. "What do you mean?"

"Stealers can help each other carry souls," Marvell explained politely. "For example, Edythe can manipulate the living world, which can be an advantage to her. I frequently work with her to answer calls."

I looked at Naya, absentmindedly playing with the edges of her braids. "There's four of you without me. Why don't you help Warren?"

It was a bold question, and I knew because Edythe made a sharp intake of breath. While her desire for manners was charming at first, I was beginning to think she would get annoyed with my outright need for answers and the horrible things I had a habit of saying.

"I like to go alone," Naya shrugged coldly.

A strange awkwardness seemed to creep into the air. I searched each of their faces for something else, something that told me they were lying, and found nothing. Their behavior was starting to feel suspicious. How could Edythe's power be any use in helping dead people? What about Naya—her lack of power meant she worked alone? And Warren, what did being able to make a magic portal do for him? My throat burned with so many questions that I began to feel like I needed a glass of water.

My hands clenched and I pressed two fingers to my temple, my forehead twisting in confusion. "This doesn't make any sense to me," I admitted. "I'm feeling lost."

"It would help if you could see what we can do. That will make a big difference," Warren promised suddenly. "If you go with Marvell, he'll show you."

My eyes moved to Marvell, narrowing slightly. "I guess I just don't understand how you tie into this. What makes you so special?"

Edythe and Naya exchanged glances, but I fixed myself on the newcomer.

Warren shook his head, interjecting. "No, telling will not matter. You need to see—"

"You know the Traveler and the Taker by now," Marvell interrupted evenly, his voice low. "Warren can travel anywhere he pleases with the twist of a hand, and Edythe can manipulate the living world to her liking. And I am the Seer."

"Seer?" I repeated, not bothering to hide my surprise and then my doubt. "As in, you see the future?"

"I don't see the future. I see *it*." The wool-clad stranger leaned in. "I see the way people die."

My mind whirled. Silence fell over the room, but I could not find it in me to look away from his face. It was both soft and strong, truthful and honest. The kind of face I imagined my brothers might have when they got older—if they could retain the kindness in them and were not hardened by growing. The kind of face that believed in a cause, and believed good could come from it.

"People...who are already dead?" I calculated.

"That's the best part," Edythe finally said, a small smugness to her voice as she leaned in toward Marvell. "He sees them before they die."

"And then," Marvell teased. "We prevent the death."

My father was a gentleman. I had known him to be kind to strangers, to his children, and incredibly emotional over his late wife. What I could remember of my mother was that she was as gentle as he was, and together they formed a united front against the terrors of my childlike mind. Before Vale and Emeric were born, my father would sit on the edge of my bed and my mother would stroke my hair.

In the darkness of my bedroom, flickering lanterns and moonlight illuminated the space, casting ragged shadows as the light bounced off of the various furniture and books I had laying around. Outside, deep in the forest where our house resided, the wind would howl and shake the trees.

"I'm afraid," I admitted once, shivering beneath the covers. My mother smiled softly, her dark eyes meeting mine.

"What are you afraid of?" she wondered.

"The noises outside. The monsters on the wall."

My father chuckled. "It's just the wind, and those are just shadows."

"But it's still scary!" I cried, reaching for my mother. Her arms wrapped around me, and she leaned a cheek against my small head.

"Hush now," she commanded. "It's okay to be scared. But we're here, and we won't let anything happen to you. Do you think your father would let monsters get you?"

I looked at him for an answer, the roundness of his face and daring smile causing me to hesitate. Not knowing what to say, I turned into my mother's neck.

"Of course not!" he blurted, and his amused voice turned accusatory. "Besides, monsters don't exist. So there's nothing to protect you from in the first place. Sleep well, my love." He reached over the bed and I felt his warm lips against my hair.

My mother's arms tightened around me, but she waited for my father to leave before she spoke again. She pushed me back into bed so that she could peer into my face. "Monsters or not, your father and I will always protect you and watch over you."

Most of what I remembered about my mother was physical. Her hugs, her smile, her voice. I had stored away casual memories like trash, only to try to resurrect them unsuccessfully after she died. Losing her had made me treat even the smallest of moments most preciously. If one thing truly frightened me it was the loss of memory, especially the final ones that I had of my mother, which were well over eleven years old. She died after giving birth to Emeric—sweet Emeric, with his ruffled brown hair and light eyes. Vale was only a year older than him, same colored hair but black eyes like my father. I was seven already when my youngest brother came into the world screaming—and my mother, screaming for other reasons, as she descended it.

The memories I did have were good ones, but the memory of monsters and protection from my parents ached me now as I faced Marvell and Edythe. Naya and Warren departed from the room once it was decided that they would not join to see me witness what it was that stealers were supposed to do. Admittedly, I was still feeling an array of reactions course through my phantom body at their earlier words.

We prevent the death.

I had to witness it. I had to know that what they said was true—and then, only then, would I fully allow the hurt and anguish to flood me. For now, my central concern was what I knew to be true: that Edythe and Marvell would become something else in front of me, monstrous creatures like Warren. It was what "carrying" souls did to them.

My body, typically flushed and warm, felt colder than ice.

My hands shook and I dug my nails into my palms to steady them. All we waited for was a calling—a type of song or wailing that Naya had explained to me earlier. When Marvell heard it, he gathered Edythe and I close to him, the three of us huddled in the living space of the cottage. The fire from the candles illuminated us yellow and orange no matter what we were wearing. Outside, the night was blacker than black.

Edythe placed her hand on Marvell's coated arm, and I did the same. I was unable to stop my quivering, but the sensation of touching Marvell soon drew my attention away. It was like spinning around and around, holding hands with your siblings or your parents in a wide field. But instead of happiness and a swirling sensation, a blurred world, you were left with the pull of stumbling forward, dizzy and halfway to the ground. The falling sensation made me stiffen. I had felt it before, more so than anyone else. It had been my demise.

While I expected something more dramatic, I was simply left with a visual of dissolving from one place into the next. One blink we were standing in the dark cottage, the next we were planted in a softly lit store. I removed my hand from Marvell to examine the hundreds of glass vases on display. Each were stacked on rows of finely crafted wooden shelves. Giant glass windows welcomed in the morning sun, and I tried to read the painted letters that stained them.

"Focus, Sonnet," Edythe murmured quietly. I turned to look where she did. In the corner of the store a rather plump, middle-aged man began to mount his ladder. In one hand he held a vibrant colored vase, clearly intending to place it on a top shelf.

"Well, you don't have to be a seer to tell where this is going," I murmured dryly.

Neither of them replied, but Marvell sauntered closer to get a better look. He looked abnormally tall and well-structured beneath the other man, his coat and shoes further proving themselves as relics of another time. Truthfully, there was nothing ghostly and monstrous about him, and my nerves began to settle. Maybe they weren't monsters after all.

Marvell turned toward Edythe and beckoned her forward. He pointed to one of the vases that was stationed on the lower shelf, a bright white one that I believed would look quite nicely in the cottage at Foxcoast. She nodded slightly, and I crossed my arms impatiently.

Then, as sudden as a gunshot, a younger man stepped into the store and slammed the door with a loud bang.

"Good morning, Mr. Reed," he announced, causing me to flinch in pain. Their voices were as abnormal as the sounds of Edythe opening windows and doors. They were sounds from beyond us, beyond my ears.

"Same to you, Lionel. The order is in the back," Mr. Reed ordered, now at the top of his ladder. He took his time placing the vase in its desired spot while Lionel hurried past him to the back of the store. A minute later, the blond-haired man emerged with a large box, smiling.

"Got it," he confirmed. Just as he was about to pass Edythe and Marvell, each off to the side as they witnessed the living interaction, the former reached over and pulled the white vase from its rest. It twirled onto the ground and smashed, pieces of finely crafted glass covering the floor. Lionel jumped in response.

From his ladder, Mr. Reed cursed. "What did you touch?"

"Nothing, my hands are on the box!" his apprentice cried. I leaned in as he placed it to the side and groaned, disappearing again to the back of the room.

"It certainly didn't jump off the shelf by itself," Mr. Reed grumbled, descending his ladder to inspect the damage.

Marvell tilted his head and Edythe moved closer, placing a hand on his arm. From his pocket, he pulled a shiny, round object and then snapped it shut, tucking it away into his pocket.

"What is that?" I asked, stepping forward. I carefully watched the space where I walked, uncertain if the glass would cause me harm and not wanting to find out for sure.

"A pocket watch. It tells time," he replied, then looked at Edythe. "It's been over a minute. He should have enough time now. Let's go."

"I know what a watch is. How did you get it?" I countered while Edythe and Marvell made their way toward the front of the store, passing through the walls easily. I followed diligently, but not willing to let my questions go unnoticed. I gritted my teeth and took a deep breath before I pushed through the glass storefront, exhaling in relief when I came through unscathed and unstuck.

The three of us stepped out into a street lined with bricks, arching upward in a steep slope. It seemed we were in the heart of a city.

"I died with it. And since I know you're going to ask, I'll answer. It seems that when you steal your soul, you can also steal the objects on your person. My watch was a gift from my brother long ago."

We started to ascend up into the city, brick buildings looming over us two to three stories high. I had never been inside a large city, and it made me itch to explore. I trailed behind Marvell, his wool coat fluttering slightly behind him as he climbed. Edythe stayed close to him, looking as formal and skilled at public outings as I imagined. Her gown slid along the ground, never picking up the dirt or grime it might have in life. The yellow glow from the morning sun made them look like real people and not just ghosts.

"Okay," I said simply. "So, what death did you prevent back there?"

"It doesn't have to be a grand show, Sonnet," Edythe sighed. My eyes narrowed on her back. "Even a simple distraction can alter the course of a death."

"So, Marvell, what did you see?"

"Not see, sense. The younger man...his delivery would be interrupted."

"By what?"

When the words passed my lips, a sudden shriek pierced the air. I cringed, hands reaching to cover my ears as my eyes went wide. Edythe and Marvell stepped to the side of the street, but I was not fast enough. At the top of our climb, where the road finally began to even out, a team of horses broke into a frenzied sprint. The carriage they pulled was dark and black, bouncing wildly as each wheel resisted the bumpy placement of the bricks. Their hooves sounded like thunder as they raced toward me.

I pulled my hands away just as they trampled me, every muscle in my body tensing in preparation for being hit. Though the horses and carriage crashed into me with enough velocity and speed to send me spiraling, I remained grounded where I stood. The light around me darkened. The inside of the carriage was a beautifully crafted masterpiece, decorated in velvet cushions and interior. What I expected to be quick was now painfully, dreadfully slow. The carriage crept in motion around me and I exhaled, my phantom heart pounding inside my ears.

Seated inside the carriage was a girl. Her russet brown, wavy hair twisted into a lazy half-do that let her waves fall down past her shoulders. Her skin was tan yet fair, and her sharp cheekbones emphasized the black liner that coated her eyes. What was most striking was the smear of golden sparkles that covered her upper face like a half-mask. Her body lounged casually, half-exposed by a red shirt which clung to her curves as her bare belly turned into the wide of her hips. Her pants were loosely fitted and made of silk, a beautiful gold that matched the glitter across her eyes and forehead perfectly. Her shirt could have been simple and plain if not for the fact that she had shrugged into it like a jacket, tying it above her navel and leaving the center of her core exposed from her collarbone down to her hips.

I waited for the carriage to leave me in the morning sun, back on the street, but I remained suspended indefinitely. The girl picked at her fingernails, several of her fingers clad in large, golden rings. Before I could find my breath, she smirked, and her eyes rested on me. I was so near to her I could tell they were the darkest shade of brown.

I stiffened.

Her eyes rested on *me*.

"Stealer," she whispered, lips pressed tightly in a knowing smile. "Do you like to tell time?" The carriage seemed to return to its normal speed once she stretched her wicked grin. It ripped through my body in an instant, leaving me to look after it empty and confused. The horses descended until I could no longer hear their hooves fading away. As I looked, Lionel emerged from the store, vision obstructed slightly by the package he held.

Edythe and Marvell moved closer, no doubt expecting more questions from me. But all I could do was stare after the carriage that disappeared, throat dry with one realization. Naya, Edythe, Warren, and Marvell were unsure if there were others like them already out in the world. They had been roaming freely for so long without a sign that there were others out there.

And I had unwittingly, accidentally, found one.

CHAPTER SEVEN

"You're lucky that passed through you." Marvell grinned, signaling me with his head to step out from the street. My hands felt sweaty as I stepped closer, the three of us now loitering.

"What's wrong?" Edythe asked, concern in her gaze as she undoubtedly caught my expression. I could feel surprise coat my features. My lips parted, but I paused. If the others weren't aware that there could be more stealers, then why had I just seen one so soon? I recalled the glittering gold of her mask, her long fingers adorned with rings, and the silky fabric that she wore. She seemed like an oddity, a mystery that my heart ached to solve.

As Edythe and Marvell waited for my answer, I was struck with the realization that I did not want them to know. For the first time I had some kind of power over them. The mystery girl could be my chance to verify what Warren, Edythe, and Naya had told me about the world.

It could mean a way to see my family again.

"Nothing," I lied smoothly, reaching up to fluff my hair. "I just wasn't fast enough, that's all. I've never been run over before."

Edythe reached out to place a hand on my shoulder, nodded, then turned back to Marvell. "Let's keep walking, shall we?"

As the two of them turned, my eyes narrowed on their backs. Edythe's compassion was frustrating, especially when I knew I had insulted her only a little while earlier. Marvell was still a mystery in himself—I was not certain, or impressed, at his display of power. I expected to feel cheated when I witnessed it. I expected to feel like he should have been there to sense my death, and Edythe there to reach out and grab my wrist before I slipped on the rocks back home. But I didn't feel that way. I felt empty.

Who knew that being dead still allowed you to be unimpressed?

The three of us continued to venture further into the city. Even though I had never seen a city in person before, I could not enjoy it properly with the new knowledge I had. Here, each building was laid out in heavy stone and brick, each roof a spectrum of browns, reds, and blacks. Chimneys blew gray smoke and curtains billowed from open windows, catching the warm breeze. As the morning turned into early noon, more people piled out into the streets ready to run their errands. Every instinct in me told me to step to the side and dodge their nonchalant walking, but I found it compelling that they could pass through my body. I wondered if I would accidentally stick to them, but Edythe assured me such a thing was not possible.

"We can get stuck in buildings. Why not people?" I murmured, shivering as a young woman passed through me. She was dressed in clothes that reminded me of Naya. "Where are we, anyway?"

"Buildings don't have souls of their own," Marvell pointed out, turning his cheek to inspect me quickly, peering over the high collar of his coat. "We're in Vena. In Pushka."

I had never heard of Vena before. Pushka was the land of innovation. I had heard that there were cities of glass, of sunshine, of steel, and of wasteland. This, it seemed, was a city of bricks.

"Vena," I murmured, pushing through the two of them. I peered up at Marvell's tall figure, catching his eyes. A flicker of warmth swirled inside of their dark coloring.

"City of time," he explained. A couple holding hands passed through us and I stopped myself from trying to react. The city had been built on a large slope, not bothered to be evenly flattened out. This left most of the roads as steep hills, and it was only until we ascended to a flat clearing that my attention focused on something other than the people bustling through us.

The clearing was laid out in tan bricks, and at the forefront of it was a massive stone architecture. The size of it did not captivate my attention as much as the beautiful, intricate clock that had been built on the outside of it. From a distance, I could see it was expertly crafted into spheres and painted to resemble dawn, dusk, and the night sky. Symbols of the sun, moon, and stars adorned it while pure silver clock hands were stark against the swirl of blue, orange, and yellows. Beneath it, massive golden doors were engraved with images of winged children.

"Wow," I breathed. "A clock tower. What's inside?"

"I'm not sure," Marvell mused, as taken aback by the tower as I was. Though I doubted it was his first time seeing it. "The clock only tolls for some, which opens the gates."

"Yes," Edythe agreed, looking somewhat bored by the conversation. Her hands came together at her waist as she watched the citizens of Vena loiter in the clearing. At its center was a gaping hole, the edges of it blocked off by silver railings. My eyes found a young boy who pressed a golden coin to his lips, then tossed it right into that open hole and looked at the clock tower expectantly. After a moment, he sagged in defeat and took his mother by the hand.

"The clock grants wishes," she murmured.

"If you toss a coin into the well and the clock tolls, the doors open for you to fulfill what you wished for," Marvell piped in with a smile. I wanted to smile back, but I hadn't taken my eyes off the little boy. He was dressed oddly to my eyes, but he reminded me of another little boy I knew. Or two.

"What's the point in tossing coins?" I said a bit too abruptly, my heart aching. "Why not just walk through the door? We're dead. What wishes could the dead still have?"

Edythe looked at me, her pointed nose twitching. "Even the dead wish for things beyond their gains."

"Well, now what?" I turned away suddenly, ignoring her comments. The curiosity in my veins was burned to ash at the new sting of grief that I felt there.

"We can keep walking if you'd like. I'm interested in hearing your thoughts on our ability to prevent death." Marvell laughed softly, inclining his head. "There's a park not too far away we could probably loiter in safely."

I balked, wanting to tell Marvell that I hadn't found his abilities to be that impressive. What did I expect, actually? For death itself to show up, cloaked in black, and Marvell to beat it off with a cane? He was a tall, coated man with eyes and a smile far too kind to truly be honest with. As much as it pained me, I could see why Edythe took a liking to him. He was handsome, soft spoken, and believed he was doing something genuinely good. So, I decided, I could not bear to tell him that I was not easily delighted at his abilities.

The "park" he spoke of was a series of white brick paths that had been laid out beneath vibrant green archways. The vines and sticks reached together to form an archway from one side to the next, providing a plethora of shadow and shade from the warm sunshine for citizens to walk under. Together, we seated ourselves under what I would call a city forest, each small movement of the leaves reminding me of the rustling leaves back home in Enya. I sprawled across the ground while Edythe and Marvell took to an open bench close together.

"So you don't help souls cross over?" I murmured, peering up at Marvell. He looked down at me with a soft gaze.

"No," he answered, lips pressing together tightly. "I have before. But it's not something that felt right to me. Each time I would come upon them it was too early, not too late. And then I realized I could sense the death to come."

"But not everybody's death," I guessed.

"No, unfortunately not."

What a strange power. And again I was left with the question of who decided such a thing. It was hardly fair. I looked at Edythe. Her hands were folded delicately over her velvet dress, wrinkle free and ever fancy. "How many souls have you...?"

"Enough," she caught my eye. I did not shrink back, but allowed myself to see the caution and the sadness that existed in her irises. "I was alone for quite a long time. When I met Marvell, I realized we could join our abilities for something different. Something better."

"Better than a heavenly afterlife?" I wondered aloud, falling backward on my hands. My dress pulled up to expose the bottom of my legs, my bare feet sliding against the rough cut brick.

"Would you not agree that life is more agreeable? Than an untimely death?" she challenged.

"I don't know. Who says it's untimely?"

My question left them both quiet, but Marvell merely twitched into a small smile. "Sonnet, you are quite the questioner. It's refreshing. That must be the essence of life still on you. I'm saddened to see you suffer the same fate as us, but something tells me you are quite special."

"Where are you from, Marvell?" I asked, though my eyes flickered to Edythe to signal that the question applied to her as well.

"I'm from Pushka," he offered warmly. "From a city called Deford, well in the south where it's warm. A coastal port, actually, where all sorts of people coming from Creo tend to land before they migrate through Pushka."

I glanced at his formal clothes and his thick wool jacket. "A jacket in a place where it's warm?"

"I am from Deford. But I died in the north on a business trip. My family, like most people in Deford, are artisans. We were very good mechanics and technicians. In fact, my brother was the one who made my pocket watch."

"That's amazing," I breathed. "I always wished I could create something. I just... well, never got the opportunity to."

"You're from Enya, right?"

I nodded swiftly, and Marvell grinned. "Enya fuels the rest of the world, Sonnet. Pushka would be nothing without Creo and Enya's resources. Your homeland has had a hand in every corner of the world. In that way, aren't you an artisan?"

I could feel heat rise up through my neck. "Thank you. I think what you're doing is admirable, at least. Both of you."

Edythe blinked at me, inclining her head at a delicate and appreciative angle.

Her keen eyes raked across my reddening face. "I'm from Pushka as well. A different time, however, but from a place that was once the luxury capital of the west. That city is long gone now, though. More people pushed east when it became clear that moving livestock through the west was more preferable. And I'm sure you can imagine that where people had money they certainly did not want their land to be covered by stinking animals on the move."

As the breeze picked up and sent the leaves above our heads rustling, I could not help but think I would only ever be able to see things through that narrow scope of life. Marvell called it an essence, but it was more like an awareness. Despite their predicament—which was my predicament now too—they had tried to rewrite it into a better narrative. A narrative of their own control, where they could prevent a death instead of merely cleaning up after one.

The image of the red-brown haired girl, her coy smile and decorative jewelry, flickered in my mind. It was only a shame that the sharp sword of mistrust not only sliced my heart, but now threatened me to keep secrets from the only other souls in the universe that knew what it felt like to exist neither here nor there.

Sprawled under the archway, I knew that I would do anything to preserve the essence that still flowed through me. I would not let go of what I had once been. Marvell and Edythe were not my enemies. But the mystery girl was knowledge I knew I had to protect, and of this I was certain. As certain as the hands on a clock tower.

I was sad to leave Vena if only because I knew that somewhere inside of it there was a girl in a carriage who had taunted me. Marvell and Edythe continued to prevent deaths and demonstrate their power for me. When I was alive, I used to wish for answers pertaining to the afterlife. Now, not even interrupting the course of death could impress me. My mind was filled with new architecture and new people, slightly shadowed by the mystery girl who wore too much jewelry.

It seemed my soul was full of surprises now. When we slipped back to Foxcoast, my phantom heart skipped a beat to think Warren might be waiting. A part of me felt connected to him despite the hesitation and fear that stung my heart. Out of everyone and everything he felt most familiar, even though Naya was proving to be a good friend and Marvell was incapable of anything but kindness. Warren was the closest piece I had to my living self. He had seen what the real me was like—flesh and blood, albeit newly ready to decay.

Edythe was a good friend too. She smiled graciously at me despite my harsh and cruel words. I kept my head down, wracked with guilt when I realized what I must do. Such words were not usually like me, and it left me wondering how much I was already changing. Was it something like what the others had gone through, change creeping in like an infection? So deadly I was hardly noticing it was turning me into a monstrous creature?

When we materialized back onto the cliffs covered in cloud and rain, I turned toward Edythe and politely asked Marvell for privacy. I kept my eyes on his back as I watched him walk right toward the white cottage, his dark coat blowing in the wind behind him. He, I decided, looked like the hero in a story.

Edythe looked at me with concern, pieces of her copper hair dancing around her temples. "What's wrong, Sonnet?"

"It's nothing," I assured her. "I'm just sorry for what I said to you earlier. I should be more sensitive."

"Yes," she said bluntly, turning her chin up. "It was a very cruel thing to say." Defeated, I looked into the lush grass beneath my feet. "However," she continued, stepping forward to rest her hands on my shoulders. My eyes lifted to meet hers. "It is a brave thing to atone for your mistakes. I know this can be hard to believe, but we truly are here for you."

Peering at me now, I wondered just how old she was. Her face had shadows of maturity and wisdom, the kind of wisdom that had no energy or space in being arrogant. It was the true, good wisdom that came from experience.

"It's going to take a while for me to trust anyone here," I whispered suddenly. I felt like a small, emotional child. I wished I could cry or scream. Instead, I looked at her, feeling so numb it made me sick. "I'm afraid of—"

"I know what you're afraid of," Edythe interjected with a shake of her head. She pursed her lips. "It is not my purpose to convince you of goodness or of safety. I can only say that this is a very different place than the world we once knew. And we are alone in it, together."

With a swift movement she patted down my hair and then pulled herself away, turning her back so that her violet gown dragged slightly across the damp grass. I watched her until she disappeared into the white cottage in the distance, right in the same spot Marvell had disappeared into.

A bit reluctantly, I followed, knowing all too well that what she said was untrue.

Inside the cottage, Warren was waiting. I scolded myself for feeling slightly relieved at the sight of him in his brown jacket and dark pants. His expression was neutral, perhaps curious, as he leaned over the back of the sofa to catch my eye.

"Marvell is quite taken by you," he greeted with a snort.

My eyes flickered to Marvell. He looked so small in the cottage. Too well dressed, like Edythe. They should be combing through libraries or admiring an artist's shop full of exquisite work to be purchased.

"I'm glad," I said earnestly. "He is very kind, and I like to be favorable in the eyes of kind people."

"You also like speaking like them," Warren noticed, some sharpness in his voice.

A slight tinge rose to my cheeks. I couldn't determine if it was from annoyance or something else.

"Perceptive," I merely shot back.

"I've been told as such."

Relief gone. He was just irritating.

Edythe stepped up from behind Marvell who had been watching us with amusement. She placed a small hand on his arm and inclined her head toward the steps, probably insinuating she wanted to go upstairs. He nodded and followed her obediently, leaving Warren and I alone.

I sighed and moved to sit on the velvet sofa while Warren moved to lean into the window that faced the sea. "Where's Naya?"

"She's out. I'm sure she'll be back." His eyes watched the horizon and I watched him, studying the shape of his nose and his high cheekbones. It was hard to believe he was the same *thing* that had grabbed me in the water. That twisting, dark creature full of teeth and death. What kind of evil lurked inside of him? Where was he hiding it?

"Alright."

"You're upset?"

"No," I said stiffly. "Just disappointed."

"What did you think of Marvell and Edythe?"

I paused and considered my answer. Would he want the truth or a watered down version of what I believed he wanted to hear? Marvell and Edythe's abilities were unique, if only a bit painful to recognize due to the fact that they were useless for me. I could not tell Warren that my thoughts were elsewhere completely—they were focused on a mystery I planned to solve.

"It was interesting," I decided on. "But kind of bittersweet."

"I can understand that. And it doesn't always work, you know," he pointed out simply. My back straightened slightly, somewhat pleased by his honesty. It was something I valued in other people, and I was beginning to realize that not even Warren could be an exception to that value I placed upon others. "Sometimes things go horribly wrong."

"Well, death comes for us all in the end." My shoulders lifted in nonchalant care.

"I would like to show you something," he said suddenly, ignoring my attempt at trying to annoy him.

"Show me what? Not more people?"

"Would you allow it?"

"Allow...more people?" I wondered.

Now Warren sighed loudly and shook his head. He turned his eyes to me, and I looked back sheepishly, caught in being naive.

"No, would you allow yourself to be alone with me? We'd have to travel like you did with Marvell and Edythe. But it'd be you and me."

"Us?" I could feel my eyebrows raise in surprise. "What is it you want to show me?"

"Just something I want you to see. You've seen Edythe and Marvell's gifts. Won't you grant me the opportunity of showing you mine?"

His words sank through me. Hadn't I traveled with him already? He was the Traveler, capable of going anywhere in the entire world. From here to the next, I had seen him rip a portal like nothing. More importantly, could I be alone with him? Did I want to be?

"I'm not sure," I looked away honestly. "I'm not just something to prove yourself to in order to make yourself feel better."

"I know that," he replied coldly. "And I have nothing to prove. Just something I want to share. With you."

I looked back up toward him. His gaze was soft and honest, so much so that it gripped my chest. Silence fell on the room. I neither needed nor wanted Warren to prove anything to me—in fact, I was already feeling quite confused at my desire to be near him the moment I had left. Yet in his presence I grew wary and easily irritated, like he could be blamed for all the problems in my world. It was a contradiction like no other.

"What else is there to do here?" he laughed bitterly. I eyed him, for once noticing the small desperation in his eyes. Perhaps he was lonely, lonely like a traveling ghost. I knew he could go anywhere he desired without a thought. He wasn't anchored to one place. But what was it worth when Edythe and Marvell were together and Naya wanted nothing to do with anyone? How long could a soul travel the world and its wonders before it grew tired of it all?

I had a feeling Warren might know.

"You're right," I nodded at last, surprising even myself. "Fine, show me."

Warren moved to reach out into the air, his fingers grasping hold of imaginary threads that held the universe together. My eyes studied far more closely this time than the first. His fingers cut through the world as easily as cutting through butter, peeling away and revealing the slight glow of a place beyond.

He stuck his hand through the glowing split in the air up to his elbow, then turned toward me. He reached out expectantly, hand upturned in order to call mine. I met his gaze, blue and lonely, then pushed myself up from the sofa. My hand slid into his and my shoulders tightened. What sort of game was I playing with him?

"It's okay," he nodded slightly. The warmth of his hand was nearly unbearable. It was a feeling I had been missing and denying myself; the welcome and warming comfort of another, someone who felt like living flesh. But as he stepped into his portal and took me with him, a small voice—perhaps the universe itself—reminded me that the flesh I touched was not alive and never would be again.

CHAPTER EIGHT

Crisp, cool wind touched my face when we passed through to the other side. I kept my eyes open as we moved like whispers, the warmth of Warren's hand giving me a sense of security. A small vibration ran through me as I traveled, nothing more.

We stepped into long, soft grass that grew up past my ankles. Before us lay a large lake, perfectly round and the clarity of it a pristine pink reflection of dusk that radiated through the sky. Surrounding the lake were four massive, rocky mountains, each with their own distinction that made them awe-inspiring. They arched upward and high, casting shadows over the painterly scene.

"Where are we?" I whispered. I could feel my legs trembling, perhaps from the travel. Or perhaps from the unknown.

"I call it Peak's Lake," Warren replied promptly. I turned to meet his eyes. "But I'm not sure if it truly has a name."

"You should have named it Mirror Lake," I scolded. Despite myself and how I distrusted him, I felt my mouth widen to a grin. "It's beautiful, like a perfect mirror."

"Call it what you desire, Miss Sonnet."

His blue gaze flashed in amusement though I sensed the sincerity that laced his voice. He was being honest, letting me change the name of a lake. His lake. Suddenly sheepish, I decided to change the subject.

"Why did you bring me here?"

Now something else flickered in his eyes, perhaps fear or uncertainty, by the way he took our conjoined hands and brought it up to toward his chest. My body stilled as he placed his other palm on top of mine, rubbing small circles into my skin. I could feel my phantom heart pick up in a nervous flutter.

"This is my favorite place, and a place I can trust myself to be honest." he began quietly.

I resisted the urge to snatch my hand away, scream, and stomp into the water. What was he doing? *He can't look at me this way,* my brain howled. *Not like he's not a monster. He can't hold my hand this way.*

I could feel my heart getting ready to battle my brain—and the heart, I knew, was a strong muscle. It would win.

"You think I'm a monster." He took a deep breath. "And I'm going to tell you that you're wrong. But a part of me wants to tell you that you're right. There are sides to me that are not pleasant...sides that I can't control."

My brain felt like it was going to ignite on fire. I wanted to stop him already and truly run away, to tell him I already knew how horrifying and disgusting he was. I had seen him when he was swirling blackness and teeth, desperate to feed on my soul and take what wasn't his. Yet my heart leapt out to see him for who he was now—just a soul as I was, desperate to understand what we were.

"I know," I retorted, voice hard. "I've seen it."

Warren's jaw flexed and his eyes flashed, the soft demeanor replaced by passion. "Let me be your monster then. Make me the ghost that haunts you. Just don't turn away from me like I killed you when all I did was drag you from the reeds."

My breath hitched from the sudden change in him. I moved to pull my hands away, but he tightened his grasp. Heat flooded my face. "What is this really about?" I demanded.

"I see the way you look at me, the way you pretend like you don't want to be around me."

"*Pretend*?" I choked. "I am not pretending."

"You do. You admire Edythe and Marvell. You are upset when Naya isn't around. Yet you treat me as though I'm the one to fear. I'm the same as *they* are. I think you pretend that you like them more than you like me."

"You just said you're a monster," I protested. I snatched my hands away and he dropped his own to his sides. "Why would I even *like* you in the first place?"

"Because we're connected," He said bluntly. His features hardened, the dark circles beneath his eyes making him seem unkempt.

I stepped back in surprise, feeling the shock on my face. My brain was suddenly quiet, her consistent hissing gone stagnant. My heart continued to beat quickly, enchanted by his words. A traitor heart.

"You're crazy," I sputtered at last. I shook my head in disbelief.

Warren suddenly smirked. I froze in fear—raw, human fear. The kind of fear that mixed with anticipation and excitement, wondering what he would do next. Not the sort of fear I felt when I had been running away from him knee-deep in a river.

His lips still pulled to the side, he blinked toward me and inched closer. "You feel it too. Don't you? I can see it in your eyes."

What could I say? That he was wrong? He wasn't. Or was he?

He stepped closer and reached for my face, the side of his finger starting at my temple and trailing down my cheek until he followed the slight curve of my jaw. Still frozen, I could only allow myself to feel his gentle touch. My eyes locked onto his, and I felt my brain begging for my heart and I to have some common sense. His eyes were a brilliant, deviant shade of blue, not even the lake could compare.

Blue like a bluebird.

"Warren," I managed to say. A warning and a plea.

He stopped, letting his hand linger near my chin. The smirk on his face fell, though his features softened. "Yes, Miss Sonnet?"

"Please don't."

He was quiet for a moment, assessing my words, then he spoke. "You have nothing to fear. Not from me. It's true what I said—let me be your monster, but I would never harm you."

I nodded slightly, reaching up to take back his hand and pull it away from my face. My eyes drifted to the dark leather of his jacket and stayed there.

How could I tell him that the trembling in my limbs was not entirely of a fear that told me to run? It was mixed with fear that wanted to stay, to tell him yes instead of no.

"How did you find this place?" I wondered, pulling away from him in order to step closer to the lakeside. Grass grazed my ankles before the ground turned to soft and cool sand. I avoided the temptation to test the water, to see whether it would be cold or warm.

"By chance. For a while I had a habit of slipping from place to place to see where I could go. I stumbled here and quite enjoyed it. It's quiet, and the lake always looks different during different parts of the day," Warren explained, no indication in his tone that he had just confessed that he felt we were connected.

The pink and blue in the water quivered slightly, small ripples rolling toward the shore as bugs and fish disturbed the surface. I was thankful that I faced away from him, noting the heat that still clung to my cheeks and neck.

"I've never brought anyone else here before," he pointed out abruptly.

I closed my eyes, reopening them slowly to process my next words and what they might bring. "Then why bring me?"

I heard his soft steps merge closer until he was standing beside me. Unlike me, he had shoes on, which prevented him from feeling the soft sand. Or testing the water's temperature, I realized.

"I meant it when I said we're connected. Something inside of me..." He paused, as though he were choosing his next words carefully. I supposed he might be, given that if he were to say the wrong thing, I had no qualms about running for the hills. "...is very intrigued and very frightened by you."

"Frightened?" I echoed, turning to face him fully. My eyes widened, nearly tasting the hesitance and painful admittance emitting from him. "Of me?"

"Sonnet, I'm not a monster. But I'm a soul with monstrous qualities," he remarked evenly, coolly. That smug and calculated demeanor turned cold, and Warren placed his hands in the pockets of his coat. Pulling it tighter, he looked out across the lake to avoid my scrutiny.

I paused. What was it that he had once said to me? That he was a soul, like me, and not a monster. But the others had cautioned me, perhaps even alluded to the truth that I already knew—that there was a side of him that was very much monstrous, perhaps even dangerous. *The worst among them.*

"Edythe has looked at the folklore—she's stolen literature, laying it out inside that little cottage for me to read over and over. It all says the same. Monsters come from some sort of underworld, where true evil crawls out of. That's not me," he continued. The muscles in his jaw flexed and he closed his eyes, seeing something that I couldn't. "I had a life. I was born, then I died. I remember it."

The question burned the back of my throat, burned me so raw that I almost felt like falling to my knees to quench it with the lake water. Manners be damned, I wanted to know right then how he had died. I wanted to know who he had been. I felt the urge to humanize him in any way I possibly could—even if it meant demanding answers I wasn't exactly entitled to.

My trembling did not stop—it only seemed to worsen at his words. They'd done *research.* Not just meek research, either, but a full investigation. He had suspicions, and so did Edythe at one point, about who they were and why they turned into *things.*

Things that I hadn't even seen. Not really, not aside from Warren. *He's the worst,* a small voice chided in my head. Whatever plagued them—what could begin to plague me—had changed him more than the others.

"When Naya died, I felt crazy. I was changing more rapidly—it started in my hands, then crept up to my arms, then my chest, then my entire self. I was afraid of what was happening and felt sick with fear. The others only have it sparingly—the darkness, I mean. So I decided to try to do something good and give Naya what she wanted. Something she begged me for every single day." Those blue eyes opened and stared off past the lake, past the jagged, snow-capped mountains. I knew they were even farther than that. Watching a distant memory unfold inside of him.

"She wanted to go home?" I guessed quietly.

He nodded once, ever so slightly. "Yes, and I honored that. I traveled with her back to her childhood home. It was a fancy city home right off a busy street. When we got there, though, it was Naya who changed. She turned empty and hollow, wandering from room to room to watch her family just sit around. She wouldn't respond when I spoke to her, and both of us were stuck there for many days. I tried to pass through the walls but they were solid."

I tried to imagine Naya with her tight-lipped smile and clear eyes, braids swinging when she tossed her head. She was the opposite of vacant and hollow.

"What happened?" I leaned forward, anxious.

"Her family started to get violently ill. It's true, you know—our presence does things to the living. It makes them sicker. They stopped eating, started shivering like they were cold, and vomited any food they could get down. I watched her sister vomit over and over on the carpets. I watched her mother scrub it over and over with a large brush in an infinite number of circles. They'd even have nightmares in the middle of night, right when Naya would stand at the edge of their beds to watch over them. I could see sweat clinging to them and terror in their eyes, like they knew something was watching over them."

My heart skipped a beat, caught up in the whirlwind of the story he told. Of what it meant. There were no friendly dead watching over humans. It was something we romanticized while we were alive, caught up in a fantasy that the beyond should be around us.

My blood turned icy, a sudden thought occurring to me. "Are you telling me this so I can stop asking to see my family?" I choked out, not being to help hide the venom that leaked from the back of my throat.

Warren tilted his chin to look at me, finding something in my eyes. Doubt, fear, perhaps even a bit of sickness myself. "Partially. But there's another part of this story you should hear."

I waited while Warren took a deep breath, filling lungs he didn't need to fill. *Phantom habits, just like me.*

"Watching Naya so empty and distant...I began to crave her," he admitted. I felt my trembling go dangerously still, my chest constricting. "It was the first time that I felt that way about a soul that had already been stolen. You wouldn't understand, of course. You haven't helped a soul cross, but there's a craving that makes you want to help them. So seeing Naya like that, I wondered if it was a way for stealers to finally get where we were supposed to go in the first place."

My mouth felt dry—drinking the lake water didn't seem like a terrible idea after all.

"I couldn't help it. I reached for her, not even realizing what I was doing, and that was when she finally broke free from whatever had her so hollow." Warren's voice turned to steel and he sighed, reaching up to tug on the blue collar that poked out from beneath his leather jacket. I watched his long, pale fingers rub the shirt's material.

"Naya likes to be alone. I can't say how many souls she's helped cross, if any at all. She's very private. But I respect her privacy." He reached out to inspect his fingers, flexing them as though they had gone stiff. "We've never spoken about what happened."

"You crave other souls?" I asked quietly.

"We all do," he corrected with a small clear of his throat. If not for the stillness of my body, I was certain that blood would be rushing to my neck at his small correction. *Of course,* I thought. *Of course all of them are monsters, not just him.* "It's hard to describe. You reach for them, hoping they'll trust you. Then they cross over when they do, and it's a rush of everything beautiful that you can possibly feel."

"Deceptive." My lips pressed tightly together.

"And addictive." After a pause, he continued. "For me, that is. Not the others."

"I haven't seen them," I reminded him with a sigh, my eyes burning holes into the mountains. "I've only seen you."

"They're more cautious. Edythe and Marvell are more focused on saving souls than helping them cross." Bitterness coated his tongue. "It used to be different, though. There was a time when Edythe would help them cross and indulge in everything that comes with it."

"I'm not sure if I ever want to help souls cross," I swallowed, feeling the lump in the back of my throat take root. A sudden intensity burned throughout my chest, igniting a fire of stubbornness. "Not if I lose the part of me that is still alive. I know I'm different from the rest of you. Marvell called it an essence, and I think he's right."

Warren took a deep breath as if to inhale the scents around him. That cold gaze fixed on me, roaming from my own eyes down to my mouth. His stony expression didn't break as he muttered, "I never insinuated helping souls cross is a bad thing. But what an interpretation, Miss Sonnet. If you don't help the souls cross, where will they go?"

I wanted to curl into myself and unleash my fiery rage all at once. His questioning made me feel like a small child—his obliviousness to what he was admitting to was making me want to slap him. "You realize what you just confessed to me, don't you? You *crave* other souls. You want to *take* them. You're describing yourself like a—"

"Not take," he interrupted, voice hardening. "We help them. When you get a soul where it's supposed to be, you get something out of it. A universal exchange."

I made a noise of disgust and turned away from him, looking down at the water's edge.

"I'm not a monster," he nearly snarled. I sensed him clench his fists—for a moment, I braced myself, feeling like he might attack me. I remembered his long, shadowy limbs and claws. I remembered white teeth, snarling and salivating—ready to eat me, to devour me, to crush me into oblivion. My body tensed.

Instead, he turned away completely, a small *swoosh* of sand as his boots kicked it up without bother.

"And if you ever try to call me that again, you'll learn the true meaning of being afraid in the afterlife."

CHAPTER NINE

Foxcoast brought back gray clouds, the sea breeze, and a chilly air that had the edges of my dress swirling. I could hear the powerful waves breaking off of the rocks below us, reaching up toward the tops of the cliffs where we stood. The lush, green grass that rolled across the flat plains was wet and sticky against the bottom of my feet.

While traveling back, I had half a mind to beg Warren not to release my hand and leave me in-between the world somewhere. I had no idea what I would do if he tried to release me and let my soul wind up somewhere of his choosing just so he would never have to deal with me again. But he did not let go of me, not even when we got back to the edge of the cliff side and stared out toward the ocean. I released him at once, the memory of his threat simmering between us.

We walked together back to the white cottage, its small exterior like a beacon among the sea of green and gray. I wanted to warm myself within its walls and even sit on the velvet couch, desperate for some sort of comfort. I began to feel the absence of Warren's touch and shivered, blaming it on the cold wind and not on my stupid, traitor heart. I followed him as we disappeared through the doors, happy when I reached the other side and found a dark skinned, glowing face turn toward me as I entered.

"Naya!" I exclaimed with a smile. My heart widened at the sight of her, her long braids draped over her left shoulder. The silver of her shirt shimmered as she moved toward me.

"I was wondering where you crawled off to," she snorted, eying Warren warily. He cast a sharp glance at her and then made his way toward the steps, no doubt heading toward his room. Probably to sulk or cause destruction. Or maybe to sneak away, already craving souls to satisfy him.

"I'm glad you're here," I sighed, making my way toward the couch. I didn't bother to fix my dress, which was hiked up to my knees—though I knew it might be because it was Naya I was speaking to and not Edythe.

The weight of her pressed down on the other side of the couch. "What happened?"

I hesitated, searching her face and eyes for anything amiss. I had been telling myself it was easier to relax around the others, but why? Even though Warren's threat was still radiating through my system, I knew I had been more unfair to him than the others. But I couldn't *help* it. Not when I was only ever seeing the others like fellow souls—and meeting him had begun with a monstrous creature, not a blue-eyed boy. I had met Naya exactly the way she appeared now, which made it easier to talk to her and be around her. Damn it, I wanted to scream. To cry. To curse. To go home.

Home, my mind whispered.

Naya had gone home—and it had made her family sick. I could only imagine what her mother looked like. Like Naya, I suspected, with round eyes and the same braids cascading down her body. Except they would be tied back, and she would be scrubbing the floor her sister had soiled again and again with her vomit.

I took a deep breath and decided it was best to be coy. *Edythe would approve of my manners,* I thought sourly.

"Warren took me somewhere and he...threatened me," I admitted, hoping I could pull away my thoughts from what else Warren had said to me.

"He what?" Naya stiffened, blinking away the surprise. "What did he say?"

"He thinks I'm avoiding him on purpose. Pretending not to like him." I murmured bluntly, casting my eyes to the wooden floor. "It's like every time I start to see him like a normal person—like us—he just ruins it."

Naya was quiet until I looked toward her, worry lines creasing on her forehead. I noticed her throat bob once as she swallowed.

"I feel the same as you," she said softly. "Edythe and Marvell are with each other, and Warren is..."

She didn't have to say it. I could see it in her eyes, in her face, in her body language. She was afraid, afraid like me. Not just of Warren, but of Edythe and Marvell too. I had no idea when exactly it was that Naya had died, but it couldn't have been too long ago. I wondered if she still had the essence of life on her, as Marvell had said was still on me. It would make sense why I felt easier with her.

The sound of high wind pushing against the cottage made me flinch, but Naya didn't move a muscle as she peered out toward the window. "As sorry as I am to say it,

Sonnet, I'm glad you're here. I can tell you're...different."

How similar her words were to my thoughts. I wanted to reach out and grab her hand, my need for touch and contact suddenly too much to bear. I could feel the stinging in my eyes—hurriedly, I reached up to dab at them. My hands fluffed the sides of my hair nervously. "Would you be able to help me with something?" I murmured.

"Not going home?" she guessed, tilting her head toward me sharply. Her eyes stayed fixed on the outside, watching the rain begin to pelt the windows as hard as tiny rocks.

A flash of carpet and retching rang in my ears. "No, something else."

Curious, her braids to the front of her shoulders as she angled her body toward me while I explained to her what it was I needed her to do.

Her eyes sparkled. "Sure. But can we do it tomorrow? I'm tired of traveling today."

Being in Vena with Naya was different than with Marvell and Edythe. Together, we sauntered the streets like two friends taking a morning stroll. The beautiful, brick architecture once again took my breath away. Even the narrow streets were made of brick, young children hopping across them while they headed to their schools. Their clothes were too thick and heavy, nothing I would have worn back in Enya.

"A bakery!" Naya sighed wistfully, hurrying her walk to peer into the glass window of a pastry shop. The windows were filled with cakes and treats I couldn't even recognize—some of them colored to look odd, like green or purple. I had never seen a cake colored anything other than white or brown. "I used to love eating apple crusts in the morning with tea."

"The cakes are...oddly colored."

"Yeah, they are," she nodded, standing up to her full height. "They dye them in cities like these. You've never seen them like that before?"

"No, but I have to admit they still look appetizing. I'm from rural lands—no cities unless you're willing to ride several weeks on horseback. And certainly no purple cake."

"You? A country girl?" Naya caught my eyes and let out a soft laugh. "I would have *never* guessed. Not with those bare feet, slipping on river rocks."

Her comment on my death did not offend me. Instead I felt my mouth break into a smile. "And what about you? I don't see anyone here wearing leather with silver silks."

She tossed her braids over her shoulder, hitting me with them in the process, then kept walking. I could hear the scuff of her boots as they dragged along the brick road, the fabric of her shirt dancing as it loosely clung to her torso. It was tucked neatly inside of her tight black pants. "Not in Vena, at least. I'm from Zarya." The pride in her voice made me smile, a small accent clinging to the way she pronounced the name. Like it was heaven, or paradise, bouncing off of her lips.

It sounded familiar to me, but after a moment of walking I gave up trying to find it tucked away in my mind. "Is it here in Pushka? What kind of city is it?"

We rounded the end of the street and came to the center of Vena, the openness of the city center now filled completely with a market. Vendors of all sorts tried to sell their oddities, and a brief glance at the closest merchant revealed several glass plates, each vivid in colors of red, blue, and orange. The woman selling them looked worried.

"Yes, it's in Pushka. It's a city of metal, and it's beautiful. The buildings are so tall they can see all the way across the land. Every home is built sturdy and strong...we import the iron from Creo's mountains and create steel."

My mind jumped to the image of a young Naya, running through streets made of sleek metal surrounded by tall buildings. "Do you visit?" I wondered, watching as the woman selling the plates attempted to persuade the citizens of Vena to purchase something. I wished I was alive and had money so that I could take one. It might even look good in the cottage, set upon the fireplace mantel.

"No," Naya grimaced. "It's too painful. I have considered moving there, though."

"Moving there?" I whipped around to face her, both of us stopped among the crowd. Their bodies passed through us, not even bothered that they were walking right through ghosts.

"Yes. But that has complications of its own...as much as I hate being stuffed up inside of that cottage, I hate being alone even more."

Her words sank through me. They didn't add up to what I knew of Naya—that she enjoyed privacy and being by herself. The others had mentioned that she spent time slipping away by herself, so where was she going? The question burned my lips, but I made a conscious effort to keep them to myself, fearful that asking them now wasn't the right time. Soon, I knew, Naya would reveal her secrets.

Or maybe she wouldn't. Maybe we were all doomed to keep things to ourselves. That was fine, wasn't it? The dead have secrets. Just like the living.

"That's true, I guess," I finally said. "I've thought about it myself. Just going back home and wandering the woods." Naya sighed but stayed quiet.

"What business do you have returning to Vena?" she mused at last.

"There," I jerked my chin. I reached out to point a slender hand toward the tallest building in Vena—the one that overlooked the center with all its citizens scrambling to buy goods. There the clock depicted a beautiful display of the current time. The different hues of blue and gold stood out against the brown building. Below, the golden doors carved with winged children were sealed shut. "My business is there. We're going to go inside of that clock tower."

"The clock tower?" She eyed me skeptically. "Why?"

"Marvell says it's off limits. But I think there's going to be something very valuable in there," I murmured, not bothering to linger away from it any longer. I cut through the city's center, Naya trailing at my heels. As the tower neared closer, I found my heart beginning to quicken, desperate to run right through it entirely.

"I don't exactly agree that it should be off limits, but what is it you expect to find?" Naya scoffed, arms crossed while she watched me assess the golden doors. My eyes scanned the intricate carvings of the winged children, expecting some sort of inscription. For doors that were supposedly meant to open to the greatest desires of those who tossed coins into Vena's black hole, it wasn't very forthcoming. It made no such promises outside of being a door.

"I don't know if I should tell you just yet," I said simply, running my hands along the smooth carvings. "You'll see for yourself if we get to the other side and I find what I'm looking for." My eyes flickered up to the clock tower.

There she was—burned onto the inside of my brain. Ring-clad fingers, bare skin, and a wicked grin. I had made the connection when I saw Marvell's pocket watch, the flash of its small fingers connecting with two distinct memories inside my brain. I had seen the mystery girl in the carriage, and she had asked me if I liked to tell time—no doubt alluding to the fact that Vena had its very own clock tower. It seemed as though she liked to play a little riddle of her own, knowing I would want to find her once more. And what better place to look than the clock tower of desires?

I hoped that I was right. I suspected she was hinting toward the place where I could find her again. And with her, it meant I could find more answers. The stealers had given up information that I could only take at face value. I was not entirely sure I trusted any of them yet. Even Naya, close as I was beginning to feel toward her, felt off-putting to me. Like each of them had secrets they didn't want to share. Like they wanted to keep me at a distance, a place where I accepted everything they said as the end-all truth.

Naya shrugged, not bothering to pry too deeply into my attempts at sleuthing. "That door is very solid. Do you think you'll have trouble getting through it?"

"I hope not. I haven't gone through any thick walls yet. How hard can it be?" I pulled back and braced myself, remembering the coaching that a certain monster had given me.

"Hard," she said quickly, stepping forward to catch my attention away from the door. "I'll go first—so you can watch me and mimic what I do. If you get stuck, well... at least you got stuck in a pretty clock tower."

I couldn't smile at her lighthearted words, not when my mind was so focused on what lay beyond the wall. Would the girl be waiting? Would she even be there at all?

Making a demonstration, of herself, Naya took a deep breath. I watched her shoulders move up and down in phantom breathing before she reached toward the door. Where my hands had fallen flat against the marble to feel it, hers slipped through entirely. I swallowed nervously, recalling the displacement of expectation from one's mind. Right now Naya would be fighting every instinct that braced her for how the solid door would feel. Instead she was willing herself to believe the door could be passed through completely—that she had free reign of its solidity.

My body went still as Naya disappeared through the door to leave me out in the open. Coldness suddenly gripped me.

Okay, breathe. Release your expectation.

I felt my phantom lungs expand to grasp the air around me before letting it out slowly. To avoid looking at the marble carvings, I closed my eyes, reaching an outstretched hand toward the door. It would be able to be passed through. It was not real and it was not solid, this I knew. I could work with that. I would never get stuck in the door or get blocked, since I had the ability to go through solid objects now...

My eyes shot open just as my shoulder pushed forward through the door. Right before my face was about to pass through, I began to panic, so close now that one of the children's arms was curved above my eyebrow. I was inside of it!

Keep going—don't panic. It's not solid, it's not solid, it's not solid. Inside of the door was pitch black, then a burst of light caught my eyes.

The beauty beyond the door was unthinkable. So much so that I nearly tripped over myself completely, pulling my entire body free at last. No celebration came from either myself or Naya, who was standing wide-eyed beside me. In front of us was an elegant room, so wide and deep that it could fit a hundred of our little cottages all at once. The floors and the walls were made of glossy marble, carvings of vines and trees swirling up on six large posts that were centered in the room and reaching toward the ceiling. That ceiling! It had been painted a dark blue and adorned with the colors of the sky, jet black to the pale break of a golden morning.

I looked to Naya, but she was far less enchanted with the architecture than I was. Her eyes had fixed on what was across the room at the very end. A good lengths away, but I could make out what it was that had shaken her quite so. There, settled upon a marble throne, was the mystery girl. Without looking at Naya once, I stumbled forward and started to make my way toward her. My feet were ice cold as they shuffled across the pristine floor, so different from the water, mud, and warm brick that I was slowly getting used to. I could hear Naya's soft steps trailing behind me, but my stride did not lack in determination and purpose.

The mystery girl's brown hair fell into thick waves past her shoulders, her navel and half of her chest exposed by the slip of a red shirt that she had tied in her middle. Her golden pants matched perfectly with her jewelry, shoes no more than soft slips that reminded me of what I might pair with my gown. She sat so regally, with her ankles folded behind each other, arms stretched outward to grip the rests on her throne.

And she wasn't alone.

Beside her, perched upon a second throne, sprawled a man radiating with so much darkness and night that I could not look away. If the mystery girl was everything exotic and beautiful, clad in warm tones, he was her cool and enchanting counterpart. Like Naya, he wore silk; however, his black shirt tucked into black pants was covered by a well-fitted jacket. Dark gold embroidery covered it completely, adorning his all-black attire with leaf-like accents. His jet black hair, sticking up slightly from the top of his head, matched perfectly with his deep set, dark eyes. The only thing fair on him was his light skin.

She was a lioness—this was her panther.

"Well," she chuckled. "Stealers do listen after all, don't they?"

Refusing to look at Naya, I felt my brain try to put together words. Sensing our shock and speechlessness, the panther pulled his jacket tightly around him.

"You didn't quite mention how beautiful the new stealer was," he laughed, a short and bleak one. Then he turned to his lioness. "Do only beautiful people steal their souls away? It's like we know we can't just *die*. We need to make a spectacle of things."

His voice was boyish and charming, different from the deadly cunning that I had expected to come from him.

"Who are you?" I finally managed. My eyes fixed upon the mystery girl, desperate to know who she was and how I had come to find her. Even more so, how she knew of the stealers...and how they *didn't* know of her. Whether or not the questions blazed in my gaze I could not know, but each of them looked at me and me alone.

They exchanged glances, the panther inclining his head slightly as if to encourage his fellow partner to do the honors of their introduction.

"Very well," she murmured, tapping her fingers against the arm rests. "My name is Kezia and beside me sits your grand leader, Leander. We are the rulers of this realm, and through our governance all who inhabit it are at our mercy. And yes," she suddenly laughed, a warm and feminine sound. "That includes *you*."

CHAPTER TEN

Kezia should have snickered afterward, casting a glance toward her panther called Leander. She should have stood from her throne and shrugged nonchalantly, explaining that she was only joking and everything she had just said was untrue. But she didn't. The lioness fixed her powerful stare on us both, willing us to accept her position as a ruler.

"You can't rule this place," I found myself saying numbly. What did I know, though? Nothing—I was brand new and they could have been dead for years and years.

"Can't?" Leander echoed, his fingers moving from his jacket to the bottom of his chin. He tilted his head to the side and looked upon me with amusement. "We *do* rule this realm. It is ours and always has been. The stealers can attest to that, can they not?"

My breathing caught and I went rigid, dragging my eyes to finally look at Naya. Her round face and honey eyes were cautious, suddenly uncomfortable. "The others know about this?"

"I don't know," she murmured, her gaze flickering between the three of us. Her face melted into something soft as they rested back on me. "But maybe it's time to explain what *you've* been hiding, Sonnet."

"I saw this girl when I first came to Vena," I turned to look at Kezia. Her painted red lips were curled into a dangerous smile, smug and proud upon her perch. "I knew then that we were not alone and what you all have told me are lies. There are other souls here—so I wanted answers. That's what I came for."

Naya would understand, wouldn't she? If there was anyone who could understand the longing I felt for concrete answers, to grip a small bit of truth to what Edythe, Warren, and Marvell had told me it would be her.

"The stealers may not know who or what we are," Leander scoffed. "But we certainly know of them."

"That is the truth," Kezia nodded.

"Are you souls or something else?" I demanded, not bothering to hide my excitement and my desperation.

"Souls we certainly are, my dear." She winked, finally standing up from her seat. I stayed very still while she sauntered toward me, just as close as she had been in the carriage. The red hue in her hair was easily seen up close, her eyes just as dark while they bore into mine. Like everyone else, she stood taller than me. "And we're so terribly sorry for your death. Leander and I felt a ripple in the realm when you decided to steal yourself away. It was quite brave of you to run from that creature."

Warren.

"Yes," she sighed, seeing the recognition in my eyes. "Souls we all are, but we are without the affliction the others have. Aside from you, of course. That makes three of us."

Naya's leather boots stomped against the marble floor. She was next to me in an instant, her braids swinging across her shoulders. "Affliction?"

Kezia's feline gaze snapped to Naya. For several seconds she merely assessed her, then seemingly decided that whatever fight she was going to start was not worth it. Behind her, Leander stood to his full height. He was tall, nearly as tall as Marvell, when he approached the three of us.

"You know what they mean," I said softly to Naya.

"No, I don't think I do," she shot back.

"Why Warren looks like...like a monster," I choked out, reaching out to grab Naya's arm. "Now that I know you're all souls, please, this is the only way we can find the answers we're looking for."

"*Now* that you know?" Her eyes narrowed, pulling her arm away roughly. "You thought we were all, what, evil?"

"I...I didn't know," I confessed, my voice quivering. The words that came rushing out next carried across the room in a hushed whisper. "Warren told me what happened when you went home—these two may be able to help. They don't have what he has."

The words were wrong. Naya's soft face turned to stone as she looked at me, her long lashes suddenly wet with fury. She laughed, the hollowness of it reminding me of the hollow that Warren had described inside of her once before. A hollowness that she had kept tucked away somewhere. My phantom heart gave a twinge of regret and panic, beating violently against my ribs.

"What else did he tell you? Did he tell you that he *attacked* me? That I looked into his mouth full of teeth and escaped with this so-called life?" She shook her head. "I'm not looking for answers, Sonnet. We're *dead.* Nothing is ever going to change that. Not talking about home, not accusing people of being monsters, and certainly not clinging on to whatever so-called *rulers* have to say about it. And it's not only Warren, by the way. If you think he's a monster and he's evil, then we *all* are."

It didn't bother her that she turned past so me so sharply her hair nearly collided with my cheek. I watched her go, leather hitting hard against marble before she disappeared back through the golden door. When I peered at Leander and Kezia, caution and pity welled in each of their eyes.

"Do you see now why I'm here?" I begged swiftly, my eyes burning. "I need you to tell me everything you can about what, and where, we are."

"Of course," Leander bowed, voice soft. "Why don't the three of us talk over breakfast?"

The hall that Leander and Kezia guided me through was every inch as beautiful and elegant as room with the golden doors. The walls were intricately designed and pure white, stretching toward a flat ceiling that served as a crystal clear mirror to the activities in the room beneath it. Accents of gold and black gave the room a rich and expensive appearance. Their palace, it seemed, was hidden right in the middle of a city made of brick.

Breakfast turned out to be an assortment of open books sprawled across a wooden table. They were accompanied by several pieces of bread, each turned sour from age. Even from afar I could see the wide circles of black and green that coated their crust. Cups of tea, long forgotten and gone cold, were scattered about. Even a solid gold kettle stood as decoration against the dark wood of the dining table.

Leander took a seat, motioning with a hand for me to take the empty one adjacent to him. Kezia leaned forward on the table with her palms, her eyes sweeping over the books. *She's seeing if they've changed at all,* I thought. *If some living person had come in to flip the page.*

"I'm sure this must be very confusing," Leander started, resting his rounded face in the palm of his hand. "Where should we start?"

I felt myself blink at him wordlessly.

"We can start with your death," Kezia decided, looking up from her inspection to catch her panther's eyes before she rested on me.

"No," I swallowed. "I want to talk about where we are, not about me. You said this is a...a realm?"

"Do you know what a realm is?" Leander wondered. I bristled, feeling my brain push against any form of teasing or scrutiny. I was surprised to find that his face was soft as he looked upon me, body relaxed and chin still propped.

"Of course I do. I'm not stupid. But I don't know how this could be a realm. Is this not death? The afterlife?"

"It is," he shrugged. "Just as it isn't."

"We are in a realm that exists alongside the living realm. Whether there actually is an afterlife we cannot truly say for sure," Kezia acknowledged. "When we died, our souls left the living realm and ended up here. Either through misfortune or something else."

"Misfortune?" I found myself echoing, picking the unusual word in order to criticize them. "What a strange thing for *rulers* of this realm to say. I would have thought you'd consider us lucky."

"You seek answers, we give them, and yet you don't believe us." Leander's mouth quivered with amusement. He picked up his chin and gestured to the books that were sprawled on the table between us. "Imagine that a single book and binding is the entire universe. Each page represents a realm. We were used to being on one page, and now we are on another."

"Another story to live through and tell," Kezia sighed wistfully, swirling one of her golden rings around her index finger.

"And in this realm you two are its grand rulers?" I stiffened, sitting up straighter. "Am I supposed to serve you?"

"Wouldn't that be a delight?" Leander chuckled, a charming and warm sound. "Would you prefer to call me *Your Highness*, sweet one?"

Warmth rushed to my face, overheating me instantly. My heart kicked against my ribs.

"Leander and I govern the realm because it is a dangerous one," Kezia explained, leaning back onto the table. I briefly wondered if she ever got annoyed by the bareness of her skin. The slight curve of her breasts, her bare sternum, and her midriff were all exposed and always would be. She would never be able to wrap even a blanket around herself when she felt like being modest.

"What do you mean it's dangerous?"

"This realm is not where we go to wander for eternity. We live in a realm full of wraiths." A flicker of muscle moved in her jaw, her lips setting into a flat line. "We meant it when we said that us three are the only souls in this realm that are not corrupted. The others have been turned into creatures—nasty, foul things that take advantage of the living."

The venom in her voice made my chest ache. What I believed, what I had accused them all of...every bit of it was the truth. Warren really *was* a monster, a corrupted soul that was once a person. That once had a life. And not just him. Edythe and Marvell too.

Naya.

"They...they said they help souls cross over," I faltered. My hands and legs began to tremble. I reached forward to grip the table for support, wishing desperately that I could knock the books out of my way in frustration. "Helping them get to another place."

"They lied," Kezia hissed. "We are not gods. We can do no such thing. There's a reason why we've crowned ourselves rulers. We are both masters of this realm because we're the only ones who haven't been tempted to devour other souls. The stealers are under the false impression that they're doing anything other than terrorizing their own entities."

Leander cast her a worried glance, lips tight.

"And neither one of you have stopped them?" I gritted my teeth, my knuckles going white from holding myself steady. "They are souls too. Naya and Marvell and Edythe...even Warren. You've let them continue to turn into monsters. Do you have *any* idea what they even look like? What they've transformed into?" My voice raised to a high pitch.

"We do, and you don't," Leander said calmly. He pushed out of his seat and lifted his hands to surrender. His prowling, charming demeanor had suddenly turned diplomatic and cautious. "You've seen...what, one of them? The worst among them?" His words made me freeze. Sensing the shift in my body language, Leander went on. "Kezia and I have tried to help them. We have tried and failed."

"What have you done?" I argued. "Other than hide in the shadows?"

"We," Leander said stiffly, "are the shadows. We are in every nook and cranny from here to Enya and Creo. We are the tiny particles of dust sitting upon the windowsill in that little white cottage, and we are the slippery rocks which kill beautiful, green-eyed girls."

"How can I believe either of you? I came here for answers, not for self-righteous talk."

"Your stealers may have power beyond your living imagination, but we are the true power," Kezia scowled, taking a place beside Leander.

I balked, wondering where in the universe the fear that was beginning to wash over me had come from. I was no subject—I had died a free soul and I would live freely in whatever realm I wanted to. These were not my rulers. They were not my king and queen.

"Under whose authority are you rulers?" I challenged. "I'm as much as a soul as you are. I am no creature."

"Show me your ruler's gift, stealer," Leander nearly purred, reaching to pull his jacket more closely. I could feel his dark caress on my cheek, my neck, right down to my ankles. "And then we will look on you as an equal."

Just as my lips parted to respond, the black-haired ruler opened his hands. From the ends of his wrists where his jacket ended a thick, blue vapor began to materialize. I watched it with both fascination and terror as it swirled around his hands like a curious snake. Then the vapor rose into the air, slithering in circles before it came for me in attack. The smoky substance wrapped around my arms and my neck, tightening so that I was bound to the chair I sat in. *It's not real,* my brain screamed. *It's not real!*

My chest began to tighten and I panicked, pushing back against the mysterious power with all my might. My legs kicked, desperate to lift me free from the chair, but the blue haze gripped me firmly. As I inhaled the substance, I felt it scrape against my throat, dryly choking me.

"We are not the only beings in this realm," Kezia said suddenly, watching the challenge in my eyes dissolve into terror and disbelief. "Leander and I were gifted with incredible power far beyond what was possible in the living world. We use it because we have to."

"They...have power...too," I rasped, resisting the invisible binds that kept my wrists from bending away from the table.

"Oh, we know," Leander chuckled, a tall menace with his dark outfit and swirling blue smoke curling around him like serpents. "But it's nothing compared to what we can do."

My eyes rolled to the ceiling, staring into the iridescent shine that came from the mirror. It perfectly reflected the room beneath it right down to the moldy bread that lay across the table. What was missing was the three of us—just absent beings, calling ourselves rulers, bestowed powers I wasn't sure we deserved. That I was not sure were even real. I closed my eyes tightly, flashes of images suddenly cutting across the blackness.

A frozen river. Bundled tightly in jackets, the crunch of boots pressed on the outer layer of the snow. It had frozen and was so hard none of our feet were breaking through the surface. It made following my footprints that much harder.

I tilted my head, turning to see both boys running past me toward the river. They kicked small flurries of snow storms as they went, shimmering like glass under the morning sun. An odd time when the wind and sunlight were warm but the temperature was cold enough to freeze the rain.

"Race you there!" one of them snickered.

"Too slow, freeze-brain!" the other teased.

I wasn't much for running, but I figured I'd give chase anyway. A broad grin stretched across my face and I kicked myself forward, knowing they'd reach the river completely before I did.

"Strange..." Leander suddenly murmured quietly. I heard his footsteps inch closer, felt him lean over to inspect me. My throat wheezed from being held captive by his horrible gift. "There's something about you...something I can sense. I can almost taste it."

An essence, I thought. Life. Something they didn't have anymore. Something I was desperately trying to cling onto however I could.

He must have seen recognition on my features. "You know what I'm talking about, don't you, sweet one?"

"Leander?" Kezia's pitch altered slightly, giving away her curiosity.

The three of us gathered around a circular stone pile, each stone smaller than the one piled before it. It was a small, beautiful decoration that we kept near our house. The grass was finally turning from green to brown, a promise of the new season. A season of birth and growth, ready to bring warmer days and joyous laughter.

We each had a handful of lavender bundles grown especially for this occasion. The first boy, slightly taller, leaned down to press the lavender between the rocks. The second followed suit, then stood up straighter and with pride.

When it came my turn, I tucked the lavender between two rocks. They were warm and hard as they scraped against my fingers, yet I knew they would caress the delicate flowers with the utmost care. When I was finished, I wiped my hands against my shirt and folded my hands in front of me.

"Happy birthday, Mom," I sighed.

Behind my closed eyes, tears pooled. No—no, I couldn't think about this. I couldn't *see* this. Water threatened to spill down my cheeks as I coughed, heaving against Leander's smoke and the memories that flooded me.

I would never again place those flowers. I should have cradled them to my chest and inhaled deeply, savoring the sweet smell of them before I tucked them away. I should have held my brothers far more closely, keeping them warm and giving them a smile that promised everything would be okay.

The universe had stolen away my life and the promise that had been given to me throughout it. The promise of an afterlife where I could wrap my arms around my mother again and patiently wait for my brothers and father to join us. Instead, I was cursed to roam in a realm full of monsters. Paradise, heaven, whatever you wanted to call it—it had been *stolen* from me.

Rage flowed throughout my veins. Rage toward whatever being had crafted this life for me—had made it a part of my grand plan to slip and fall. I did not die of sickness or unfortunate health. My body was strong, my mind was strong, and I had more to offer the world than to disappear like something insignificant. My undoing had been so simple it was maddening, an injustice that burned through every inch of me.

"You can't hold me down," I choked, opening my eyes with a snap. My teeth made an awful scraping noise as I clenched my jaw, fingers now hooking deeply on the wooden table. The smoke around me tried to curl more tightly. Leander's eyes scanned my face in surprise. I could feel the world around me beginning to quiver like an earthquake, building up power that felt like the beginning of an explosion. But all I could see in the back of my mind, the back of my eyelids, were memories of a life I refused to let go of.

"And why can't I?" Leander argued, eyes narrowing in focus. More smoke coiled from his body to race toward me. It danced in the air, searching for the best way to enter me, before plunging for the kill.

"I am not a monster or a wraith or a creature. You can't control me." The air around me began to quiver.

"You're nothing," Leander said simply. His voice was even as he hurled the insult toward me and my anger latched onto him like a leech. "Just a girl who slipped on a rock, destined to be as corrupt as her little friends."

I opened my mouth to scream, but no sound came out. My memories of life were replaced by different ones—Naya's face, Warren's eyes, even Edythe and Marvell. Except they were holding onto each other as delicate and proper as always. Monsters? No, just souls.

Souls like me.

The vibration around me ceased to exist. Then, it ignited in ripples. A flare of light erupted, burning my eyes. I blinked rapidly against it, catching glimpses as the blue smoke got caught in the light and fizzled out with a snarling hiss right where it hovered. They were like snakes being thrown into a fiery pit of light and wind. As Kezia and Leander began to reappear, I felt the release of my anger disappear with a harsh pop, their hair tossed and eyes wide with surprise.

What was most interesting is that they weren't looking at me at all. Their eyes, as round as saucers, were fixed on the table. Before, the books and journals had been sprawled out as though someone was doing unfinished research. Now the wooden table lay clear, and I didn't have to look up toward the mirror to see that they all had been swept off the table where they now lay dormant on the floor.

CHAPTER ELEVEN

The rulers quickly fixed their expressions. First Kezia, then Leander. They dragged their eyes toward me and accessed me in a new, different light. The surge of power that flowed through me left me feeling anxious, my legs bouncing in anticipation. Now freed from the vapor that tied me to the chair, I stood and flexed my fingers.

"How dare you do that to me," I managed, throat still dry.

Briefly, Warren came to my mind. He had once said that the only being able to alter the living world was Edythe. I had seen it with my own eyes—her power was certainly something to be envious of. I never imagined that I might have a part of it too. In fact, I was not even completely sure how I had managed to do it.

"I asked to see your ruler's gift," Leander cleared his throat, reaching up to fix his hair. He rotated his neck in a faux display of releasing tension—I half expected to hear a sharp crack from his muscles that stretched beneath the skin. "And you certainly delivered. What secrets *are* you hiding, sweet one?"

Secrets, my mind echoed. I met his expression evenly. No doubt they would see the surprise echoed in my own eyes, but they thought I had secrets. And with secrets came power.

But could I truly pretend that I had any idea how this all worked? That I knew what had just happened?

"That light you displayed," Kezia murmured, pressing a ring-clad hand to her chin in thought. "Was certainly something that my own power responded to."

I waited patiently for her to elaborate, but Leander already began to question her. "What did it feel like?"

"A powerful caress, like something was pushing back toward me," she said at once. "It felt very different than the hands of the stealer. Typically that feels as though it should—someone reaching *out* of the realm. This felt like someone reaching *in*."

"What are you two talking about?" I demanded with a hiss. "I'm standing right here."

"I'm sorry," Kezia perked up. She cast her eyes down toward the books, unable to ignore the fact that a few had been blown away to different pages. "One of the stealers has a similar gift. She would be able to move any object in this very room—"

"Yes," I interrupted. "Her name is Edythe."

Leander's eyebrows raised. Kezia nodded in agreement, crouching down to the floor. "But that's different. Edythe has worked very hard to master that gift, and when she does it, I can always feel a press in the realm, like tapping on my shoulder. And I know exactly which shoulder it is anywhere in the world."

I stared at her, unable to comprehend what she was confessing. Then it hit me, like cold water falling over my head to quench anything that was left of anger. A ruler's gift—fit for a lioness queen.

"If this realm is a page in a book, then I am its author," Kezia explained, running a ghostly hand over the books and journals, which she could finally read beyond the pages she had seen over and over again. Then she stood, her silky pants shimmering with gold as her muscles twitched beneath the fabric. She looked at me full of pride and dignity, every inch of her feminine features conveying what I would expect a queen to convey. "I feel every inch of this realm as it lays across the living world. I can sense when powers are used and when new souls step into it."

"And me...what just happened?" I pressed.

Kezia nodded slightly, stepping closer to inspect me. I was so close to her now that I could reach out to hug her if I desired—instead I only stared with caution. My breathing was still ragged and my throat still burned from the raw vapor of power that Leander had washed over me.

"Leander is right," she said after a moment, reaching out to grab a piece of my dress. Delicately she began to re-tie the small bow that had come undone there. I wasn't sure how long it had been untied. When she was finished, she patted it down and then pulled her painted lips into a smile. "There is something about you. Something different."

I said nothing, staring back into her dark, amused gazed.

"And I apologize for Leander's behavior. We may be rulers, but we are just. And we should not have done that to you," she continued, looking back toward her panther.

He shrugged indifferently. "I can see a light inside your eyes. I saw it when I saw you inside the carriage. I called you stealer, but you are far more than that. This power of yours only proves it. We wish to protect you now."

"Protect me?" I repeated. "How can you do that? And from what?"

"This place is our home. Very rarely do the politicians of Vena come in here to disturb us, and it is quite the luxury. There is an open room at the top of the clock tower that you can reside in. It looks over the entire city of bricks," she offered. "It's a joy to watch the young children toss coins into the pit, then grow old and bring their own children."

Stay here with them? I hesitated, uncertain now about my idea to come here at all. Whether it had been right to do. They had not imprisoned me, despite their unfriendly welcome by using their own powers. But how far was I willing to put my trust in them?

Back at Foxcoast, Naya was sure to tell the others that I believed them all to be horrible, evil creatures. It was unlikely that they would show me any more appreciation or warm smiles.

Isn't this what you wanted? A voice chided me. *To be free of them?*

Yes. Yes, in a way. What I wanted most of all, though, was to go home. To see my father and my brothers. I had believed Warren when he told me the story of Naya, and she did not seem to deny that the experience was unpleasant. She did, however, state that Warren had not told me the entire truth.

This was not a realm of wraiths, I decided angrily. This was a realm of liars.

"Okay," my voice hardened. "I'll stay briefly. But I have more questions and some ground rules. No using your powers on me—and I promise not to use mine on you." I looked toward Leander specifically, his mouth twitching into a playful smile. Even Kezia met my words with a wicked grin.

"Excellent!" she nearly purred, touching my elbow in a friendly and excited gesture.

What none of us seemed to comment on, or even realize, was that I had power, yes, but I had no place in threatening with that power. Not even I knew what it was or where it had come from. Even as we avoided stepping on the books for whatever reason while we exited the room, we each agreed that we were equals.

"It's a pleasure to meet you, Sonnet," Kezia said simply, an afterthought to all that had happened.

My eyes moved to the back of her shirt, small pieces of fuzz caught in the dark velvet texture. Her reddish brown hair was thick and wavy, bouncing while she took step after step. I had been following her to the room that I would stay in for the time being, trying very hard not to think about all that had just unfolded in front of me.

Not only did I have some sort of power ready to explode at any moment, I had met the mystery girl I longed to hold over the rest of the stealers' heads. I expected to feel proud and determined, no longer bothered by the monsters that tried to tell me how my new reality worked. Instead, I began to feel the weight in my heart that told me somewhere Naya was telling them all what I had said and done—telling them about Kezia and Leander.

"You as well." My feet stuck to the cold granite of the staircase. It was three times wider than the staircase back at Foxcoast, inside that little cottage that sat on the edge of the rainy cliff side. Even more elegant, the walls were painted an ancient and stark blue coated with unlit candles.

"I think I detect a bit of Enyian on your tongue, actually. That is where you were from, correct?"

"Yes," I whispered.

"My grandmother was born in Enya before my grandfather stole her away to Pushka. You could only imagine her surprise to see the lands of innovation." She laughed, both dainty and daunting. "Enya...land of the wilds."

"Of thickets and trees," I finished for her, longing. Enya truly was a place of good farmland and thick forests; no large clearings or cliffs like in Creo. And certainly no cities like in Pushka. My phantom heart gave a small twinge.

"Enya is a beautiful land for certain. I was born here in Pushka, though—in Vena, actually. Though when I died, I pledged to visit there as often as I could."

"And have you?"

"Yes, many times. One thing about death is that it makes you appreciate, certainly. But it will surprise you as well. I have never lived a day in death where I was not still excited to see all that the world offers. In some ways, I am glad my soul resides here where I can take as long as I need in order to see it all," she said boldly.

At the top of the stairs, there was a single wooden door. We phased through it to reveal a room large enough to host sixty people at once, by and by larger than any sort of room I had ever stayed in. A large bed was pushed in the corner covered by white sheets and quilts while a writing desk sat not too far away. What was most enchanting was that the room opened up to the outside, not confined by a fourth wall but left open—the backside of the clock tower. I felt my jaw go slack at the mechanical heart of the clock, smelling the pungent scent of oil and rust as it filled my nostrils.

"Amazing," I breathed. I imagined the wooden boards might creak beneath my steps but they didn't, not as I wandered closer. There were small openings between the mechanics and structure that allowed me to see to the street below. The market was still bustling, unknown to them that a soul like me was watching from behind the hands of their city's astronomical clock. Warm wind blew in from the openings and caused me to shiver.

"You are welcome to stay as long as you'd like." I turned just in time to see Kezia rise from a slight bow. "And we do not expect you to stay in this room alone. Feel free to wander our home—though I must tell you that beyond the throne hall and the dining area, there is not much."

"Then I should tell you that I am not an expert at passing through thick doors and walls. I'll probably stay here." I sighed, then tilted my head. "You know, I was told that the pit the citizens toss coins in is meant for their wishes. That the golden doors to this place are meant to open to their greatest dreams."

"Oh yes," Kezia nodded. "However, it is unlikely to ever happen."

"Why not?"

The lioness stepped alongside me to peer out into the market, her eyes moving from person to person. "Because this is formally known as the Hall of Inquiry. The coins they toss go into the pit, which is actually connected to the underground room beneath the throne room. Every several months Vena's representatives will collect the coins that the citizens throw."

"That's terrible," I felt myself say. "They sell their goods in the market then toss their coin in hopes their wishes will be fulfilled."

"It's only terrible if you still think about life in that way." She shrugged, turning toward me. "In death, we are free from the burdens of coin or material. Let the living toss their coins. Let them hope and dream."

"False hopes, false dreams," I pointed out.

"It depends," Kezia raised her eyebrows, "on what they wish for."

Finding no other commentary, she bid me to get accustomed to the room and gave me my privacy. I stood behind the clock tower, unable to pull myself away from it. I stood there so long that the vendors had begun to pack away their things and the citizens stopped tossing coins into the well. When night began to creep upon Vena, I found the eerie sounds of the city as they creeped up into the bedroom to be unsettling. Deciding to curl upon the bed, I felt something that I had not felt before in death.

Loneliness snaked up my back and clutched my chest tightly, threatening to unravel me completely. Not only was I in unfamiliar territory, I knew that I may have lost the few souls I had began to trust. Even when I closed my eyes and pretended to sleep, I could see a purple dress as it scraped along the grass. I could see dark braids that swung with the turn of a head, and round eyes. A long blue coat and a silver pocket watch flickered, entwining with the purple dress. Edythe and her bluntness, her hard eyes and freckled face that bounced when emotions crossed her features. Naya's sunny disposition and the way she laid across a bed with me just like this one to listen to my story, no hint of malice in her. Marvell, who I knew the least, yet could sense loyalty radiate off of him in waves.

I did not dare think of the other one until I could bear it no longer, the memories flooding me—the scent of a leather jacket, that plain face that wasn't very plain at all. Those blue eyes, bluer than any sort of blue I had found in a person my entire life. The very flesh-like, warm hand that pressed to my temple and my cheek, lighter than I ever had been touched before.

I hated him. I hated myself for even considering for a second that I missed them.

Missed *him* in particular. The monster that had crawled across the water toward me with his jaws flapping and hands reaching. How I had felt when I was pushed beneath the river, kicking and fighting against him. When the surface broke and I expected the most horrifying, terrible face I could have ever seen. The relief that flooded through me when I saw that he was a boy—a blue eyed, straight-nosed boy with brown hair peering down at me with concern.

Somewhere in the realm and not inside my head, the clock's hands groaned while they moved from hour to hour.

It felt like so long ago. In fact, I could not even recall how many sunsets and sunrises I had seen since then. And now I was with two more souls. Not stealers, but rulers of the very realm. The power to choke me, silence me, to hold me captive. The lioness queen and her panther, two felines with a taste for royal distinction.

I held up my hands to inspect them. *Something* had burst from them. Light and wind, destroying Leander's unsettling ability and breaking through to the living world. I wondered if I had some sort of power before, like the rest of them—but I never imagined I actually would. That I could and that it was possible. I was too average and plain, too immersed in the life I had lived before. A life where nobody had special abilities and we were each born and destined for something. A life where I slept, I ate, I wandered, and I loved. I would hug and push and play and write and dream. Dream like the citizens of Vena did when they tossed their coins into the dark pit.

A terrible sound emerged from me. It pulled and ripped open my chest, causing me to gasp. I curled inward, hoping to keep it sealed inside, but could not help it any longer. Tears spilled from my eyes and I cried violently, my face swelling against the flat pillow. Not certain what was real and what was not—what was inside my head or outside in the realm or in the living world—I wept. I could hear a small voice ask me what was wrong, what I was missing and what I was crying over.

"I just want to go home," I replied, turning my face into the sheets.

CHAPTER TWELVE

If I could dream at all, it would have been of my family. So instead I tried to remember every part of them I could so that they would never slip away into faded, distant memories that I could not reach. I thought of my brothers and their faces, boyish and child-like in every way. They had not turned into sharp angles and the hint of a man's roughness—that would come in time, when they sprouted in height and in character. I always believed they would look like mirrors of my father, with his straight nose and pointed chin. My father, who looked so much like them and never, not once, discouraged me from the gift of looking like my mother. After she died, I used to wonder whether he was tormented by my face, whether he wanted to see me at all or preferred that I stay hidden away.

The cruelty of having children, I believed, was when someone died and you had to look into the face of the one-half that had been left behind.

My tears and puffy face were long gone when I ventured back down into the room full of books and covered by the mirrored ceiling. The books were still strewn about the floor, permanently swept aside from the force of destruction I had brought down on them. Even the golden tea kettle had rolled down onto the floor, perhaps even showing signs of a serious and permanent dent.

I found Leander alone in the throne hall, resting with his chin one of his hands. His closely spaced and hooded eyes calculated me while I approached him; his thin line of a mouth curling into a smirk.

"Hello, sweet one." He folded his hands in his lap, the dark black of his outfit looking positively royal against the marble structure of the throne.

"Do you mind if I sit?" I asked hesitantly, not sure what their own rules and regulations were.

"Not at all. Come sit beside me and let me tell you something," he invited. I mustered up what little courage and drive I could find in my hole of a chest in order to make an effort to look at ease. I climbed onto Kezia's throne and ensured that the thin slip of my dress would not ride up past my calves. Surrounded by so much cold and marble I felt bare, perhaps even more so than Kezia might feel. Leander might have been used to looking at her skin, but I wasn't about to give him something else to fawn over.

"I am deeply sorry for yesterday," he began. I was so close to him that I found his eyelashes had a small hint of blue shimmer in them. Or perhaps they were so black my mind was playing tricks on me. His hair, too, had a straight shine to it that was like a raven's wings. His expression was soft while he spoke, and I nodded, willing to accept his apology. "I can sense something exciting in you, something I have not recognized in quite a long time."

"What is it?" I murmured, inhaling quickly. "My powers, do you think?"

Leander inclined his head. "Perhaps. I used my abilities to push you and I shouldn't have. A soul that can burn as brightly as yours is a precious thing. I can only hope you do not lose that brightness within you."

His entire demeanor was dark; his powers capable of rendering me useless and pathetic. I had made a spectacle of burning his vapor right where it snaked toward me, but I knew I could not do it again. "One of the stealers called it the essence of life."

"The essence remains in all of us until we are corrupted," he said politely, though he showed no signs of contradicting what a stealer might have told me. "Kezia and I both have it—but your stealer friend is right. Nothing as powerful."

I studied him, reaching up to pull back my hair and bring it away from my face. "Maybe it's because I'm newly dead."

He met my eyes and barked a laugh, shaking his head. "No, what you showed yesterday was far beyond. You have a gift, and I hope you learn to use it and use it well."

"Well, you all look the same to me," I sighed, leaning back against the throne. Its coolness pressed against my back. "I don't see the essence on anyone."

"It's not something you see," he said suddenly. "You feel it. Here, give me your hand."

I looked toward him, my phantom heart quickening. I looked at his open palm, stretched out to meet mine, and looked into his face for confirmation that he was serious. Truthfully, my curiosity got the better of my modesty and my shyness—I placed my hand in his, noting the smooth feel of his palms.

He must have never worked outside during his living, I decided. His hands felt like a polished rock and mine felt far too fleshy and rough. Gently, he pulled me forward to place a hand against his chest. Leander held it there firmly while a flush crept toward my neck and my cheeks. Pulling away would be rude and uncalled for, so I was left with no other decision than to stay there with a fresh blush.

I hope he doesn't think I find him attractive, I thought wildly. *Well, he's quite attractive actually, but I'm not—*

A sensation pulsed through my palm and quieted my thoughts. Leander was careful to keep his face turned away from mine, avoiding anything that might seem like a flirtatious gesture. In that way he reminded me a bit of Marvell, gentleman-like and honest.

A quiver or pulse of energy flowed from his soul and into my palm, so familiar and dear to me that I could have said I felt it all along. It reminded me vaguely of the quivering and vibration that I had felt when his vapor surrounded me and held me against the chair.

I met his eyes and nodded in understanding. It truly was something that could be felt and not seen, something that remained within us no matter when or where or how we passed on.

"How did you find out about your gift?" I whispered, pulling my hand away slowly.

Leander pursued his lips, looking out toward the golden doors as if in thought. "I had met Kezia in this realm. She told me how she believed she was put here through her own invention. It was a theory at the time. She wondered if I could feel anything different about myself—and when she began to annoy me, I wished that I could make her stop. I wished that I could make her do something else than to bother me. Of course, I feel grief when I think of it now, as Kezia was the first soul to step into this realm. To finally meet a soul that could see her and speak to her...certainly she felt overwhelmed and excited. She walked an entire continent to find me, following the pulse of where her own power felt me moving."

"Kezia was the first," I whispered aloud. "How long have you two been...?"

"Dead?" He tilted his head, bringing his eyes back toward me. "A very long time. And time does move differently in death. I scarcely remember."

We sat in silence. Rather, Leander allowed me to sit in silence in order to process my thoughts. I wondered if it was really true if Kezia had created this realm. It certainly was a possibility, if she had the power to feel it completely all across the world. Was it possible that she had died and fought so hard to remain somewhere, anywhere? Part of her power was bursting open a realm, a page, entirely?

"I can see your head turning," Leander snickered. He pressed his hands to his chest in order to smooth down the fabric. "Don't spend your afterlife here trying to figure out the how's and why's. If you do that, you'll end up a hollow shell that seeks answers and never gets them. Just like the living who fret about the beyond and watch their own lives pass by."

Solid advice, I decided. But there were a few more things I wanted to confirm with someone other than a stealer. "Is it true that we can become tethered to a place?"

"Yes," he replied nearly instantly, motioning with his hand to look around. "Kezia can feel the realm, but she cannot travel through it. We have become so fond of this hall that we rarely ever leave it or Vena. That is why your stealer friends don't know about us, but we know about them. We try to...keep tabs on them, in a way. Their corruption is a tragedy."

"They're not dangerous," I whispered roughly. Guilt washed over me like a plague, suddenly aware that I had called them such horrible things. Monsters, creatures...and right in front of Naya, thinking she would understand. Why couldn't she see I just wanted answers? That I couldn't trust them completely?

"Maybe not," Leander agreed. "But they are horrifying. We have seen them—in Kezia's emotions and interpretations. She feels them moving around the realm, taking souls. She can feel when they change and when they don't. And we've seen them here in Vena from time to time. Their corrupted forms are quite terrifying."

I nodded, but my thoughts drifted. They drifted to the little white cottage on the coast surrounded by gray clouds and drizzling rain. The intense smell of sea water mixed with damp grass and mud. My ankles tickled by long grass blades and then smeared with dirt. So different from this clock tower palace and city of bricks.

My mind was completely occupied by Naya's behavior and the aggressive way she reacted to me the day before. I wondered where her anger came from, whether or not she had it stored away for certain circumstances. I saw her in my mind as someone gentle, all round eyes and soft face with a tight-lipped smile. It was far different from the blazing, snarling person that she had become when I confessed that I thought she was a monster.

"Are you listening?" Kezia wondered. She folded her arms across her chest and peered at me from the side. We had been walking together under the warm Vena sun, my feet scraping against the rough edges of the cobblestones.

"I'm so sorry," I said quietly. My hands smoothed down the ripples in my dress in a flutter of nervousness.

"You're the one who wanted to hear about Vena," the lioness pointed out quickly. "If you were going to find it boring, I would have suggested we do something else. Like jump off a building."

My eyes found hers. "What do you mean jump off a building?"

As she started walking again, I followed her, swallowing every time a citizen of

Vena fluttered through and around my body. The streets were busy in the afternoon, when the sun was the hottest and the people were taking breaks from their work. Most people of Vena, I'd come to learn, were merchant sellers. They liked to find things from other cities to sell and trade, perhaps even try to make themselves. Blankets, vases, and especially jewelry. It made me question how much of coincidence it was that Kezia resided in Vena, knuckle-clad in gold and a glittery mask.

"Anything you wanted to do in life now awaits you in death. There are no consequences to whatever you want to do," she snorted.

"No consequences at all?" I quipped, my eyebrow raising in question. Kezia's painted lips pulled together in grim understanding.

"Not for us, anyway. We are not wraiths that try to take pleasure in consuming the living." Her nose wrinkled in disgust, the golden shine on her nose illuminating like a diamond. I could see that same sun reflected the red tones in her brown hair.

"Is that what you think they do? Consume?"

"I know that's what they can do. I've seen it. And I can feel it. They're monsters—and they're filling up this realm like they own it."

"You really hate them," I accused.

Kezia's eyes flickered across the stores we began to pass. She seemed truly interested in the different trinkets that loitered in the windows. "I hate anything that is a danger to myself or to the living. The stealers might have you convinced they are your friends, but you're just another one for them to destroy."

Her words stung me. "I feel terrible that I said those things to Naya. Out of them all, I feel like she and I were becoming friends. I hate to admit it, but it hurts me that she thinks I believe she's a monster."

Kezia was quiet for a moment. Then she turned toward me, a flash of savagery on her features as she looked down. "I won't force you to believe what I know is the truth. But you have something very unique and, dare I say it, powerful. If you're not careful, you can easily be manipulated by these creatures into thinking they deserve your sympathy. They'll destroy you too."

My chest tightened. This what was I wanted all along—an escape from the so-called stealers. An escape from their strangeness and their adamancy about what was the truth and what wasn't. But being away from them all had poured loneliness into my heart. My fear about the unknown and the distrust that I had for them faded more and more with each passing minute.

I moved toward one of the storefronts and leaned against the glass, vaguely recognizing the outline of plates and bowls that were on displayThe shoppers inside did not notice that I stopped to block their view of the street, unaware that two ghosts lingered so near to them.

"I don't know," I admitted, unable to look at Kezia. "There has to be something else that I'm missing here. That *we're* missing. You said this is your realm, right? Why can't you control what happens to the souls inside of it?"

The ruler began to study her rings intensely. At last she muttered, "I don't have *all* the answers."

Her response made my hand fall through the glass, steering me down on top of the merchandise. I tensed and braced myself for the disaster, briefly wondering how I was going to pay for the damages. Instead I passed through them completely and wound up halfway sticking out of the display. With a sigh Kezia wandered over and offered a hand, pulling me from my mishap.

We decided to keep walking, Kezia returning back to her narration of Vena and its history. Built by people who wanted to live and contribute to the wealth of everyone around them, determined to create a city that would be sturdy enough and classic enough in its nature that it never decayed or fell apart.

Heat rose to my cheeks as I tried to fake my interest in Vena. A city that I had only been in twice—and here I was, already bored of seeing it. By the time Kezia and I returned to the Hall of Inquiry, I wanted to run to my temporary room inside of the clock tower. I wanted to smell the thick scent of oil and machine. To watch the people of Vena toss their dreams into the dark pit in the center of the city. Instead, I lingered with Kezia and Leander. Each of them took a seat on their thrones and left me sitting on the marble floor, gazing up toward the ceiling of stars that reminded me of the astrological paintings hung in the cottage at Foxcoast.

CHAPTER THIRTEEN

I watched the sunrise three times from the back of the astronomical clock and watched citizens toss their coins into the pit of Vena. I wished desperately that I could call out to them and tell them to save their wishes and dreams for what they knew to be truth. I selfishly wanted to tell them not to hope, to use their coin on what they could see in front of them. I had a sensation very much like one in life where you wished you could go backward in time. Perhaps not even longer than an hour, but just enough so that you could tell yourself what you knew in the present. Sometimes an hour or so was more than enough to completely change the reality of your world.

I sat in the white-sheeted bed alone for the third morning, this time briefly thinking that it was the late afternoon in which I died. It seemed so long ago that I had forgotten how hot the sun had been despite the hour. I wore my lightest gown because I had wanted to wash up and prepare for bed early, finished with my duties. If I had the chance, I would have told myself to savor it all. The feel of the water. The press of the rock beneath the arch of my foot. Even the falling sensation before my head cracked against the sharp edge of the rock. I wished that my past self could have known they would all be feelings worth more than any other treasure.

In death, there was nothing to be lost. Nothing except the essence of life which, as of now, seemed like I held in far greater supply than anyone else.

The clock hands groaned to signify the changing hour. I stretched my phantom body, permanently looking like I was either going to bed or just waking up, and recalled what I wanted to do today. It wouldn't be easy and it certainly would mean venturing into the unknown, but I knew better than to go against my heart. My brain might be the reliable one, but my heart knew how to win an argument.

Before I wandered into the mirror room to check for Leander and Kezia, I paused as their voices carried through the elegant space and drifted into the small hallway that opened to the staircase. My feet felt cold against the floor, anxious with anticipation.

"We certainly can't force her to stay here forever," Leander said, a hint of disapproval coating his tone.

"Can't we?" his partner teased. I stiffened.

Silence. Then, "No, we can't. What is in her is far more powerful than anything I expected. Letting her go would be a shame, but being forceful will only make her resent us."

"I don't think you understand. If she can do what I think she can do, then we need to make a move. And now, before it's too late."

"I disagree with you, for once."

"You don't disagree that there's real danger now, do you?" Kezia snapped. I could hear the urgency and tension in her voice, as well as her controlled effort to keep her volume down.

Leander sighed. I could imagine him fixing his jacket to avoid responding. "Of course there is. I'm not blind. I have my own ways of sensing this realm."

"And you noticed it, didn't you? The difference between them," she replied, eager.

"Yes. Sonnet is equally powerful, though the exact opposite of the other. Her life force is incredibly strong." At the sound of my name, my phantom heart quickened.

"I think she can do it." I heard a shift in Kezia's voice, like she just moved from sitting to standing. "The question is when and how."

They were talking about *me*. I suddenly felt guilty, like I was spying on not just a conversation but a private conversation about someone's true nature and true thoughts about me. Not particularly wanting to hear anything more about my own abilities or what they thought, I made a loud show of coming into the room.

I found Kezia and Leander sprawled on the floor of the mirror room, expertly curling themselves around strewn journals and moldy bread. They didn't seem to mind, small smiles on both of their faces as they rejoiced in the pleasure of being able to read new pages. I made a mental note of asking Edythe to steal books for them, maybe even tearing the pages out so they wouldn't need her there to turn them.

They nodded in greeting. "Good morning, Sonnet," Kezia acknowledged brightly. "Did you enjoy your room and rest?"

"Yes," I said automatically, already accustomed to her referring to privacy as rest periods. I did wonder what they did during the night, though. Perhaps they walked together around Vena. "I did. And are you two enjoying your...read?"

"We've already read these new pages at least fifteen times," she chuckled. "I just hope the next representative of Vena doesn't come in here and put them all back on the table closed shut."

"That would be unfortunate," Leander agreed in a murmur.

An awkwardness fell between us. Not bearing to stand it or reveal that I had been listening to them silently, I cleared my throat. "So I was thinking of going home today," I said simply. They both did not dare look up to catch my eye, feigning a deep interest in what they were doing.

"Is that so?" Leander wondered. "Where is 'home,' exactly?"

I blinked. I really did call it home. "I mean, back to Foxcoast. I wish to tell the other stealers what I've learned."

"Do you think they will believe you?" Kezia challenged, rising to her feet. "They have been in this realm for a long time. I doubt they will give any authority to someone who has only been here for a short while."

"Don't you agree they should know of their *rulers*?" I shot back, folding my arms. Leander snorted, picking himself up to tower over us.

"Will they be kind to you when you return?" she tried instead.

"I hope so. I don't think they are dangerous. I know you think they may be wraiths but...I think they should, at the very least, know the consequences of what they are doing. You think they enjoy being monsters, but I don't think they do. Not in the way I've seen them operate." My mind flickered back to Marvell and Edythe, each holding onto each other. Each with a look in their eye that said they wanted to be better than what they were.

"We are fair and just, so we shall not stop you from going where you want to go," she decided with a sigh. The golden glitter on her face twitched in something like sorrow, though it passed as easily as it had come. She reached out to place her small hands on my shoulders, giving me a faithful squeeze. "When will you leave?"

"I wanted to go there soon. I'm not sure if there's any sort of difference in time, but I hope it's not dark."

"It shouldn't be," she encouraged. I watched her carefully, looking for any sign of panic that might suggest she didn't want me to leave. Wasn't she just talking about forcing me to stay?

"I'm tethered to that place now, whether I like it or not," I explained, looking at Leander. His face remained impassive. "I've decided that running from that tether will not do anyone any good. And I need to give the others the opportunity to better themselves. I don't want any more corruption."

"Then safe travels, sweet one," Leander supplied, reaching out to touch the bottom of my chin. I felt myself smile in response. Who knew that in three short days the soul that had made myself explode in strange and unusual power would be a new companion. And the mystery girl—the power I had wanted to keep to myself.

It made their secretive whispers a bit more alarming.

Kezia hugged me tightly and released me just as quick. "If anything goes wrong or happens to you, don't fear. You are a soul with immense and valuable power. Whether you can tap into it or not, you are a soul that carries the essence of life within her. That much is true and cannot be stolen from you."

"Don't worry about losing it," Leander continued from beside her, his eyes mirroring that same blaze of dedication. "Nothing can ever truly be lost."

Their words brought a burn to my eyes. I swallowed the thickness in my throat and nodded, turning away from them. I stepped over each of their books, even the gold kettle, and passed into the throne room. My feet pressed flat against the marble, and with every step I felt more and more certain of my decision.

There was no doubt in my mind that as much as I had missed my true home with my family, my phantom heart longed just as much for the newly found friends I had made. The heavy weight of knowing that they had confided to me, trusted and accepted me, pressed on my insides like a boulder. What had I done to return the favor?

Nothing except call them monsters. I lost faith in them, even admitted to being terrified of them.

I *was* terrified, though. But I would be terrified with purpose. This was a realm full of corruption and full of lies. I would not run from my companions inside it, not when all we had was each other. I crossed the floor with the thrones behind me and took a deep breath just before I passed through the golden doors, this time not fearing how thick the walls were. I was the master of my own soul, and nothing could trap me or weigh me down any longer. I reached, already shoulder deep inside the door, and prepared myself for facing the most certain, and potentially dangerous, unknown.

The inexplicable pull I felt toward a land where the hills were covered by lush green grass, gray clouds, and dirt paths was like allowing myself to drift toward the place that called out to me most. It wasn't my own home, where I knew my family resided, where I had been born and where I had died. The roots that had been planted within me were rooted beneath the small white cottage settled along the coast of a cliff side, surrounded by the souls I childishly and naively run from.

Closing my eyes and letting the universe carry me back toward Foxcoast was simple, much more simple than resisting its memories and its friendly caress. When the city of Vena had long gone quiet and the scent of oil filled my phantom lungs, my heart would feel the soft graze of a land faraway that promised a familiar feeling of safety and protection.

How strange, I thought. When I had allowed my soul to weep in longing for my companions and comfort, which home had I been calling out for?

My feet slid into warm grass, surprising me. The sun was high above Foxcoast today, no clouds in sight. A golden glow hugged the landscape, and dry dirt, not mud, kicked up with every step I took along the path that arched along the top of the cliff side. The salty, warm wind kicked up from the side of the cliffs and rustled my curls, pushing them away from my face. I tilted my chin back in order to catch the comfort of the sunny rays, thankful that even in death I had the opportunity to sunbathe.

The little cottage with its black accents sat where it always was, perched near the edge of the coastline. I faltered for a second before picking up my pace, my brain telling my heart that I could expect everything but kindness from them. They all deserved to push me away and consider me a traitor to their hospitality and their welcome. It would make little sense for them to continue their loyalties with me. Would I become an outlaw, some sort of vigilante soul caught between the rulers of the realm and the stealers that corrupted it?

I took a long, steadying breath before I pushed through the front door, sunlight and wind stopping to reveal the brightly lit and musky living space. The mantel and fireplace remained the same, and I could see that Edythe had opened the window to let the breeze sweep away any sort of dust or dirt that may have accumulated.

My body stiffened at the figure stretched along the golden sofa. His feet were kicked up on the armchair, one leather arm resting behind his head. His light brown hair was pushed to one side, and upon my entrance, his closed eyes flickered open to meet my own.

Warren looked the same—the same but different. He seemed exhausted, if it at all was possible to see the physical effects of exhaustion. Even his fair skin seemed to have a sickly hue as his eyes widened and he pushed himself up from the sofa, features softening.

From the way I had left things, both with Warren and Naya, I prepared myself for anger. The fear that coiled up my spine and snaked its way into my heart was enough to cause a sharp pain of regret ripple through me. How could I even begin to express all that I had learned in such a short amount of time? Three sunrises was all it took for me to learn the truth about the life that we now lived and discover an additional, surprising truth about myself. Looking at him now, how could I even begin to make him understand?

"Sonnet," he murmured. I reached into my mind somewhere, scrambling for something to say back to him. Instead, I allowed him to saunter closer to me, close enough that I could smell leather mixed with fresh pine. A boyish, human scent that nearly intoxicated me. I peered up at his face and swallowed the small lump that latched itself to the back of my throat. "Where have you been?"

"I was in Vena," I admitted hurriedly.

"I was afraid. With the way we left things, and you not coming back...I was thinking you might have gone somewhere and gotten yourself stuck. Maybe even tried to get back and lost your way," he admitted, his brow furrowed. "I don't know what I would have done if you had gotten stuck somewhere, stuck in a house or a building or even in something else that was solid—"

I reached out to take his hand in my mine, trying hard not to flinch at the confusion and pain in his eyes. "Warren..."

"What is it?" he inhaled, grasping one of my hands in his. His pale thumb stroked the back of my hand in small circles. My traitor heart nearly jumped out of me, thrilled by his touch. I felt myself begin to tremble. How could he be so kind to me like this? After all I had said and done, how could he be looking at me like this, as though I hadn't acted like a monster myself?

"I've said such terrible things," I admitted, dragging my eyes away so I could stare at the blue fabric on his chest beneath his jacket. I could feel my legs quivering, giving me away for the anxious and silly fool I was. He stayed quiet, patiently waiting for me to finish while I gathered my courage. "I've avoided you. I've pushed you away."

"It's okay," he breathed, tugging our hands so that I would fall against him. His height was just enough that I could be tucked beneath his chin, our folded hands the only thing preventing me from resting my cheek against his chest.

"No, it's not," I croaked, feeling all my courage and determination crumble into a weepy disaster. I hadn't expected this, not even for a second. Not when he had threatened me and not when I had accused him. I had placed them all inside a box to appeal to my own emotions and theories, not once considering that they could all be corrupted souls like they were. Souls that needed help and someone to fight for them, to help fix them if they could be fixed. "Because everything you said is *true*. I know there's something between us and it scares me too...well, it's a horrible feeling. And I'm terrified because I am afraid of you too. Being around you scares me and not being around you feels like it's going to ruin me."

"Sonnet, you—"

"Just listen!" I begged, squeezing his hands. I tilted my head upward toward him, allowing my voice to become a soft whisper. I could feel the burning tears begin to leak over the edges of my eyes. "Please, listen to me. There is nothing more that I want than to hold onto the life I had. And as much as I try to deny it, I can't deny that you *did* pull me from that water. You never...You've never given me a reason to doubt you or push you away. I've just been using you as an excuse to deny the truth of where we are and who we are. And I'm so sorry."

Warren did not smile. He merely used our hands to brush away the tears that raced down the sides of my rounded cheeks, then he brought our hands to his lips. He pressed them there softly once, then twice. His eyes faltered, drooping down like he was sleepy despite the brightness that existed there.

He finally smirked. "When I pulled you from the water, I saw something in you that terrified me. Our skin touched and there was light and life inside of you.

It burned so strongly that something inside of *me* told me to stay far away from *you*."

My eyes lingered on our hands and his lips, watching them form the words as he spoke them.

"But I cannot keep myself from you. We are connected somehow. I see your beautiful, earthy eyes whenever I close my own. What I said beside the lake is still true. I would never harm you, and I would be the king of your nightmares if that's what you wanted."

My heart gave a twist of pain. "No," I shook my head. "I'm still afraid, but I'm more afraid of not being able to help you. There is so much I have to tell you."

"Can it wait?" he wondered.

The question was in my eyes. *For what?* But Warren did not wait for it to reach my lips. He released my hand and instead touched the sides of my face, angling me upward so that he could press his lips against mine. I stood dangerously still and quivered, trembling like a young girl.

Warren was so careful and steady as his mouth folded around my own. I was filled with every inch of him around me and could not help from reaching up toward the back of his neck, clinging to him desperately. He was warm and solid, and kissing in death was what I had believed it to be in life. My soul reached out toward his and collided, the two of us savoring the smell, the taste, and the feeling of each other in a mutual agreement as ancient as the stars. Whether we were bodies or forms or just illusions, together we had found each other.

I let out a small, breathless gasp and Warren pulled away. His eyes darkened and his own lashes were wet. His chest heaved with a large inhale before he pressed the side of his temple against the top of my head, arms tightening around me like he was suddenly afraid to let go.

"You deserve so much more than all of this," he murmured aloud. It was the most sorrowful I had heard anyone speak in this realm, let alone the one soul who I believed was incapable of anything but destruction. "More than what I am and what this world has offered you."

I stiffened and pulled away from him, peering up at him. "Warren...I've found answers. To the questions about where we are and why we are."

"You have?"

"Yes," I nodded, then began to pull him toward the sofa. "But first...what have you heard from Naya?"

Naya had not returned to Foxcoast.

It was hard to process—I had expected her to run back here and tell the others what happened as soon as she could. Instead, Warren informed me that nobody had seen her for several days. A sick feeling curled inside of my stomach and I gripped Warren for support. We sat side by side on the sofa, the sound of the waves below reaching in through the window and touching our ears. Their consistent push against the rocks reminded me of the way my thoughts drifted and collided, again and again.

"It's because of me that she didn't return," I mused, and Warren waited for me to elaborate. "When I left with Edythe and Marvell to Vena, I found someone. Another soul."

"What?" he hissed.

"I swear to you, Warren. She was inside a carriage that passed through me when I was standing on the street. I didn't tell Edythe and Marvell because...well, because I thought you were all liars. I couldn't trust what you all told me, not without a chance to verify it. I saw her as an opportunity to get additional answers to the questions I had. I'm sorry."

"Is that where you've been?" He stared, temper rising. "I've been worried sick about you and you were off chasing someone around Vena?"

"I *found* her, Warren. And someone else too. Her companion. We are not the only ones who exist here. There are others." It suddenly occurred to me that I had not thought to ask Kezia just how many others that might be. They claimed to be the realm's rulers—how large did they know their kingdom to be? "Her name is Kezia and his name is Leander."

"Why have they appeared to *you* so suddenly? We've been around for a long time. Even Edythe has been dead for more than a hundred years," Warren questioned, his eyebrow arched. "Why have they suddenly appeared?"

"I'm not sure," I admitted poorly. "But here's what they told me..."

So I began to confess it all. How Naya had managed to get me back into Vena, similar to how I had gotten there through the help of Marvell and Edythe. Speaking of which, they had began their own search party for the two of us—Naya in particular, since they had a better idea of where her hiding habits might be.

I told Warren the "affliction" that Kezia and Leander believed plagued them all, and how they called themselves the rulers of the realm. Rulers because they were not corrupted and one of them believed she was the creator of the realm itself. He was dangerously quiet while I recalled my story, even as still as a newly carved statue when I confessed that I had caused something to happen through the buildup of my own memories and life. The light that had burst from me combined with the powerful wind, and the suggestion that I truly had an essence of life far greater than anyone else made Warren's eyebrows raise in shock.

"It makes sense," he murmured at last, causing me to let out a breath of relief. "I believed I could sense the same thing within you. You are so strongly connected to the living still, even though it has been some time since you died."

I wondered just how long it had been, but decided to keep that question for another day. "You're not angry with me?"

"Of course not. You had questions and you sought answers. Though I'm skeptical that I'll be calling anyone my ruler anytime soon."

I breathed a sigh of relief, then carefully studied his face for any sort of masked rage. I found none, just the sharpness of his cheekbones and straight narrowness of his nose that did not quiver in the slightest. "Do you think it's true, then? That you've been corrupting yourself?"

Warren leaned forward to rest his elbows on his knees, head down while he formulated what he would say next. Silence fell between us before he murmured, "Maybe. I don't see how that could be possible, though. If this is a realm, why is it here? And how can souls pass through it at all?"

"They explained it to me like the universe was a book. One page is for the living. This one is simply a different page. We have jumped from one to the next without noticing, maybe even on our way to get somewhere better. We call each other stealers because we steal our own souls—we're unlike the others, for whatever reason. We get stuck here instead."

"We put ourselves here," Warren pointed out. "Any soul that I've met, newly dead in life, is always distracted. If you leave them to their business, they just stare off. When you touch them and help them cross through you, they finally leave. A stealer is always bright eyed. They hardly even notice they have died."

He had a point, I realized. Why would souls linger until a stealer helps them cross? They shouldn't need help at all. I sighed, leaning back against the sofa and pressing the back of my neck into its fabric. "Perhaps we're just destined to be ghosts."

I felt his hand lay itself over mine to give me a gentle squeeze. "It's a fine theory, Sonnet. But I don't think even the rulers of this little realm have all the answers."

His words chilled me. How could it be possible that in death there was nothing to settle the anxious and determined mind? Throughout our lives we are caught up wondering what the rest of the universe is like, past the stars and past the grave. Never do we think for a second that we might be left with just as much to wonder about, perhaps even something to be bitter about. Words like *peace* and *rest* are used to no end, not once insinuating that the afterlife should be a place of worry or suffering.

How wrong with assumption the world lives.

I turned toward Warren, not quite knowing how to respond, when a sudden groan filled my ears. At first I thought it was the screech of wind pressing against the cottage or something that had escaped the soul beside me. But he was quiet, suddenly looking at me with concern. The groaning filled my head and I began to panic, fearful that my eardrums might burst. A high-pitched scream bounced inside of my skull and I leaned over, gritting my teeth.

"Sonnet?" I heard Warren ask, distant.

"Someone's screaming!" I wailed, pressing my hands over my ears. "Do you *hear* that?"

His hand shot out to grip my wrist tightly, pulling my one hand away from its attempt to block out any noise. His eyes burned into mine when I turned toward him for answers.

"I'm right here," he promised in a rush. His long fingers felt like metal clamps against my skin. "I'm right here."

His words were caught up somewhere, lost beyond a veil as I felt my soul get pulled somewhere else. *No!* I wanted to protest. I had just found my way back home to Foxcoast, I didn't want to go anywhere else. The world dissolved around me, quick and efficient as a single blink before I peered up into the bright, blaring sun. The cottage had gone away, replaced by an open field with a wide girth for wagons and carriages to use to their leisure.

I looked to my right and saw it—an upturned wagon. The horses had run off and gone. They likely broke free from whatever sprint had caused such an accident. I felt myself gasp, and I recognized what had been making so much wailing and screaming. Beneath the wagon was a body that had been broken nearly in half, spine and ribcage jutting out unnaturally while the hips and legs twisted beneath one of the wagon's corners. Next to the body, an identical twin crouched and stared off toward the distance, mouth agape while its wails soared across the realm.

I stiffened and looked toward Warren. Warren, who had grabbed my hand in understanding even though he wouldn't have heard what I had. Warren, who had kissed me so delicately and confessed that he felt connected to me. Warren, who was now looking at the soul with a hunger I had never seen.

Whose bright blue eyes had turned to solid black, and stepped toward the wailing soul with a shimmering, shuddering form on the verge of transformation that caused me to scream.

CHAPTER FOURTEEN

I had come to terms with what I felt for Warren—his very presence and existence alone had become such a comfort to me. Even knowing that he was corrupted, perhaps even a different creature entirely, could not deter me from facing that realization that I needed him.

But when the edges of his body began to shudder and vibrate, blackness leaking from him like an overfilled tea pot, I felt nausea roll through me. True and solid sickness that made my phantom heart turn cold. I couldn't breathe or think or even move. The king of my nightmares was inside of him whether I liked it or not. Did I foolishly think I could ignore just how much the lurking destruction within him frightened me?

Flashes of a tall black creature twitching with teeth swam across my mind. Despite the flat, cleared field that we now stood in alongside the road, I heard the sensation of water fill my ears. *No,* I wanted to scream. *No, not this!* My body fell downward—my knees having given out so quickly and irrationally that I scrambled for the green grass around me.

I recoiled away from the mass, still very much looking like Warren. *For now,* a small voice whispered inside of my mind. My eyes widened in terror as he stalked forward, every inch of him like a predator. Silky blackness swirled up and down the length of his brown coat like it was searching his soul for an opening.

Kezia was a ruler of truth, I decided at once. They really *were* corrupted. Awful, hungry creatures that were desperate to satisfy their cravings for other souls. There was nothing that could have shaken the terror from my body in that moment, gripping me so harshly that I felt trapped. My phantom limbs and bones, each trembling like I had never trembled before. Like I had been thrust into a frozen river with a monster that wanted to push me downward, downward, downward...

Nothing except the flicker of movement that reminded me what Warren was stalking toward. Or rather, who.

The broken body that was soaking in its own blood, the pure white of its bones sticking out from the unnatural angles of its contortion. Beside it, its soul stared off into the distance, unaware of itself and where it was. So different than I had been when this had been me. It opened its mouth to wail, and the sound sent my head down toward the grass, blades cutting alongside my temples.

I forced myself to look at Warren, who had stopped in front of the soul, oblivious to the graphic nature of the death. To him, I supposed, it would mean nothing. Nothing except for another soul to take, to corrupt himself with. His body gave a jolted spasm and his legs turned into black curls of night. The very sight of it caused me to gag and hurl, hoping there was something inside of my stomach I could reject. Even bile would be suitable.

But nothing came out except a wretched sound that burned my throat. I was a phantom, a ghost, a soul like the one wailing beneath the king of my nightmares as he transformed. I could still hear the river's current in my ears as I jumped to my feet, forcing myself to look anywhere except the black fire that was consuming the blue-eyed soul I had kissed only moments ago. My eyes locked onto the crouching soul and its agape mouth.

He was a middle-aged man, I discovered. I could see the fine wrinkles beginning to form beneath his facial hair. Hair that was blond like the fluff that sat on top of his head. My eyes burned while I looked at him, getting closer and closer until I used myself as a shield to protect him. His gaze did not pass over me and he seemed to be elsewhere, both in spirit and in mind.

I couldn't let Warren corrupt himself any more. Not when I had vowed to protect them, maybe even save them if they could be saved. The sickness that flooded me was a combination of my own fear and terror, certainty of what Kezia had told me drilled right down to my core. I needed to stop this.

My eyes burned because I was crying. I could feel the tears brimming, threatening me to go back to a place of curling along the ground and shrinking away from what I feared. But I couldn't let Warren take this soul—for himself, and for the man who had just died. This was a *person*. A person who had ended in tragedy with his body torn nearly into two. The edge of my gown was soaked in the red blood. It smeared along my ankles like a tiny artist had tried to make sense of the events unfolding.

With Warren behind me, only the lifeless soul staring into the distance could see just how much the king of nightmares had shown of himself. I still crouched between them, ready to use myself as a shield if necessary.

A low, threatening hiss sounded from behind me. I could feel hot breath down the back of my neck, the sensation of something peering over me, making the hair there shoot upward. My spine tensed and I reached out instinctively for the soul, longing for companionship that might stop the roaring water in my ears or the fear rolling off of me like waves on a shore. The breath that escaped me was short and ragged. I tried to find the man's eyes, to tell him that everything would be okay because I was here.

I reached—and made a horrendous mistake. My hand collided with the soul and he turned to look at me, desperation and relief in his eyes as they fixed rightly. A jolt of electric tension bubbled inside my hand and then swept up my arm and into my neck, then my brain. Warren had once said that helping souls cross was blissful, something to be desired and something that he craved. So much so that it seemed he could not help himself from turning into a walking nightmare in order to have them. But I felt no release.

I felt nothing but coldness as the soul faded from existence. One minute my left hand had been tightly grasped around his wrist, and the next, he was gone. Like a blink. Like everything else in this afterlife. Only the upturned wagon and the body, still very much twisted and dead, served as evidence.

My eyes cast down to where my hand had been resting...and I froze. Nothing, not even my phantom heart, so much as twitched. My fleshy, light bronze hand was now replaced with long, slick, jet black fingers that arched upward like a claw. Veins bulged from the back of it and curled around my wrist, ending as though I had stuck my hand into hot tar and decided to pull it out before it reached too far. I held the hand up toward the sun as if to inspect it more, making tiny movements as though to prove that, yes, this was my hand. My eyes caught the bit of sharpened nails that grew to a point before the transformation completed itself.

"Kezia was right," I said, my voice like ash.

Blue caught the corner of my eye, just enough so that I could find the confidence to face him. Whatever nightmare he had been turning into was gone. There stood the soul I had grown to trust, his usually styled hair slightly messy. I could still see the lingering effects of the transformation where the muscles in his cheeks flexed. He seemed guarded, eyes searching mine for any indication that I was going to run.

Instead, I nearly collapsed into him. His arms reached out for me and he held me upward, my feet gone slack. I held my blackened claw away from me, glancing at the broken body that lay beside us.

I had never seen a dead person like this before. When I saw myself, it was like I had been sleeping face down in the water and mud. *This* was morbid and sickening, far worse than anything I even had seen in animals. The butchered head of a deer tossed aside while my father gutted it. A squashed mouse with its stomach beside its body.

Those were the only horrors I had ever experienced.

As if sensing my discomfort, Warren began to pull me away. I let him, suddenly noticing the dark green grass stains and red hue at the hem of my dress while he walked us further from the scene.

"What happened?" I wondered dryly. Warren swallowed in response.

"Sonnet, I'm sorry—"

"No, tell me," I shoved him away, whirling on him.

"I can't help it. I just crave it—I told you that, that I—" he stuttered, reaching up to pull his jacket closer. A jacket that, had he been living, he never would have needed. Not with the way the sun was coming down.

"It's *true*. You went after that soul. You *wanted* to take it, to corrupt yourself. Do you not even *notice?*" I spat harshly. The anger and hurt that bubbled inside of me was nearly uncontrollable. I could feel it creeping in on my heart, which finally began to find its footing. "I stopped you...and look what happened to *me*."

I showed him my hand, clenching it tightly into a single fist. His eyes darkened and focused on my face, a hardness to them that surprised me. "It happens to everyone. It was only a matter of time."

I recoiled like I had been slapped. "Excuse me?"

"You knew what would happen when you touched that soul," Warren said coldly. "You knew that you would turn into something else. It's a price to pay. This is how the universe works, Sonnet."

"Are you not even sorry? Or thankful?" I hissed, stepping closer to him. How ironic that only moments ago I had been cowering in fear, overcome with emotion that made me flinch. Right now, when he looked like this—and spoke like this—I had no fear in fighting back. "I stopped you from getting worse!"

"Maybe," he shrugged. The nonchalance of it made me throw my hands into the air.

"What do you mean 'maybe'? And what about that soul, Warren? Where does *he* go? How does he benefit from any of this?"

"He gets to be gone, that's what," he scoffed, folding his arms. "Free of the living. Free from being like us. He goes somewhere better."

"I don't think so," I said, my turn to be cold. "I think I just *destroyed* him completely. I think that's what you've all been doing. Kezia and Leander are right, we're turning ourselves into wraiths."

"Well, aren't you a loyal subject, Miss Sonnet."

I stared at him, studying the twitch in his cheek and the set of his jaw. The way his eyes were so unlike how they were before, when he had looked at me just before he pressed his lips to mine. The softness in him had melted away like ice beneath the polarizing sun. Unable to help myself, I let out a small laugh of disbelief. His expression did not change where he stood with his arms crossed.

"Turning into that creature...it changed you," I accused, my tone suddenly wondrous. "Are you disappointed that you didn't get to feel your *rush*?"

Warren snorted. "Don't be ridiculous."

I smiled dangerously. "You are...you're not being cold or cruel or evil at all, are you?" I stepped closer to him, unable to control my sudden desire to tease him. My lips parted as I leaned into him, peering up into his annoyed and hardened face. "You're *jealous.*"

Warren blinked slowly, then reached out to grip my blackened hand by the wrist. His other gripped my jaw, the pad of his thumb coming down to flick my bottom lip once. "And you're being bold."

"I'm surprised you didn't settle for something more threatening," I felt my eyes flutter slightly. "Isn't that what you do best? Threaten and scare people?"

He was silent. Just as I supposed, that was confirmation enough. He added, "You as well, it seems."

His words made me pause. He was right—this wasn't me. Not this flirtatious, dangerous version. When I envisioned approaching him, I thought about hitting him. Not crawling up to him as though the dead body a yard away did not begin to attract birds, or that my hand had not just transformed to a blackened crisp.

Seeing the change in my eye, Warren dropped his hands. I turned to inspect my new form and found that it had disappeared, melting back to my usual normal.

"We need to go see Kezia and Leander." I turned away, not quite believing what had just happened. What I had done.

"Yes," Warren agreed quickly, already reaching into the universe from here to Vena. "This should be interesting."

✦ ✦ ✦

The lioness and the panther were perched on their thrones, not looking the slightest bit surprised or bothered by the way Warren and I both stormed through the clock tower and into their marble domain. My feet slid along the cold floor like gliding across ice while Warren's shoes echoed throughout the empty space. It reminded me distantly of the sound of Naya's boots when she had walked away. My heart gave a slight twinge of regret thinking about her.

"Hello, sweet one," Leander said simply, the ebony darkness of his suit still perfectly matching his eyes and his tousled hair. His charming aesthetic looked dangerous alongside Kezia, adorned with her dark red velvet and gold silk pants that shimmered slightly. Gold caught the light on her rings as her fingers danced impatiently. "Back so soon?"

"And with another stealer," his companion said stiffly.

"Slipping in and around as you please," Leander murmured, his eyes set upon

Warren. Assessing him, perhaps wondering if he was prey or predator. I shivered to think about Warren's dark form, the king of nightmares clashing with the ruler of the realm. "Such a unique gift. One you have used well and to your own advantage."

"What brings you back, Sonnet?" Kezia wondered, her eyes particularly warmer as they moved from Warren to me. I was struck with the sudden recognition that I was unsure whether or not Kezia and Leander were truly friends. I did not consider them my enemies, though I disagreed with their policies. Just as I disagreed with the stealers'. Yet I felt connected to them all, each in their separate ways.

"Something's happened," I confessed. I kept my gaze on Kezia, already feeling the weight of Leander and Warren as they studied me. "When I left before, I had told you that I wanted no more corruption. Warren now knows everything that you have told me. I admit I did not believe you completely, not at first. But now I see. We truly can be corrupted."

They waited patiently for me to elaborate, and I nervously flexed my left hand. I thought of the way that the man's broken body had been twisted and the flash of his white bone had surfaced. How his blood had pooled and been absorbed by my gown—my gown, which had been covered in grass stains and blood, long gone once my mind had been elsewhere occupied. I thought of the sickness that rolled over me in waves at the sight of Warren twitching and transforming into the thing that lurked inside of him, the thing that repulsed me beyond reasonable measure.

I brought my hand up and found that black claw arching upward, my fingers extended and nails pointed in a piercing tip. Its dark veins bulged, as though phantom blood was thickly coursing through it. I inhaled sharply.

"What have you done to her?" I heard Leander demand. Blue smoke began to plume at his hands, already snaking toward their target: Warren, who took a step forward and narrowed his eyes in challenge.

"No!" I nearly hissed, stepping in front of him protectively. "It's not his fault. I touched the soul."

The smoke stilled at the halfway point, waiting for the deliberate and quick commands of its master. But he only paused, his fair face the perfect mask of fury. "You protected him."

"I don't need protection," Warren retorted, pushing me aside. I faltered, suddenly afraid that it was a mistake to bring Warren here. Kezia and Leander believed they were corrupted souls who could not be redeemed. That there was no use in them, perhaps not even enough to warn them that every time they helped a soul cross they lost a part of the life inside of them. "And I'm not corrupted."

Now I whirled on Warren. "Yes, you are. You are refusing to believe it because they are saying it. But I'm saying it too. Don't you see? *This* proves it."

"This proves nothing. This only proves *exactly* what happens to us. It's a give and take of the universe. I thought you understood that?" he snapped.

I knew him though—knew him well enough that I saw a brief flicker of hurt behind his crystal blue eyes. I pressed my teeth to my bottom lip and studied him carefully, beginning to see Warren for who he was and what he must be feeling.

My eyes glossed over the casual comb of his hair, the thick lashes framed around his round eyes. His light skin and his sturdy body covered by the weight of the blue shirt and the jacket. A soul like me who had questions for as long as he had been dead. Questions that I was finding answers to. People that I was finding after he had spent his entire death thinking he was alone. Being lonely without company, only the stealers. Never being able to go home or talk to anyone else. Not until a dead girl by a river in Enya ran from him.

"Warren..." I whispered, watching as Leander's smoke snakes began to fade. "You've thought for so long that you were doing right. If there's a way to take any of what has happened back, I would. I would in a heartbeat. It sickens me to think what I've...what I've done to that man. He was a person, and I know that. He probably had a spouse and children waiting for him...but we can move *forward*. I know it's possible. If you, if the others, even me...if we're corrupted, I know there's a way to undo it."

His eyes swept from Kezia to Leander then back to me. "And what if there isn't?"

My throat bobbed. But it was Kezia who suddenly rose from her throne, her slender body stepping down from the dais. "While your little chat is endearing, there is something I wish to say. Sonnet, to you especially. I am so sorry for what has happened. You left us in perfect shape, and I cannot help but feel like I am partially responsible in some way for what has happened." She leaned forward to take my hand, and I felt my brow crumble at the sight of it. It had returned back to normal, gone with the lingering thoughts of terror and carnage.

But then her sharp, feline eyes turned toward Warren. Her beauty matched with her ferocity made her suddenly commandeering, hints of the ruler she called herself peaking through as she addressed her new subject. "You very much *are* corrupted. But it is beyond your character or your fault. We've allowed this to happen to you, and it is time Leander and I, as rightful rulers of this realm, put an end to it."

My eyebrows raised in surprise, but Warren looked skeptical. I briefly remembered his adamant rejection toward the idea of rulers—the mere thought that the afterlife could be governed or ruled by anyone or anything felt wrong.

"One of the stealers is wreaking havoc on the living realm," she said icily. "Possessing bodies as they live and thinking they can get away with it. Every time she slips into a new living body, I feel like I'm going to be sick." The lioness turned, glancing briefly at Leander. His impasse made it hard to tell if he knew what she was talking about.

"What do you mean, possessing people?" I stilled. "That's...monstrous."

"No, that's corruption," she shot back boldly, climbing back up toward her throne. Instead of being seated, she turned to look at Warren. "The work of a ruined creature, determined to destroy everything it touches."

"Nobody can do that," I protested. "Edythe and Marvell...they wouldn't. And Warren— I mean, I was with him—"

"It's that little friend of yours who you brought here before," Kezia scolded. "But that's not all. Your Traveler here has been letting it happen. They *all* have. They've been lying to you."

CHAPTER FIFTEEN

I felt her name like a kick to the stomach. I felt their betrayal, their lies, seep through me like poison. The world seemed to slow down at once, the Hall of Inquiry no quieter than before, yet it felt deadly silent and as delicate as a bird's wing when I turned upon Warren. My voice had been soft and gentle before, but now I was fueled with rage.

"What does she mean?" I gritted my teeth. It was the only way I could remain calm, to keep from ripping that brown hair from his head. Warren did not seem affected by what had been revealed—like Leander, he was particularly skilled at hiding his true nature.

"We didn't know that," he nearly growled, then stared at Kezia. "You're misguiding her. Tell her the truth."

"The truth is that this stealer has been using her abilities to possess bodies. She controls them and does whatever she desires with them. Then she leaves them to their destruction."

"It's unnatural," Leander said evenly, finally revealing that he had known such a thing as well.

"And exactly what we had been trying to protect you from, Sonnet," Kezia added.

"Warren, is this true?" I breathed, nervously wringing my hands together. Naya? The sweet-natured girl I had always expected to be cold and closed off was anything but? Her gentle demeanor and warm attitude had been a comfort to me long before I had found comfort and sense in Warren. It was Edythe, her rules and manners, that had always unsettled me so. But even then I could not imagine for a second that the stealers I had grown to know, now that I was a part of and tethered to them, would deliberately cause such destruction.

"Marvell, Edythe, and I noticed that she was getting angrier...more irritable, maybe," he explained at once. "We thought maybe it was something else, but this isn't something...are you positive it's Naya?"

Kezia folded her arms. "This is my realm. I know what goes on in it."

"So you are a liar then too." My throat burned. "I brought Naya here, and you didn't say a thing. Why bring this up now if you've known?"

Her eyes sparkled in response; however, it was Leander who replied. "There was no corruption in you. Protecting you first was a priority. The moment you decided to go back, we should have put a stop to it."

"I have the freedom to go where I please," I muttered. "You wouldn't have been able to stop me."

Leander looked at me squarely, reminding me that they did have the power to stop me. And what if they had? I certainly would not have become corrupted as well.

"Do you know how many living have died because of this?" the lioness spat, dragging my attention toward her. "Many. When she slips from their bodies they start to lose their minds. They start killing each other and killing themselves. Soon entire cities will be waging war. Maybe even the continents. You'd stand aside and let innocent living people die?"

Her words reminded me of Warren's story, how he had witnessed their presence do terrible things to Naya's family. I could only imagine how it might feel to have a dead ghost, a soul, slip into you while you are still alive. To possess you. It made me feel lucky I had never been possessed by anyone—not that I knew of.

"Then why haven't you stopped her?" Warren accused.

"Because we can't find her fast enough. I can trace her, but I have no way of getting to her in time," Kezia hissed.

I envisioned the small flicker of thought that ignited in each of our brains while she spoke. But I was the one to finally turn to Warren. "We can track Naya and put an end to this. She doesn't know about corruption or anything. This is a chance to do something right. To save those who still have a life to live."

Warren looked away, casting his eyes toward the marble floor. "All this time we thought she didn't have anything special about her. But she could possess someone completely. Why didn't she tell us? This doesn't make sense."

"We need to tell Edythe and Marvell too. The second we can, that is. Do you think they're back at Foxcoast?"

"I imagine so."

"I can get her to stop," Leander said suddenly, rising from his throne to join his companion ruler. "With my ability, I can render her paralyzed. It is a grand gift indeed that she has, but not everyone uses their gift in the ways we expect them to. She needs to be stopped."

I felt stung. Stung from the truth of my own thoughts. I had called this a realm of liars, and it really was. No matter what I uncovered or how many answers I seemed to get close to, something would turn the tide against me. Not only was the king of my nightmares also the closest thing I had to feeling not alone, but a soul I considered a dear friend had turned into another kind of monster. There were so many blurred lines and titles—the rulers, the stealers, the wraiths, the liars. It was hard to keep track. I felt the weakness inside my phantom pit of a stomach. I wanted to crawl onto the marble floor, to just lay there and let everything be as it was.

But I had to push forward. I promised to save the corrupted if they could be saved. The least I could do was tell Naya—to tell Edythe and Marvell as well. They had a right to know that while they believed themselves to be doing good and making change, they were destroying the ounces of humanity and life that still burned within them.

"Does possessing the living turn her into something terrible?" I murmured aloud. Warren saw the fear and uncertainty in my eyes. "Will she be as corrupted as you?"

He didn't flinch from my words, stepping closer to finally take the liberty of bringing me into his arms. There were no words to express my gratitude toward the gesture. Here, in front of Leander and Kezia. Here, after I had been rude and demanding and he had just discovered things about himself and his friends that changed his whole world. As close as I was to Naya, I had only known her for a short while. It pained me to think what Edythe, Marvell, and Warren might feel. It was like experiencing death all over again.

"Don't be afraid," Warren whispered against my hair. I wrapped my arms around his leather jacket and buried my face in it. "Nothing will hurt you."

"That doesn't answer my—" I swallowed.

Warren cut me off. I suspected it was because Kezia and Leander were listening. "We'll do what we can. Where is Naya now? Are we able to find her?"

"She's in Enya, actually," Kezia said stiffly, her eyes roaming the nature of our embrace. I briefly remembered her hostility and disgust toward the stealers. What could it mean to her now that I was clearly willing to befriend and get close to them? "The homeland of our dear, bare-footed Sonnet."

"And the forest," Leander sighed.

I pulled back to look up toward Warren. "I wonder what she's doing there."

"I guess we'll find out," he said frankly.

I nodded in understanding, bracing myself for what he was about to do next. He used two delicate fingers to rip into the air beside us, revealing a space that was so narrow and so long that he drew a thin line from the top of his head to the bottom of our shins. I had seen it before and no longer feared such power, knowing all too well that it would be over before I could even contemplate the workings of it.

Kezia and Leander, however, had never experienced it. Their curious eyes widened and reminded me of when I had set the room aflutter, distracted deeply by the new pages of their journals and books.

"As much as I hate to say it, you both will have to touch me in order to ensure you don't get lost anywhere," he muttered. Kezia suddenly grinned, nearly skipping down from her throne. She dramatically reached out one of her ring-covered hands and pursed her painted lips.

"Don't get used to it, creature," she warned with a purr.

"Oh, I won't, *your highness.*"

"You can call me mistress, if that's what you want."

Warren ignored her. Leander followed obediently, standing taller than all of us. He placed a pale hand on Warren's shoulder, and the latter did not wait. I clung to Warren as he guided us through the slip of the opening, a faint warmth covering my body from head to toe as I passed from the Hall of Inquiry to Enya's thick wilds in a matter of seconds.

Enya was my homeland. Standing on its grassy floor once more and seeing the wide, tall trees it was known for made my heart skip a beat. They were so tightly packed together and sky high, maybe even taller than any buildings that had been created by the living. Their forest floors were damp and nutrient rich, allowing for perfect agriculture and relief from the harsher seasons. Only Enya experienced the harsh snow season and the different variety of dry and wet climates.

I was able to forget the reason we were here once the world came alive in front of me. Small brown rabbits bounced around happily, blissfully unaware that four souls stood in a realm that was so near to their own. They would be safe here until a predator came along, like the sleek black foxes that slipped in and around the bush.

Sunlight was blocked by the canopy of trees up ahead, just enough so that small beams of light made the grass look like it was glowing. My feet felt like they were stepping on cool fluff, warming significantly when I stepped on the spots where the sun broke through.

"Beautiful," Leander murmured. "I haven't been on Enya for quite some time."

"I think I like the cities better," Kezia replied with a shoulder shrug. "An Enyian accent is cute, but it is easy to forget that these wilds belong to isolated folk."

"Isolated?" I echoed, turning to face her. They each looked so unusual—Kezia's exposed skin and silky pants paired with Leander's dark suit embroidered with gold. It was like bringing gold and silver coins to a merchant who only traded in livestock.

"What do you mean?"

"Pushka is quite civilized," Leander replied smoothly. "It is no secret that Enya is more rural."

"Rural, of course. But we're civilized," I argued, crossing my arms. "Just because I'm barefoot, doesn't mean we all run around kicking up dirt and not bothering to put on clothes."

Kezia let out a sharp laugh. "I meant there are no tall buildings, no carriages, not even dense cities where people gather. Isolated means lonely, doesn't it?"

"I was never lonely." This was starting to feel as though they were criticizing my home continent—my people, in a way. Even though people from all three of the continents could travel, I wondered why Enya was the one considered the most uncivilized. "Yes, people are more spread out. But we still interact, we still teach each other and have friends."

"Maybe you forget from being stuffed up in Vena, but Creo is rural too," Warren said to Kezia. I dragged my eyes toward him, monitoring his expression. He looked out of place too, with his leather jacket. But certainly less so. "It's the land of sea and lakes."

"True, true," Kezia murmured, her eyes dancing beneath the glittering gold mask of glitter that spread across the upper half of her face. "Where would Pushka be without Creo?"

"Exactly," I said stiffly. "I've heard the dirt in Pushka couldn't grow a flower."

"Let's not get caught up in where we are, but rather why we are here," Warren scolded, catching my eye before he looked around. "Enya is small, but I doubt Naya is here to enjoy the scenery. Where would she be? How are we even going to catch her?"

"I can feel where she is," Kezia reminded us, already heading in a direction of her choosing. I watched her go, noticing the way Warren's eyes rolled at her words. Even I had to admit that her theory of creating the realm was not something I was particularly invested in.

She and Leander may have been right about corruption, but I suspected the world had far more secrets and answers than we would ever discover. Creation of an entire realm simply was not something I could imagine a single person could do. It seemed more likely that Kezia simply had the ability to feel the world around her, to sense when it was breached and what went on inside of it.

With no other option, we walked in silence, following Kezia's pursuit. Even Leander had nothing to say, merely studying the different vegetation and then the way my feet sank into the mud alongside him. Kezia and Warren, despite being strangers and not particularly fond of each other, spoke quietly about the continent and the ways of travel.

Even though I was from Enya, I never traveled much farther than my own home. Dying young was a tragedy in itself if only because there had been little time to actually grow and leave the nest. My father, however, had ventured all over Enya. He had told me little things about it, like how the continent looked very much the same no matter which part of it you walked to. How the animals and the people never changed, each incredibly trusting and willing to help their neighbors. There were towns and villages, but nothing that could be considered a city, no residence where strangers might pass each other on the street. The communal feeling that came out of Enya was a grand unification of knowing that the land had to be protected and the other two continents would hardly survive without our export of food and livestock.

Pushka would have its soldiers and its ambassadors where they built the biggest cities and argued over policies and laws. Creo would always have its massive mountains and beautiful lakes hiding the most wondrous of animals and adventurers.

At last I murmured, "It's possible Naya isn't doing this on purpose. Making the living world start murdering each other doesn't sound like something she would do."

"There's no way to know for sure until we find her," Leander said calmly, placing his hands inside the pockets of his dark blazer. He looked down toward me and smiled warmly, voice quiet. "Have you practiced your little gift at all?"

I could feel the heat flush throughout my neck from being put on the spot. "No, but I did tell Warren."

"And what did he think?"

My eyes narrowed. "Do you actually care?"

Overhead, the rustling of leaves distracted us both. I watched as vibrant green leaves floated down from the canopies and were carried away by the wind.

"Yes," Leander said carefully, then he paused. His eyes moved toward Kezia's back before they drifted back to me. "My own abilities are far more than being able to entrap your soul—and by that I mean make it stay in one place. I was able to sense the essence on you and I am able to sense an essence on others. Or lack of it."

I remembered the hushed whispers of Kezia and Leander in the mirror room, the urgency and tension in their voices as they consulted one another.

"And you noticed it, didn't you? The difference between them."

"Yes. Sonnet is equally powerful, though the exact opposite of the other. Her life force is incredibly strong."

I tried not to react to the sudden memory. He had been talking about Naya and I! Not only that, but he was talking about our life essence. Leander had known the moment he saw Naya that she was corrupted—perhaps entirely without a life essence.

My eyes found Warren up ahead. He pointed toward the top of the tees with his right hand and murmured something quietly to Kezia. Her glittering mask twisted up on part of her nose, her mouth curling into a wicked grin. With every step she took, her red-tinted waves bounced off of her back and swayed side to side in nearly perfect harmony with her hips. I was not a jealous person, but I could still feel the way Warren's grip felt on my face and his lips pressed downward against mine. It shamed me to admit that I wanted that sensation and experience unique to me and me alone, even if I doubted that Kezia would ever see Warren beyond a corrupted wraith.

Truthfully, the lack of criticism or prejudice they openly held against him had nearly impressed me. I could not forget, however, that their true loyalties were with themselves. Only I truly believed the stealers deserved to be saved from corruption, if they could be. In the end, it was Kezia and Leander who had allowed them to continue to destroy their souls.

"He lacks a life essence," I whispered in realization.

"It seems that way. Something lost."

I looked at Leander and frowned, watching him leap over a cluster of vines. A phantom habit like anything else. Ahead, Warren turned back to make sure that everything was alright. I noticed that he had his own new habits, like checking backward to ensure that he could keep his eyes on me. I met his gaze and smiled slightly. The tension in his body visibly softened before he made a motion for us to catch up to them.

No life essence, a voice whispered. I imagined that his brown hair had turned jet black and his clothes, his body, shifted and shimmered into the creature I knew Kezia and Leander would expect to face. The creature that terrified me beyond reason, that could make my knees fall weak and my soul remember what it felt like to fall in a dizzying spin toward death.

Monsters and corrupted souls—they were the same things. Maybe they weren't, though. I wondered if any stories my father had told me, any documentation written in any sacred or ancient text spoke of real monsters. Maybe they didn't exist in this realm at all, but the living world had seen them. Somewhere, horrible creatures *did* exist to cause chaos. To cause destruction and death and the end of the world even.

But those creatures were not corrupted souls like Warren. Not souls like Naya or Edythe or Marvell. No matter what Kezia or Leander believed to be true, I knew they were not monsters doing monstrous things. They were souls who had lost their right to live and then lost their only ability to hold onto what was left of what they had lived.

Just as Leander and I picked up our pace, I shook my head and whispered back to him, "Nothing can be truly lost, remember?"

He gave me a knowing wink.

I sauntered up alongside Warren, nearly tripping on a bit of tangled vine that clustered near my ankles. His arm reached out to steady me, his warm hand curving beneath the spot near my elbow. I noticed his eyes move to my neck, where I realized there was likely still a reddening blush from Leander's little questions. Remembering the way Kezia had laughed, I deeply hoped Warren wouldn't think anything of it.

"There's a town nearby. We need to be careful," Warren said, mostly to me. "We have to be careful about who we interact with. Four souls around the living at once can be trouble."

"We passed through Vena with no problem. Why would there be a problem here?" I pointed out.

"A larger city gives more breathing room," Kezia explained, crossing her arms. "If the town is small and there are fewer people we put ourselves and them in danger. We can't take any chances that someone might screw up, like getting transfixed or trying to snatch a soul because they can't help themselves."

"I can help myself just fine," Warren scoffed. "You two act like you're the exceptions to everything."

"We are," Leander grinned, reminding me of the dangerous panther counterpart to his lioness queen. "We've never corrupted ourselves. We know how to keep the living from being affected by us. But do you?"

I sure didn't, and Warren merely met Leander's gaze with a hardened glance.

"Can you help yourself if a poor soul calls out to you?" Leander went on, a razor edge to his voice. "What if you stare too long at the living and forget yourself? Getting transfixed can make time move faster. By the time you open your eyes, the living you're looking upon can be three generations ahead."

"Not to mention how it'll feel when you watch them get sick and die," Kezia nearly purred. "Losing their mind all because of the weight of your soul watching over them."

"That can truly happen?" I jutted in, uncomfortable with the way they were treating Warren. Treating me, perhaps, without even realizing it.

"It can when you're a wraith," she declared, meeting my eyes. "A monster that lurks and tells them they should be afraid."

Warren suddenly pushed onward, picking up his speed so he could walk ahead of us all. Leander made a small noise of disapproval and Kezia merely shrugged, dropping her arms to let them swing. I lifted my hand to inspect it, then pressed it against my chest and held it there tightly.

CHAPTER SIXTEEN

In the western part of Enya, tucked away among massive tree trunks and beneath thick canopies, is a small village called Grethel. There, the people live in houses very much like my own—constructed with stone and wood, guarded by fences and their inhabitants' weapons. They live closely together and spend their days maintaining their relationship with larger Enyian towns that govern the continental trade. Grethel, however, is not made up of farmers. Instead, they are blacksmiths.

The scent of fire and metal filled my nose as we wandered into the village, the hard-knuckled citizens not turning a single eye toward us as we passed around and through their horses and bodies. The women wore loose clothing, sometimes pants and sometimes dresses that allowed them sanctuary from the humidity. The men wore clothing that protected them from their work, thick leathers and fabric so they wouldn't get cut or burned.

Kezia and Leander moved like silent, unseen monarchs ready to demolish the town and colonize it for their new castle. Warren looked like their brute, well-dressed enforcer with his boots and leather jacket. If the people of Grethel could see me, they'd likely recognize me as an Enyian. In every inch of my movements and the way words flowed past my lips, I was Enyian. The very soil beneath my feet seemed to hum in understanding, reminding me that I was dangerously close to my family in the south.

Not one soul with me seemed to notice the things I did. Perhaps they thought it, allowing it to remain within themselves like I did. Or perhaps they didn't care and had been long enough dead that it no longer occurred to them. Kezia looked around and sighed, then turned toward Warren. He had been quiet ever since they had blatantly mentioned that he had the capability to turn a single village mad, worse than any of us. His eyes remained fixed on the ground.

"She's still in Enya. I just don't know where." The lioness threw her head back. "Why would she come here?"

"You're asking the wrong person," Warren answered.

"Very helpful. You're lucky you had that power given to you or else you'd be outright useless."

"Sonnet and I could have done this on our own," he snapped, those blue eyes burning with anger. "You two should have just stayed in your tower and played pretend like you always have."

"Pretend?" Kezia laughed darkly. "And let a wraith ruin everything? I don't think so."

"We would have been happy to stay at the Hall of Inquiry, but letting people die didn't seem like much fun." Leander placed a protective arm over Kezia. She shrugged him off.

"But letting the stealers corrupt themselves? Now *that* was fun," I hissed. Three surprised eyes turned toward me. I shook my head and moved away from all of them, scanning over the different stone buildings that made up Grethel. "You two need to stop acting like we're the enemy. There are no enemies here."

"Of course not. No corrupted soul can take the place of our ruling," Leander said smugly.

"But she's right," Kezia clenched her teeth. "Let's just try to focus."

"You're the one who's getting frustrated," Warren said coolly, then turned to address me. "Maybe Naya can't control where she's going. It's possible. If she's transforming, even severely, then she might not realize what she's doing or where she is."

"That happens to you?" I asked.

He paused, and I suspected he was trying not to glance at Kezia or Leander. "Yes. Sometimes."

"Enya isn't a very big continent. It's all small villages like this, maybe even a few towns. If she's anywhere here, it wouldn't make sense." I pressed on my head, wondering if I could will the answers to my phantom brain. But nothing.

"We should find somewhere to be alone, away from the living. No houses. Our presence will disturb them. The sun will be going down anyway," Leander suggested, then inclined with his head for us to follow. I stayed close to Warren, placing one of my hands on his shoulder for comfort.

"I don't suppose any of us can see in the dark?" Kezia wondered out loud, turning to follow her companion.

Leander led us past several stone buildings before he at last smiled to himself. He motioned for all of us to follow, heading toward a building that was tucked away privately behind a garden. The new structure was taller and wider than any of the houses. Curiosity ignited inside of me while I watched Kezia and Leander disappear through its aged and weathered wooden door. I held tightly onto Warren while we followed, silently hoping that I wouldn't get stuck and make a fool of myself.

When we emerged and found ourselves inside, I burst out in a tiny laugh. It was a tool shed, rows and rows of large smith tools hanging dangerously alongside several gardening tools. The smell of damp mold and dust filled my nose and made me wish desperately that Edythe was with us, for several large windows adorned the walls that made it possible to see out and upward toward the tree canopies.

"Is something funny?" Kezia questioned.

"Yes, actually. I would have never thought that ghosts would be hanging out in my father's tool shed when I was alive. I wonder what the owners would think if they could see us."

"Probably that two stuck up rich people were coming to knock it down," Warren muttered, gesturing to Kezia and Leander's adorned wardrobe. Even in the dark shadow of the shed, the golden mask that the lioness wore glistened when she moved. Leander's nightly suit, however, was even darker than the shadows.

"You'll feel right at home, then," Kezia responded to me, ignoring the small quip from the Traveler. It was possible that she even found his words to be a compliment considering the lavish, marble built clock tower she kept herself hidden away in.

"I doubt it. We may be in Enya, but our shed was never this big." My voice quieted.

"We need to figure out a plan, and quickly," Warren murmured suddenly, stepping away from me so that he could lean against one of the wooden pillars that held up the roof. Above him dangled a variety of cutting tools that, if they fell, would slice him in half entirely. If he wasn't already dead, of course.

Kezia spun on her heel and faced the three of us, lifting her hands like she was about to surrender. Her eyes closed and her chest heaved long and deeply. "I can feel that she is still in Enya. She's not moving, though."

"Can you tell if she's herself?" I asked, not quite sure how anything truly worked.

"How do you know she's in Enya but you don't know what village or town she's in?" Warren accused. Leander shot him a harsh look. "Or did you two expect me to bounce everyone from town to town until we know for sure?"

"I don't expect anything from you," Kezia corrected, dropping her hands. "And yes, I *can* tell that she is not completely in this realm. She's taken control of a body. But she's not moving, which I don't understand."

"She could be sleeping," Leander proposed.

Despite the fact that the three of them did not look convinced, I nodded quickly. "You know, you might be right. It was Naya who explained to me that we don't dream.

123

Do you think she can dream and sleep when she's taken over a body?"

"So she possessed a body just to take a nap?" Kezia's eyebrows raised. She took a page from Warren's book and leaned against one of the pillars that stood closest to her. Her long fingers twisted the rings around her fingers, her eyes staring off into some sort of deep, thoughtful trance. "I've laid in plenty of beds while I've been dead. That doesn't mean I'm itching to sleep in one again."

"Who cares about the why," Leander pulled his blazer closer to his chest with a clearing of his throat. "This stealer is corrupt, and right now she has control over the living. The longer she spends in that body, sleeping or not, the more deranged it's going to be when she tries to slip out of it. For herself *and* for the body she's using."

I swallowed tightly. This couldn't be Naya—not the one I knew. Not the one I had laughed and teased with. Not the one I had laid in bed with and told of my childhood, my family, and how important it was to get back to them.

It seemed ironic that I would be back in Enya to chase her down and not my family. Grethel was in the west, but my home was in the south. It wouldn't be hard to go there without needing water or food or even shelter. The wilds were thick and confusing, but I had all the time in the world. I was dead, which meant I was limitless.

I knew it wouldn't be possible. I could not leave Warren with Kezia and Leander, not when they couldn't care less what happened to him or why. He was as limitless as I was, yet he had been dubbed a monster by the so-called rulers of the realm. I promised myself I would save them all from themselves and I meant it. The only difference was now it seemed that Naya would be the first I had to save—before, I thought it would be Warren.

"We need to get Edythe and Marvell here," I declared, catching Warren's eye. Now that I really looked at him, he seemed tired, perhaps as sickly and tired as when I had reunited with him at Foxcoast. "We will need their help, and they need to know about the corruption. I know they have their own methods, but I think it's best if they travel with us."

"You're right," he agreed, pushing off of his wall to saunter closer. He took one of my hands—the corrupted one, by chance—and brought it to his lips. He pressed his warm kiss against my knuckles, peering at me from behind their ridges. "I won't be long. I'll explain first, then bring them both back."

"Can I trust you to tell them the truth?" I whispered, searching his eyes for any sort of deception. I found wickedness, admiration, and hardness swirling all at once. He nodded stiffly, then looked at Kezia and Leander.

"Your sweet one will be safe with us," Leander promised, sticking his hands into the pockets of his slacks. "We've hosted you before, haven't we Sonnet?"

I ignored him, pushing Warren to get going. "I'll be fine. I'm in my homeland, remember?"

Something flashed in his eyes, unrecognizable to me, before he dragged two fingers from his head to his waist. A faint glow emitted from the traveling portal he made.

"This town is Grethel, don't forget. We'll be right here when you come back," I promised hurriedly, wondering if it really meant anything at all to him.

He didn't reply. Instead, he pushed one arm and shoulder through the portal before he disappeared completely. The world closed behind him like nothing had ever happened, like his soul did not just step through a fold in the universe, leaving the rulers of the realm and myself alone again.

Every second that passed brought me to the conclusion that there was a real possibility that Warren might never return. What if it had been too much for him? Traveling with two souls who had kept themselves hidden away from him, determined to make him see that he was a corrupted wraith feeding on others with no remorse or reason. Only I knew otherwise. I might have agreed with Kezia and Leander's knowledge of everything that happened in this realm, but I knew that no stealer was a deliberate monster. Not even Naya, wherever she was. There had to be more to the story that I had missed—a story that Leander and Kezia themselves had never gotten to read. Not in the way that I had and did.

"So you haven't had any other displays of power?" Leander mused, not bothered by the fact that he had to sit on the floor. Each of us were sprawled near each other, me with my lack of care as my gown hiked up toward my knees and Kezia leaning against him. He had one arm draped over her shoulder, lazily albeit protectively. The sight of it made me feel colder.

"No." My voice felt raw. We spoke here and there but for the most part seemed to be waiting for Warren to return. "It doesn't matter, anyway."

"Of course it matters. You were able to move those books, to reach into the living world," Leander said quickly. "That's marvelous."

"Well, what's so special about it? I can't do it all the time. I'd be surprised if I could do it again, actually."

Leander glanced sideways at Kezia, some unspoken conversation passing between them, then leaned forward toward me. "I mentioned earlier that I would be able to help Naya with my abilities. It's true that I can stop her, but what has been happening goes beyond having the ability to jump into living bodies."

My heart picked up speed and I wrapped my arms around myself, rubbing away the coldness I now felt. The sun was getting lower in the sky, causing the windows to turn a dark shade of blue. It was only a matter of time before the moon became our only source of light. I highly doubted anyone would be putting lamps in their tool shed for the loitering ghosts.

"What else are you planning to do to her? We just have to make her see that what she is doing is hurting her. And she needs to know about helping souls too. We can't let her corrupt herself anymore," I said swiftly, meeting Kezia's colorless eyes.

"Corruption is a dangerous, dark thing. We both believe that your abilities allow you to do something which we can't. Your life essence is so strong. Perhaps it's possible for you to force Naya out of a living body," she murmured.

My gaze moved from her to Leander, searching each of their expressions for further elaboration. They waited patiently while I collected myself, the tightness of shock rendering my cheeks stony. "Are you saying you want me to be the one to control her?"

"We don't know much about her and we certainly know next to nothing about how her being in a living body works. We *do* know that it's causing her to corrupt herself and making the living lose their lives. You seem to be some sort of bridge between this realm and the living one," the panther shrugged.

"I don't know what to think," I admitted, leaning to rest the back of my head against the pillar I leaned on. "Edythe is far more advanced at moving and touching things in the living world. I think she might be the best bet."

"Maybe," Kezia said, and the harshness in her voice made me look over. She threw off the arm Leander had dangled over her, brushing her palms along her silky pants. "But Edythe won't be able to do what we need her to do. What we're going to ask you to do."

"What are you asking me to do?"

The lioness and the panther looked at each other once more. It was Kezia who continued, her shoulders squaring as she faced me completely. "We want you to practice your abilities. Practice them so that you can direct them on your stealer friend when the time is right. Leander will render her immovable, then you can envelop her with as much power as you can."

"What is that supposed to do?" I asked, not bothering to hide the tinge of anger that laced my words. They were expecting me to attack my friend with a power I couldn't begin to describe. Their method treated Naya like a criminal—she was only someone who was doing something she didn't understand was wrong. If she was as corrupted as we believed, even to the same scale as Warren, then there was nothing to say she would be any different than she always had been. Perhaps she was angrier, but anger alone didn't make you dangerous. I envisioned that we would find her and explain the consequences of her actions.

Leander and Kezia seemed to think we were on a mission to punish.

The two of them studied me carefully for a long, quiet moment. Then Kezia parted her lips, swallowing before she spoke the next words. "You know what they are and what they have become. They are wraiths, as much as you don't want to believe it. Helping them is not an option anymore, Sonnet."

"What do you mean not an *option*? What other options are there? I thought we were going to find her to talk to her and tell her she needs to stop."

"It won't work. I can *feel* her. I can feel how strong and powerful she is, like a storm moving through fire. Our only option is to destroy her."

Despite her powerful and determined words, Kezia did not look happy. A deep line had set on her forehead and her knuckles turned white, the rings on her fingers nearly bursting as she constricted her hands.

Destroy her? They wanted to kill someone who was already dead?

"You waited until now to tell me this?" I accused, my eyes flickering between them. Ice washed through me and stiffened my phantom bones. I imagined them shattering like ice—even more, I envisioned myself leaping from this very spot in order to destroy *them*. "Now—when Warren is away? Because he's just as corrupt as Naya? How can you say these things? You don't even know Naya. You don't know Warren, either."

I hurried to my feet in order to look down at them, taking several steps away in an attempt to restrain myself from actually pouncing on them. I could feel the instability rising through my mind and heart, willing me to kick and punch and scream.

"You walked with him," I snarled, my voice rising. I pointed an accusing finger at Kezia. "You *smiled* and talked to him. You let him use his abilities for your own gain and then you plot his...his—"

"Death?" Leander finished, rising to his feet as well. Kezia followed suit, neither one looking particularly threatened by me. "Hardly. When they are destroyed, who knows where they go."

"What happened to being fair rulers?" I snapped. "If you want to lead this realm, then don't destroy your subjects. Warren was right not to accept you and feed into your delusions. You're just two souls who think you're better than the rest of us."

"We *are* better," Kezia hissed, stepping forward to close the distance between us. She stood taller than me and looked down, those black eyes like coal against the shimmering gold mask that ran along her upper face. "And you were too. Until you let them tell you how to live in this realm. Until you believed their words over ours and trusted them. And look what happened."

She reached for my wrist and yanked it above our heads. Before I could snatch it away, to punch her like I had been planning to, I saw what she was drawing my attention to. My left hand had transformed, quivering inside of Kezia's iron grip. The skin around it was veiny and pulsing, like the very anger inside of me was being fueled by my black-hand heart.

I let out a choked sob, angry tears pooling in my eyes. "Let go of me," I begged, tugging my arm wildly.

"You let yourself be corrupted, Sonnet," she scolded, her own eyes glistening with a new wetness, as though the coal had been left in the rain to glisten and shine. "And I let it happen to you. *We* did, by letting you go. You called being with them *home*. It's our fault. And we know we have to destroy them. If you're not careful, it'll happen to you too."

"You're wrong." My tears trickled down my cheeks as they raced toward my chin. "I won't destroy them. I can't kill anyone again. I already...I already took that man. I won't get rid of my friends. Corrupted or not—I can't let them disappear. There has to be another way."

"There isn't any other way. You are all wraiths."

"So you'll destroy them? And what about me—if you didn't think you needed my power, would you destroy me too?"

Kezia let go of my hand quietly, no longer fearing that I might hurt her. I covered my face, turning away so that they wouldn't see just how much I had been holding from them. I felt the unnerving presence of someone else entering the shed and heard boots as they scuffed against the floor.

Without quite looking, I flung myself into their arms, desperate to get away from Leander and Kezia and all the nonsense they forced me to think about.

But the arms that wrapped around me were not covered in leather.

They were wool.

CHAPTER SEVENTEEN

The Seer continued to step into the shed, his arms tight around me while he shuffled us to the side so that more bodies could pass through the door.

I looked up into his surprised and somber face. The warm smile I had grown used to now only a pitiful half curve. "Marvell," I breathed, pulling back slightly. "I'm so sorry. I thought—"

"It's wonderful to see you again," he chuckled. His eyelashes fluttered lightly as he took in the smear of tears on my face, glancing over my head to give Leander and Kezia a calculative stare.

A flash of copper caught my eye and I looked at who had walked in behind him. A weight lifted from my chest, familiar longing forming inside while I reached for her. Her velvet gown was soft to the touch, even through the thick skin of my corrupted hand. Edythe squeezed me tightly, placing her own hands on my cheeks to dry them.

"Oh, Sonnet," she tsked, shaking her chin slightly. The freckles across her nose bounced while she took in my appearance. "Are you alright?"

"Much better now that you're here," I admitted. Without quite worrying about whether it was proper or polite, I grabbed her into another hug. "I missed you so much. Both of you."

"You did?" Edythe asked. I could sense the doubt in her voice. Of course, I thought. She would think that I was still my old skeptical, disapproving self. How could she have guessed how much had changed about me? How the stealers had become souls I trusted?

"I did," I said certainty, then moved to show her my hand. "I'm so sorry. Warren must have told you what has been happening."

"He did. We can address that as the time comes. For now—and I know this will be hard—but avoid any soul callings that you hear. It will try to sweep you toward it, but you must fight it," she commanded. I nodded while she stepped away and placed her hands together, chin raised as she looked upon Kezia and Leander. She moved to place one hand on Marvell's waiting arm.

Standing across from Leander and Kezia, they looked like poised diplomats waiting to discuss their next move. It was an interesting dynamic—I'd almost say that they were mirrors of each other. Edythe and Marvell looked like two sophisticated, elder siblings of crowned royalty. Kezia and Leander looked like the troublesome younger siblings determined to lose themselves in the pleasures of mischief.

"You must be Kezia and Leander," Edythe said politely, albeit obviously. "Our rulers, I presume?"

"You'd presume correctly," Leander smiled. Even though his height matched Marvell, I applauded him for being able to look unbothered under Marvell's intense and protective gaze. "But lucky for you we're not the groveling type."

"What shall I grovel for?" Edythe inspected her nails briefly. "Only a king or queen worries about being dethroned. I have nothing to seek penance for. My name is Edythe and this is Marvell."

Marvell blinked twice. His lips parted to speak but another set of boots caused a distraction. Warren shuffled in, passing through the door so easily I wondered when I had really gotten used to it. The sight of him made me reach toward him, surprised to see that my hand had transformed back to normal. Ignoring it, I slid my hands beneath his leather jacket and pressed my cheek against his blue collared shirt.

Marvell and Edythe watched us closely, their features softening. The Seer especially looked taken aback, though neither commented on my warm and friendly embrace toward a soul I routinely fought with and blamed for my death. I looked up into Warren's face and frowned. His skin had taken on a sallow hue and his eyes, once bright and blue, had turned a dark and dull shade that blended in with the coming darkness of the tool shed.

"Are you alright?" I whispered. He smiled and pressed the tip of his nose against my forehead, breathing in deeply.

"Don't worry about me. What happened? Your eyes are red," he whispered back. The concern in those eyes, as dull as they were, made my chest tighten. *This is who they wanted to destroy.* Leander and Kezia could not see him as anything more than a monster—a lost cause that getting rid of would make their life easier.

For now I decided to keep it to myself. If their greatest weapon was me and all they could do was render other souls unable to move, then Warren and Naya weren't in any danger. I would never agree to their wicked solution.

No soul, living or dead, would have me to fear. I was no emissary. I had been born and died with freedom in my veins. Not even corruption would squeeze the right thing out of me.

"You know me," I offered weakly. "Death makes me emotional."

The moonlight cast in through the windows while I watched the thick layer of dust that coated them glow like fireflies. I stayed close to Warren, watching his lips move while he conversed with the others about the best course of action. There was no more doubt surrounding my heart in order to protect it. I would do whatever it took to protect him, even if the very core of him frightened me beyond reason.

Nothing could change the fact that it had been Warren who had pulled me from the river. Who reached in through its current and held me close, looking down on a scared and frightened girl. I could only imagine the kind of strength it took to do such a thing. The idea of someday coming upon another dead person made me feel weak. Seeing animals dead was an eerie and curious experience, even if those animals had been small ones. A mouse, a squirrel, even an occasional bird. The sight of their tiny organs and bodies never became any easier. I highly doubted that one could ever get used to seeing the gruesome insides of *human* bodies, addiction or not. Empathy and humanity did not die with the physical body. It lived on.

At least in me it still did.

My eyes dropped to my hand. It was normal and fleshy, showing no signs of being able to change at all. Where was the man's soul that passed through me? How could it be possible to exist all at once and then not at all? Life itself was so fleeting and tragic, moving too slowly and too quickly all at once. How could it be possible that in death there was no justice or peace—not for any of us.

He could have been a husband or a father. He could have been nothing. But he had been a person with a smile and a voice and a conscious. The sight of his gaping and wailing soul filled me with sudden dread. What was worse? Being stuck in an afterworld realm like this one or being rendered to nothing more than stardust?

Warren turned his eyes on me. "Are you ready?"

"What?" I blinked.

"We're going to head out now. Kezia thinks she's close," he explained, ignoring my blatant obliviousness to what was being talked about. "We should get to her before she moves on."

"Okay. Are we walking?"

"Not this time. We'll travel north of here. That's where we think she might be."

Edythe and Marvell exchanged a hesitant glance. Then, without fear, Marvell faced Leander and Kezia. "Isn't it possible she'll go back home once she's done? Why do we assume she needs to be tracked down? We should have waited at Foxcoast for her."

"And let the living world continue in jeopardy?" Kezia scoffed. She folded her arms, the muscles on her abdomen flexing with each movement.

"Naya probably won't go back home," I said quietly. Each of their eyes turned to me expectantly. "I got into a fight with her, and ever since then she hasn't returned to Foxcoast. It's probably me she doesn't want to see."

"What did you say to her, Sonnet?" Edythe wondered. There was a flash of disapproval in her eyes. I felt my own annoyance flare inside of my stomach. How long would it take for her to realize that I wasn't an enemy? I was one of them now, in every way—dead, corrupted, phantom skin and bones tethered to the same place they are.

But now it was my turn to feel angry and ashamed. At myself. What I had said to Naya wasn't about her specifically, it had been about all of them. Warren especially.

"Well," I began, keeping my eyes on the floorboards. "I confessed that I thought you all were monsters. And then I told her that I understood you were souls, but you had been changed somehow. I also told her that I knew she had visited her family once."

The room was quiet before Leander sighed theatrically. "Oh, the drama. To think I died to get away from it and wound up always in the middle of it anyhow. Let's get going, shall we?"

My eyebrows raised just as he pushed his way past all of us, signaling to Warren that it was time for him to use his ability. With a hardened glance, I watched as he reached into the folds of the realm, the world, and then reached his hand out. Toward me. Like I was the one thing he wouldn't want to lose, others be damned.

I snatched his open palm and shivered when Edythe hooked my arm with hers then placed a fair hand on Marvell's dark blue arm. Kezia's strong fingers gripped my shoulder with Leander holding onto her. Warren guided me through the opening and I gave a slight pull, the weight of the others making me push myself through.

When Warren pulled me through to the other side, it was pitch black, the green grass taking on a blue-gray hue while the moon towered over. We were in an open field—a foggy one that brightened my cream colored dress against the haze of the atmosphere. The field had a slight incline while I strode across it, keeping Warren and the rest of the stealers behind me while they continued to pass through effortlessly.

The icy breeze cut through my hair, pulling it away from my face while my feet slid into the fresh, damp soil that covered the plain. *A growing field,* I realized. The clean, vibrant scent of the open plain erased any smell of metal and dust that had settled inside of my nostrils. The sharp scent of rain and wind brought me to the present moment in front of me.

Small indents in the soil caught my attention. I slowly followed them, admiring the oddly shaped prints that had been left for me to discover while my feet dragged softly against the ground. Ahead of me, a flash of tan moved in the corner of my vision, and I dragged my eyes away from the prints. My lips parted as I studied the creatures peering around the open plain for any hint of danger.

There, as though six ghosts had not just stepped onto the growing field, a herd of deer grazed on the new grass that poked through the soil. The largest one, with his horns arching like giant branches off of his head, seemed to meet my eyes. He stared for several seconds then turned away to tend to his herd, scanning the tree line.

It was my first time close to a deer that didn't run when I got too near. I could not help myself from stepping closer and closer until I was nearly immersed in the herd, the deer around me flicking their tails in peaceful delight. I couldn't help but let out a small giggle of laughter, every instinct inside of me telling me to stay as quiet as possible. But it would never be needed because I was dead. I was no longer part of their world.

I could see the swirling black and brown in their eyes and the bit of russet that mingled on their backs beneath their tawny pelt. The antlers of the largest one were coated with light fuzz, pieces of it dangling like it had been rubbed off.

"They're beautiful, aren't they?" Warren smirked from behind me, causing me to jump. I let out a small gasp and looked beyond him—the others were moving in the opposite direction, trudging down the plain instead of up it like I had.

"Where are they going?" I asked tightly, the sight of Edythe and Marvell disappearing with Kezia and Leander making me nervous. Who knew what she would try to do when my back was turned.

"I told them to go ahead. I saw you take a little detour," he murmured, placing his hands inside of his coat.

"They are beautiful," I declared at last, reaching out like I could pet one. My fingers inched dangerously close before I dropped them, defeated. I would never be able to touch them.

"I'm still not used to seeing them like this. They used to run whenever you got too close. I would see them all the time in Creo. We call them branch deer because of their antlers."

My head jerked toward him, my body gone still. His words flowed through me, and I searched his face for the answer to the question I didn't have to speak. The wind whipped against my hair, pushing the curls into my cheek like they were hugging me closely.

"Yes," he nodded stiffly, sensing the question that bubbled inside of me. An unspoken question that he knew I would want the answer to. "That's where I was born. And that is where I died. I think it was early morning. I just bought a new shirt because I could finally afford a nice one—well, let's just say if I knew I was going to wind up in it forever I would've picked a different color."

I waited patiently while he collected himself, the deer stepping carefully around me.

"I bumped into a man and I guess he decided to punish me for it. Maybe he was having a bad day—or actually, maybe he saw my shirt and decided enough was enough. I come from a poor town in Creo where we used to work cutting roads into the mountains. It's a labor job, the kind that takes a real toll on you. The advisers were pretty wealthy men from Pushka who used to dress in fancy clothes and tell the workers what to do. I think this guy was a worker, because when he saw me he just... lost it. He started punching and kicking me. All I did was walk down the street. He came at me so aggressively, I just thought I did something wrong. I didn't realize I was dying until I couldn't breathe. Blood was filling into my lungs and it suffocated me."

I stared at the stony, calm expression that covered his features. It wasn't fair. How could taking someone's life be so easy? I wondered where that man was now. Did he get to live with his family and his conscience, not bothered that he was a murderer? What justice would be served when he died? Who would he have to answer to? Nobody at all? Warren had been *murdered*.

And I had the audacity to call him a monster. I had accused him of taking *my* life.

"Warren," I whispered carefully. "I need you to know something." His eyes met mine, a small muscle in his cheek flexing. I stepped forward, slipping my hands beneath his jacket to feel the warmth that radiated throughout his phantom body. "I don't blame you for what happened to me. Why I'm here... I don't know if there's any meaning to it. I can't even be sure if we're going to find all of the answers we are both searching for. Maybe Kezia is right and we're just dead. And that's that."

"And that's that," he agreed, reaching up to brush the hair from where it had stuck to my lashes. "If this is all there is, forever, then I can live with it. I was nothing in life. Nobody missed me when that man beat me in the road. I was just some poor kid trying to find a purpose. I put on a fancy collared shirt and thought it would give me something. A better attitude, a better outlook, a better reason for walking around.

"We are in the end of our lives. Yet we live on. And who's to say we stop here? When I was alive, I wondered if my parents were out there somewhere. In the sky, in the stars, or if they were alive too. I didn't know them. But still I wondered. And I'm standing here now, with you, *still* wondering."

My chest constricted, and the tightness in my throat gave away my weakening willpower to not cry. But his words struck me, so deeply and so emotionally that I thought perhaps we were meant to find each other. I never met anyone, living or alive, who could ask the same kind of questions I did. When I died, it felt like I had been cheated—I never considered the beauty of still being able to wonder and dream, to look to the stars and the world around me while maintaining my ability to question it all.

"I was thinking...what's worse—to be stuck in this realm or to be stardust?" I confessed, my voice cracking.

"Above all, I think we were always meant to be stardust. What if this is just another stop along the way to getting there?"

I leaned in to kiss him then. He met it with such desire and appreciation, his hands and body moving so gently against mine. Here, in the north of Enya. In the night with nobody except the moon to see us, her light illuminating the smoky haze and the deer that couldn't be bothered.

"What kind of monster are you?" I whispered, drawing away to look at his eyes. He avoided me and pressed his forehead against mine, his hands sliding down the length of my arms.

"The kind that adores you," he confessed with a fierceness that surprised me. "I may have had nothing in life, but I have you now. And I would wander this entire world as a ghost with you if you let me. I know I frighten you—I know I'm a terror and a nightmare. I see you shake and gag whenever you're near that other side of me... but I adore you."

I let him kiss me again. Never had my heart been so receptive to words before. Never had my brain been so fooled into thinking the heart was right. What entity, what ruler of the universe, decided that it would allow a soul to still care and love? Even when it had been corrupted, torn apart into shreds and transformed into a king of nightmares. Who granted the ability to carry it with us when all else had been lost? And would we keep it until we turned to stardust?

"Please know," I whispered once more and pulled him close, placing my hand against the center of his chest. "I will do everything I can to protect you. To save you. If that's what I can do and what it takes. I might be afraid of you...but I don't think I can lose you, either."

Warren was quiet, considering his next words carefully. "I keep hearing the souls calling out to me," his voice hardened. "It's difficult to resist them, Sonnet."

I looked up at his face to see the fear and embarrassment that rested there. "Warren, you have to. I know you don't want to believe it, but you don't have to be corrupted anymore. You don't have to crave anything anymore. Just resist."

"They're getting louder," he shook his head.

"Don't answer them, Warren. Whatever you do," I pleaded.

His eyes moved toward the deer, and I turned just in time to see the flash of tawny colored pelts bouncing beneath the moonlight. They leapt over us, powerful hind legs making them look like spirits slipping in and out of the fog. Their tails flickered while they did so, kicking up small tufts of dirt behind them.

"They look like ghosts," I murmured quietly, watching them leave.

"Yes, they do." The monster beside me agreed.

CHAPTER EIGHTEEN

O ur travel had been for nothing. When we joined the others, Kezia quickly informed me that she felt a disturbance in the realm. This time, it hadn't come from Enya.

We were on the wrong continent.

Somehow, Naya had been able to move quickly and swiftly almost as though she were traveling like Warren. The stealers concluded it would be impossible, that only Warren had the ability and the name of the Traveler.

"Naya can travel," I remembered suddenly. The silver chain of Marvell's watch stuck out slightly from the inside of his coat, distracting me. Its shiny coating reflected the moonlight—I briefly remembered my fascination with it, the single piece of the living world he was able to take with him. It had crossed over like a soul itself. "She was the one who took me back to Vena."

"What?" Edythe nearly hissed. She blinked quickly then made a show of fixing her elegant dress so that it sat perfectly along the ground like it was a grand ballroom we were standing in and not the thick of Enya's forests. Clearing her throat, she murmured, "What do you mean she *helped* you travel?"

"It was like traveling with Marvell...at the time I assumed she answered the call of a soul and just ignored it. I didn't think much of it, to be honest. It was dizzying and it just happened." I shook my head. "I'm sorry, this is my fault. I should have mentioned this sooner."

"Regardless, you understand how big Pushka is, don't you?" Marvell sighed, cupping his chin in thought. "She could be in any of the major cities. Each of them are incredibly unique and have citizens in the thousands."

"That's certainly where I'd go if I felt like possessing people. Somewhere with an entire lot to choose from." Leander perked up, snapping his fingers toward Warren.

"She *would* go back to Pushka," I realized, looking at them eagerly. Each of them looked worried and tired, perhaps even afraid. But Edythe was the most expressionless of them all, her physique and stature giving off a propriety I would never compete with. And neither would Kezia, the self-declared ruler of the realm. "Because that's where her home is. That's where her family is. Not to possess people, but to see her family again."

The acceptance in their eyes was like a dagger to me. *Of course* Naya would want to go home. Out of them all she had been the only one who could understand my innate desire to reunite with my family. Her cold shoulder toward the subject, the secrecy of what had happened when she did, and her blatant disapproval for being dead nearly proved what her ulterior motive was.

Happiness and sadness began to flood me all at once. Happiness because I was right. Naya was no monster, not the kind that was evil. Sadness because all my friend had wanted was to see her family again—and now, two souls standing around me wanted to destroy her for it. I longed for the answers to my questions. Did she know what she was doing? Did she care? Was I right? Did she simply want to see her family somehow?

"That's a fair assumption," Edythe said at last. "But we don't even know where Naya is from."

"She's from Zarya," I pointed out. Their shocked expressions made my temper flare out and I couldn't help myself from snapping at them. "You mean nobody even thought to ask her?"

"She's a private person," Marvell admitted calmly. Edythe's eyes dug into my skin. I could already sense the lecture I would get from my outbursts. "Quite honestly I'm a bit shocked she told you. Why you and not us?"

Hurt flashed in his eyes but I ignored it. "Because I had an interest in her. And we both know what's it's like to long for our families more than anything else."

"We had families too," Edythe said with a disapproving scoff. "Why do both of you act like you're the only ones wanting to go back to them?"

Leander pressed his lips together to hide his amusement. I ignored Edythe, hiding myself from her criticism. "Warren has been to Zarya before. He's been to her house, even. Isn't that right?" I asked.

Before he could answer, Kezia clapped her hands together. "Okay then, let's go. We don't have time to stand around and start criticizing the kind of small talk we've had with each other. She's from Zarya, who cares? It's a metallic city. It's a large city, stealer. Do you think you can get us as close as possible?"

I could see the irritation riddled on Warren's face. As much as he and I butted heads, it was nothing compared to the disdain he felt for Kezia. A part of me couldn't blame him. I only hoped he never got a chance to figure out that she wanted him destroyed completely. And that she wanted me to be the one to destroy him.

"Yes. But with all of us around, we're bound to start making her family sick. Naya and I were only there for a short time, and they were hardly able to live in their own house," he said coldly.

Kezia paused. "Did one of you get transfixed?"

"Transfixed?" I asked. "You mentioned that before. What does it mean?"

The lioness cast her gaze downward. "Yes. It happens when there's a lot of emotional energy in one place for both the soul and the place. Like a home, or where someone has died. The soul becomes transfixed, almost like a trance. And it becomes frozen without purpose."

"That's what happened to Naya." Warren murmured. Edythe and Marvell looked toward him, their faces twisting in disbelief. I even saw pain crack the surface of Edythe's freckles, her nose wrinkling slightly.

"You've seen this happen before?" I asked Kezia, unable to handle the curiosity that burned through me.

"Once," she said simply, meeting my eyes. "The transfixion was so strong I crossed an entire continent to break it."

Leander said nothing. It occurred to me that I had been calling them lioness and panther, rulers, and on occasion king or queen. But they were not together in any way other than partners. The touches and friendliness had been rooted in deep trust and companionship. Kezia, whether she created the realm or not, was alone. She had trekked for as far and as long as she needed in order to find someone else she could be with. The true devastation of being dead wasn't being dead at all. It was loneliness.

And the seven of us, Naya included, were together. I couldn't know if there would be others. If there were others Kezia and Leander knew about, kept hidden away like prized secrets. But to me, in the moment, there was only us.

"Then we will have to be careful," I said, determined to let no soul be transfixed again. I would protect them all—even Naya's family, if they were there. There was no reason they needed to be subjected to the sickness that would course through them because they were being haunted. Worse, because they were being haunted by their own family member. "We can try to draw her out and away from her family if she's already there. But if she isn't, then we need to distract her. I can distract her—"

"And I'll draw her out if she's already inside," Warren offered. Nobody moved to contradict him, so it was decided.

The Traveler made another cut into the realm, his eyes fluttering slightly while he did so. I moved to grab hold of him, wondering when this would become normal and whether it was possible to actually rest in peace.

Zarya was unlike anything I had ever seen. There was no vegetation that decorated the massive city made of metal structures and pure glass. Their streets were cluttered and busy, so fast paced I thought time accidentally sped up somehow. But no—the people of Zarya simply moved quickly, so hurriedly that they didn't stop to take in everything I was able to take in from the other side.

The tall buildings cast long shadows across the black paved roads. I had no idea why roads wouldn't be dirt or even brick, but their flat tops helped different people push and shove into each other without a second glance. Signs for clothing, shoes, and accessories for purchase made it easy to understand why Naya had died in the outfit she was in. The dark pants and silver shirt blended in seamlessly with everyone else. While it wasn't practical for farming or raising animals, it was likely perfect for a night out in the city where everyone wanted to wear the latest and greatest.

None of my companions were interested in Zarya, though. While I was captivated by the new world, Warren was already inspecting the tall buildings.

"It's one of these," he declared to himself. "I tried to get us as close as possible."

"Very helpful," Kezia scoffed. "Did all that corruption ruin your memory, stealer? Try to be more specific."

It was Leander who cut her a glance. Indeed, he did look unsettled and uneasy with his glistening temples and unruly black hair. But not even his sleek outfit adorned with gold embroidery seemed like it came from Zarya. Why was he on edge?

"You should have stayed in Vena," Warren shot back. "Let us handle this, since she's *our* friend, not yours. It would have been quieter and less annoying—"

"Wait," Marvell said. He put out his hand to cut both of them off, tilting his head slightly to the side.

"What is it?" Edythe said, her attention come alive in full force.

"Someone's...about to die." Just as the words left his mouth, a man from the crowd around us reached out for the stranger who had been keeping pace next to him. The woman he grabbed was young, her bright red hair falling in braids down to her waist. Her skin turned a chilling shade of red as her assailant's fingers clawed at her throat.

"He's going to kill her..." I stammered, uncertain what to do. What *could* we do?

Kezia let out a gasp, gripping Leander while she watched. Their compassion for the living was far beyond anything they felt for those of us who were already dead, I thought wildly. Several people who had been sauntering past broke out into a run, terrified of what was happening. Others began to help the woman by clustering together and attacking her assaulter all at once. The frenzy around us segregated into a small circle, leaving an open space in the road closest to us.

While my eyes watched the chaos unfold, a flash of braided hair caught my attention. It looked so similar to Naya that I thought I was hallucinating her among the crowd. My eyes scanned the flicker of human flesh and clothing as they scrambled against each other. Then, emerging from the chaos, was a young girl—younger than any of us, with her face still showing traces of youthful fat. Her dark brown hair was pulled into a tight bun at the nape of her neck; her clothes a dark gray color that matched the rest of the city's aesthetic. She happily strode away from the crowd as though she were oblivious to it entirely, setting for the opposite direction.

"There!" I pointed. "That's her! She's...I can't believe it. She's *inside* that girl. That has to be her." I stared. Only Edythe moved into action, racing for the living girl. It would have been humorous if it had been any other situation. Edythe, racing in her violet gown, dragging it beneath massive metallic towers. When she got close enough, her small hand reached for the girl's clothing and pulled. She pulled and pulled—and it *worked*. It worked because Edythe was the Taker, capable of touching the living world like she was alive herself. The girl, stopped by an invisible force, seemed to understand her predicament immediately. Her eyes glazed over the emptiness in front of her, then rolled backward toward her skull. I blanched, afraid to keep watching but unable to tear myself away.

I had promised to be a distraction, but could I really be one now? She had possessed a body and taken it for her own. What I was witnessing and watching was far beyond what I believed to be possible. It was worse than possible; it was unnatural. Each of us sensed it now, and I could tell from the others' frozen expressions. Even Kezia, who had claimed to feel the power and chaos caused by it, looked fearful.

Edythe's tight grip did not let go. She said nothing while the girl's eyes rolled backward and she began to choke, saliva pooling inside her mouth and leaking out the corners. Then she convulsed, and no citizen in Zarya moved to help her. The ones who ran away in terror did not come back, and the ones who had it in them to help someone were already trying to make sense of the violent mess that had blossomed without reason.

I expected Naya to remove herself from the body of the girl, to face us and explain what game she was playing. I planned to tell her all that I knew—even more so, to apologize for the way I had made her feel. I couldn't allow her to believe that I thought she a monster. Even now I thought she was simply misunderstood. So when the physical body that hosted Naya began to quiver and convulse, I took a few steps forward while I waited for the warm soul I knew to emerge.

But what came out of the girl's body twitched. It twitched and oozed in a way that reminded me of the king of nightmares. Like a spider emerging from its nest or egg. Long arms with sharp claws forced themselves out of the living world, pulling the rest of its body with it. But there was no phantom body to the soul at all—it was a mass of swimming black matter. Its face was a stubby, flat construction of spiky teeth. There were no eyes, but its head had a dark skeletal look to it that was perfectly round and bald.

The sight of it pulling itself free made me keel over, smooth arms catching me just as I hit the paved street. They stayed around me tightly—whoever it was had knelt with me. And I wasn't the only body to hit the ground. The girl it had crawled out of, dangling from Edythe's fist, hit the street with a thud. I did not blame Edythe when she dropped her; there was nothing else she could do besides watch the wailing soul appear alongside its body.

Movement made me turn and look—and then I pressed my head to the ground, nails digging into the hard surface. My entire body began to shake, and I considered myself lucky that nausea didn't roll through me. There was no gagging or heaving this time—no water in my ears, either.

But it may have been the hands that wrapped around me. Then the second pair of hands that helped bring us both back to our feet. I leaned into them both, surprised to see that it was Marvell and Leander. Marvell had caught me the first time, and now Leander stayed close, his eyes meeting Kezia's. For some reason I doubted that they had imagined it would come to *this*.

I forced myself to look, to *really* look, and see what was happening. My hands gripped onto the two tall men who held me, forcing them to stay in place while I finally allowed myself to inspect the king of nightmares. I had only really looked once and that was when I had died. The second time I deliberately kept my back turned, my body quivering from the idea of what I might see.

The uncontrollable sobs that began to rip from my chest nearly tore me apart as I took in its form. It looked strangely canine while it hunched forward with its massive claws, just a shadow of broad shoulders and curved back. I could see now that its elongated teeth, white as pure bone that I once witnessed inside a dead man's body, were nestled inside a muzzle. The king of nightmares remained eyeless, its entire form just an ethereal mass of swirling dark. Where Naya was all skeletal terror, the king of nightmares was mongrel ferociousness.

Warren was.

The realm and the entire world seemed to go quiet before Naya turned to grab the wailing soul with her twitching claws. There simply wasn't enough time to intervene. There was no expectation that she would do such a thing, no plan that we could have put into motion while her claws gripped the soul and did something terrible. She pulled at it, tearing it into tiny pieces. My eyes widened as the young girl's soul couldn't be bothered to care while Naya tore its phantom limbs, spine and shoulders breaking loudly, and then absorbed the soul entirely.

I had seen first-hand what happened to newly dead souls that stealers touched. I had touched one myself and watched him disappear entirely. But *this*? This was gruesome, cold darkness that I refused to believe.

Naya. How could *Naya* be the one doing this?

"Stop!" Edythe begged, unafraid of each wraith she hurried toward. The skeletal darkness arched backward and let out a warning hiss, the length of her arms much longer than Edythe stood tall. Yet still the Taker yelled, this time begging Naya to stop what she was doing.

"You don't understand!" she continued. "You've corrupted yourself! Don't you see what's happened to you? To both of you?"

Naya knocked Edythe out of the way, sizing up the king of nightmares with a high-pitched squeal. The dark violet blur that was Edythe spiraled and hit the street with a thud. In the living world, people were already beginning to step on her, horrified by the dead body that the wraiths hovered near.

Warren responded, leaping onto Naya in an attempt to get any part of her within his jaws. Their spine-chilling appearances were enough to make me want to vomit, but watching them together was nearly impossible. Only shock kept me from looking away, just like looking at a dead body and trying to grasp that it was only a shell. Their black bodies were like smoke and mist all at once igniting in a plume of tangled teeth.

I could hardly tell who was who while they shrieked, the long snout of Warren's canine-like form snapping inches from her thin and skeletal neck.

CHAPTER NINETEEN

I couldn't blink or breathe until Leander let go of me, reaching out with his hands to produce his paralyzing vapor. The smoke slithered and snaked its way toward the wraiths, bouncing in anticipation for a new victim. It would be only seconds before they were each frozen in place, choked down by the same dry smoke that confined me to the chair in Vena.

"Sonnet."

My name broke through the chaos but sounded far away, a desperate attempt to bring me back to my new reality. Hands ripped me from the safety of Marvell's grasp and I pulled back to meet the glittery mask of gold adorning jet black eyes.

"You have to do it," she begged me, looking less like a vindictive snob attempting to destroy my friends and more like a girl without any other options. "It's inside of you and I think you can use it as a weapon."

"I can't," I argued, attempting to pull away from her. "You don't understand, please—I can't do that. Not to them—"

"Do you think they want to look like this?" Kezia demanded, her hand reaching up to fist the collar of my gown. I felt it hike up from my ankles, exposing the shakiness of my legs. "They don't want to be like this. If you truly care about them, you'll do something!"

Kezia could not have known how her words affected me. I felt them settle inside of my brain and weigh me down like a stone dragging me to the very bottom of a river or lake. The lioness was a ruler of truth, one that sickened me to my core. Because I knew that both Warren and Naya were missing something the rest of us still had. Something that made us who we were: stolen souls with the ability to still care, protect, and love.

Warren and Naya let out a deafening series of snarls that made me jump.

I thought about Warren. The handsomeness in his face that I had failed to acknowledge when I first met him. I thought about the way he had pulled me from the river and what that might have took, what emotions went through his body as he looked down into my face. A stealer—someone new to speak to, to understand, to ask questions with. He had shown me arrogance and fear from the very beginning. But he was a soul. A soul that had been taken from the living world too soon, like each of us.

The feel of his lips on mine. The wetness on his lashes when he confessed that he could not stay away from me, despite the instinct inside of him that told him to run. The shaking confession he gave to me when he admitted that he began to crave souls and how that terrified him. These were things a monster should not care about. These were things a monster or a wraith could not understand.

A memory flashed inside my mind. Warren and I among the deer, my palm pressed against the center of his chest. Placed there deliberately for a reason—the same reason that Leander had taken my hand and pressed it against his. The flicker beat of his phantom heart, the same phantom heart that made him still feel warm. And the emptiness within it, the cold absence of what each of us took with us when we died.

I knew the moment I placed it there that his life essence was gone. It had been lost in the mission to help souls cross over, lost in the realm and all that it left unanswered to him.

And Naya...a girl with warmth in her veins. A girl with a soft side that surprised all who met her, me included. The gentle look in her eyes whenever they met mine. I had never pressed a hand to her chest, but if I did I knew there would be nothing. Just a hollow space in her heart where she should have kept the hope and joy of being alive.

"No," I said firmly. Kezia's eyebrows raised in surprise, but it was not her I was talking to. I reached for Leander and pushed him away from his focus on the wraiths. "Use your powers on me. Not them."

"What are you talking about?" Kezia cried. I could see Marvell scurry off toward Edythe, dragging her away from where the wraiths tore each other to shreds. The side of Edythe's face had twisted into a substance like sleek, black oil. The bit of skin that was visible on her arms had turned just the same, reminding me of what my hand could transform into. My heart kicked inside of my chest, fear sharpening as she suddenly twisted to meet my eyes. The brown shade of them had turned jet black, hiding the whites. I trembled, reaching out toward Leander hurriedly.

"Leander," I begged. His cool gaze met mine and he nodded once, already throwing out his hands so that the smoke would target me. It spilled from the cuffs of his blazer and struck me. I inhaled it willingly then sputtered and choked, my phantom muscles convulsing wickedly. My eyes glanced toward Warren and Naya.

I made a promise to protect them.

"What can *you* do?" the panther said, a steel edge to his voice. "You refused to use your power. How can you help them? How could you help us?"

I waited patiently for the fury to envelop me, but none came. No, I needed more. I needed *something*.

"*This* could have been you. You were from Enya. You had a family, didn't you?" he tried again. The smoke washed over my eyes, drying them out so much that it stung when I blinked. I let out a painful cry, suddenly afraid of what I had agreed to. I had no idea if this would even work. And the longer Warren and Naya fought each other, the more danger they were in. The more danger the living world around us was in.

"You're a filthy, disgusting wraith. A creature." Kezia's voice broke through the smoke. I began to cry, both from the smoke and from their words. Despite the tactic they used, and I knew this was a tactic I *wanted* them to use, the words still hurt me. They still stung the gentleness that lived inside of me. "You don't deserve to be here. You deserve to be ruined like they are."

No you don't, a voice whispered.

A voice that I began to recognize. It was strange and murky, the same whisper that had been in my head all along. But it couldn't have been.

Sonnet..

My mother. It was my mother's voice. I let out a scream of delight and sadness. Was she seeing this? Could she see what had happened to me?

I am so sorry.

I tried to think what my mother had to be sorry for. Nothing—it was I who was sorry. Sorry I had slipped in the river. Sorry I had befriended stolen souls. Sorry that I had become one of them. Sorry I stolen myself away. Away from the place where she was.

"I want to be with you," I cried out. If Kezia and Leander could hear, they gave away nothing. Not even insults were hurled at me. "I'm so sorry I did this. I'm so sorry I didn't get to live my life. I'm so sorry you died too."

I'm happy to see you where you are.

How could she be happy for me? I was stuck in a realm full of monsters and wraiths and lies and truth. I never found peace.

You've held onto what it means to be alive. You've felt the grass. You've kissed the wind. Do you remember your brothers? Your father?

I made to laugh but instead choked, my throat twisted and raw from the blue vapor that swirled inside of my mouth. How could I forget my brothers? My father? I would never forget them. When the world became nothing more than stardust I would remember it all. To forget was to kill, and to be forgotten was to truly die.

"I'm trying," I rasped.

Try harder. There is still so much life in you. Do not let death carry it away.

I tried to focus on the whisper of her words inside of my head. I tried to place whether they were coming from far away or if they were coming from directly inside of me. Either way, I took them in full stride. I promised to find a way to save the stealers if they could be saved. I still didn't know if that was possible—but what was inside of me, the life I held in my heart, was more than enough.

We are never really gone. We are never really alive. We are just moments, Sonnet.

It reminded me of what Leander had said. Nothing was ever truly lost. Nothing could ever really be destroyed. The universe might have made us believe that the life essence inside of us could disappear, but we were souls. Souls *are* life's essence.

The air around me was calm. The suffocation in my throat and lungs went bland even though I opened my eyes to see the swirling blue smoke still trying to find its way into my body any way it could. I did not look at Kezia, Leander, Marvell, or Edythe.

There were only two souls that needed what I was about to do. What I was about to unleash.

My feet made no sound as I dragged myself across the flattened pavement, the edges of my dress flowing behind me. The fear that was able to paralyze me far worse than anything Leander could conjure was long gone. It had been replaced by the intensity of my new role, my new understanding of what my purpose was. Warren and Naya's massive forms did not look at me, not even when I sauntered close enough to see the iridescent, oily shine of their new forms. The coldness that radiated from them felt like standing on top of snow, a freezing breeze pushing my hair and gown back with each striking movement. They hovered and loitered, too determined to prove themselves as the most terrible. I wondered if this was how Naya was able to travel so quickly—a phantom, a terrible ghost that could move across the lands in search of its prey. If somehow I had closed my eyes, distracted and dazed, from the truth of how I had traveled with her.

"I don't think you two are going to like this," I warned loudly. They each finally turned toward me, jaws open and absent eyes crawling over every inch of me. I thought briefly of how it would feel to be torn apart by these wraiths. These corrupted souls that were my friends.

The king of nightmares unhinged his jaw, a warning that he could swallow me in one gulp. The blast of his shriek hit me, just a black wind that brought forward what was buzzing inside of my chest and my soul.

Then I closed my eyes and let what had been hidden inside of me break free.

The wraiths let out a wail so high-pitched I re-opened my eyes far sooner than I expected, nearly jumping out of my skin. The light that emitted from me blinded them, their heads shaking and bouncing in an attempt to rid themselves of the bright cloak. I moved for Naya first, the terror I had felt at the sight of her replaced by the desire to do what was right. I could not destroy them. They didn't have me to fear. But they would have me to remind them. To remind them of what it felt like to be alive; the flicker of a life essence that kept us from losing ourselves forever.

Without an essence, there would be no reason to look back on the living world fondly. No reason to think we had any meaning at all, anything that suggested we were more than human beings who lived for a short while then were gone forever. There had to be meaning in something, in anything. The feel of grass. The touch of wind. The sound of the sea as it tossed and turned. I was overloaded with it. I had far too much, built inside of me like a direct connection to the living realm. It was all flowing through me too rapidly for me to grasp. This time, instead of keeping it, I would tie it to something else. To *someone* else.

My hand grasped Naya, a slimy and scaly feeling all at once. One massive claw wrapped around my neck and I gasped, choked not by smoke or shock this time. Her hand lifted me from the ground, but I pressed deeper, hand flat against the ridges on her body that acted like a ribcage. A haze of blinding white light kept the three of us inside a protected bubble, one that was causing her to tremble fiercely.

"Naya—" My eyes burned, my voice a painful rasp. "I know you just wanted to see your family."

Her round head tossed backward, the pressure around my neck nearly unbearable. Was it possible to die *again*? Would she pop my head right off and leave me to spend my eternal afterlife in two pieces?

"I know you wanted to see them…to go home again…and I'm sorry—" My eyes bulged, windpipe cut off as Naya drove her squeezing to its furthest. Had I been a real body with a real beating heart, I suspected I would have been long dead. A flash of light erupted from my palms, and without hesitance, I directed the blast toward Naya's chest, my aim true and steady. Naya dropped me at once and I bounced off the pavement, phantom skull cracking against the blacktop. A faint smile touched my lips, knowing that I had struck where I had meant to.

The bright shield around us still stood, but Naya began to shrink, coughing and sputtering a deep black substance that made me stare. Only Warren's sudden movement made me look away just in time to see him tear the largest slit in the universe I had seen so far. It looked like the rabid, sudden rip of a wild bear or wolf. Indeed, the canine-like swirl of darkness let out a powerful scream and then dove through the portal, desperate to get away from all the light and danger.

"No!" I screamed. He was part of this too. I needed to give what he had lost back to him. There couldn't be just one—I had meant it to be for *both* of them. With courage I never thought I had, I scrambled to my feet and threw myself toward the darkness before it could disappear through the portal.

And felt my body press against the king of my nightmares as we stumbled together.

CHAPTER TWENTY

I had lived a life and then lost that life, reduced to the mercy of a slippery rock that the universe had created and set for me. I'd been dragged from the water and the reeds by a monster, one I had been convinced was out to destroy me. I found companionship and familiarity among strangers who had lost their lives as ridiculously and randomly as I had. We nestled inside a small cottage on the edge of the coast where the gloomy atmosphere dampened the grass and ignited the sea. I developed the courage and willpower to hold onto life's essence and face the creatures that terrified me beyond reason.

It was all pale in comparison to the achievement of falling through the world with Warren. There was hardly anything to hold onto. His slimy body felt like thick, frozen oil. Then we collapsed in a single blink, my eyes widening as we fell right down into water.

I had only been underwater once—when he had pulled me from beneath the river. Even then my entire body hadn't been submerged. Beneath the surface now it was quiet and silent, small pieces of vegetation floating around me slowly as though they were suspended in time. No bubbles or disturbance in the water signified that we had fallen, but I still felt like I was floating. My dress and hair bobbed around me, dragging my attention to the soul that was staring back at me.

My heart soared at the sight of him. There was no reason to hold our breath or try to not speak, but we did it anyway. We simply looked at each other until I smiled slightly and he swam forward to meet me, every inch of him the Warren that I had come to know. Not the monster. Not the king. But Warren, with his dark hair and his bright eyes.

Our lips found each other beneath the water, his hands going to my waist and mine reaching behind his neck. There would never be a reason to pull away or stop kissing, but I thought I would have to resurface eventually. It was only when the water around us began to vibrate that I noticed light had been bursting from us both. I could feel every good and pure thing about life still blossoming inside of my chest. The life essence that had terrified the king of nightmares leaked out of me and into him, lighting up the water like a submerged lighthouse.

My mother was right. Her whispers had said we were moments, not alive or dead. And *this* was a moment. A moment that reminded me of the excitement I felt when I would laugh with my brothers. When I discovered snow for the first time. When I hugged my family. When I simply felt the warmth of the sun. When I merely existed. Not just survived or went through the motions but saw each and every thing that made being alive beautiful.

There were still beautiful things. And there was still so much to look forward to.

Warren released me and smiled, taking my hands so he could bring us back to the surface. My head broke free of the water and I laughed, allowing myself to be pulled toward the shore. Just when I found the smooth rocks beneath my bare feet, Warren pulled me closer. Both of us stood soaking wet, the admiration in his face impossible to ignore.

"Did it work?" I whispered. He closed his eyes and leaned his forehead against mine, arms tightening around my waist. Without waiting for his answer, I pressed a palm to his chest. The phantom heart beat kicked against my palm. And behind it...

"Something's changed," he murmured, opening his eyes once more to look down at me. "I feel like...like there's some sort of meaning again. Or some answer that I've gotten but don't know what question it belongs to."

My cheeks began to wet with more than just water. "That was me. I answered you. The life inside of you—inside of Naya—was gone. But nothing is lost forever. You just needed someone to put it back inside you."

"Life essence?" he echoed, shaking his head. Small droplets bounced off of the strands of his hair.

I nodded. "It's inside all of us. It's what makes us souls. It's what makes us have meaning. Yours was gone—lost somehow. Maybe from corruption or maybe something else. So was Naya's."

"I didn't feel like I was lost before," he confessed.

"I don't think it's something you really realize. You just forget how to appreciate the moment and the beauty that is a moment. Living or dead...it doesn't matter." I sighed.

Warren was quiet. My eyes peered past his head and toward the mountains. They were mountains I recognized, having seen them before. The sun was beginning to set, casting a golden glow on the peaks in the distance, shadowing the clear lake like a smoky blanket. The sound of the water brushing against the sandy shoreline sounded peaceful.

"We're at Peak's Lake." I blinked in surprise.

"No," he insisted, a heartbeat later. "We're at Mirror Lake."

I could not help but tilt my head back to laugh. Allowing me to rename his own lake…an infuriating, monstrous soul determined to make my heart flutter and my blood boil forever.

"Warren," I began seriously, my laughter dying out. A shadow flickered over his face, fearful of what I was about to say next. It seemed like he wanted to protect what little joy and life we were experiencing in the moment, hesitant to let anything disrupt it. "I need to tell you something."

He nodded briefly, and I took a breath to steady my nerves. "Kezia and Leander…I know you don't trust them. That you are skeptical of them. And that's fine. But I also want you to know that, despite everything, I think they had good intentions. But you deserve to know that they wanted me to destroy both you and Naya."

"Destroy us?" his jaw clenched. "They thought you could get rid of us somehow?"

"I guess so. I told them no, that I would never do that. I vowed to protect you, to save you all if I could," I admitted. "And I've done that. I'm just not sure if it really worked or not. I guess we won't know until we go back."

He blinked slowly, lips parting as if to say something. A moment went by before he finally sighed, reaching up to pull some of the sticky hair from my temples. "I ran because a part of me, wherever the corruption lives, knew what you could do. The life that is still inside of you…it's been dangerous to me all along. I couldn't help what I did. I hope you forgive me. Making you run after me like that. Knowing how much it terrifies you…" he drifted off, swallowing loudly.

"It's okay," I murmured. My hand tightened against his shirt and his chest, liking the way that the small flicker of essence inside of him seemed to call out to me. "I…I'm not sure if I'm afraid anymore."

"No?"

The ghosts of whispers swirled inside of my phantom brain. "I think I heard my mother's voice speaking to me when I let Leander use his power on me," I murmured, recalling the faint memory of her voice. Had it been real or had I imagined it?

"I don't think that's possible," he said honestly, surprise on his face. I wondered if he had even noticed that Leander's vapor had suffocated and choked me while he challenged Naya for a taste of the soul that she had killed. It was brutal honesty, a kind that pointed to rationality and reason for doubt. I couldn't hate him for such a thing, not when I admired the truth so deeply.

"You're probably right," I shrugged. "But it was there. Something was there. And I owe it everything. I don't know if I could do what I did again." The bright light that had poured from me, searching for any sort of darkness that it could devour, was now gone.

"Hopefully you won't have to." Warren found my eyes and I saw a determination inside of them. Someone who seemed to want to make a difference. I wondered if he would be able to control himself, if he could ignore the calls of souls across the realm as they died. There were millions of people in the world, so vast and diverse it would be impossible to keep track of them all. How did they all find a place to go? What was our purpose, really? Were we just stuck souls that truly had stolen ourselves away? Would we ever have answers to those questions?

"We can't let anyone get corrupted. Not anymore," I said at once. I remembered the long snout of his canine-like face, his eyeless face and body leaking with a black haze. He and Naya were like black holes trying to see how much they could swallow, even each other. "No more *helping* souls. No more getting swept away to them. We have to keep fighting. We have to remember what it was like to live and hope and dream for things."

"I agree with you, Miss Sonnet," he said pointedly. I pushed him playfully, hoping he would see just how serious this was. Then I pressed my fingers to his cheek, feeling the warm and fleshy feeling that lingered beneath my fingertips. "The life inside of me...I'll never let it go out again."

It was time to go back and confront Naya.

When we returned, the street was a different kind of chaos. The living world had blocked it off completely, though many people chose to stop and stare. The young girl's body still lay on the ground, destroyed by whatever Naya's corrupted presence inside of it had done. Time seemed to move slowly while healers, people skilled in medicine herbs and medical inventions, hovered over her, not even bothering to protect what little privacy she had left.

The sight of her laying in the street made me shiver. It made me thankful I had passed away so quickly and so isolated. The only witness to my death were the rocks, the river, the trees, the sky, and Warren himself. Perhaps the birds continued to fly overhead, none the wiser that a human had just met a youthful end. Perhaps a fish or two swam by, confused by the unusual behavior that had been exhibited. Then again, at least that young girl had people who were able to identify her, move her, and protect her. For this girl, it would not be her family that stumbled upon her. It would not be her father or her younger brothers.

It made me wonder whether death could be felt. We were all energy, all connected—did the young girl's family feel a strangeness in the air? Did they feel her physical body when it collapsed in the street? Worse, did they feel when she had been torn apart by Naya? Would they even know or understand, or would they continue to think that their daughter, sister, or friend, had gone to a place where they would live in peace?

As we stepped back into Zarya, Edythe and Marvell were holding each other. I had never considered Edythe a girl who would want to be held, but her eyes were turned into Marvell's wool coat. His arms wrapped around her, dark lines etched on his face while he watched the pair of souls huddled on the ground. Kezia stood away from them, focused entirely on the body that lay in the street. She had displayed such a desperation to protect the living world, I could only imagine how much it would bother her to see that someone had died. Someone we could have protected earlier had we not dwelt or bickered. Her head shook back and forth slightly.

On the ground, Leander held Naya in his arms. *Leander.* Sure enough, he rested on his knee and had pulled Naya onto his lap to keep her from touching the blacktop. She had returned back to normal, her long braids swinging slightly as they framed her round face. The silver and black of her clothes paired nicely, resting against the dazzling and lavish outfit that her protector wore. Her eyes remained closed, like she was sleeping, but I knew that could not be true. It was Naya herself who told me we could not sleep. That we could not dream.

"What happened?" I asked, hurrying over to where Leander held her. His cool gaze met mine—covered by the mask of composure, but I was certain there was worry that swirled inside of his irises. "Is she alright?"

"She collapsed and returned back to this once you dove after the stealer," he murmured, low enough so only the two of us could hear. "What happened to you two? Are you alright?"

"Yes...for the most part," I replied. "Do you mind if I...?"

Leander said nothing, loosening his grip on Naya so I could kneel down and shuffle closer to her. So gently and with so much calamity I thought I would never be capable of, I pressed my palm to the middle of her chest. Her shirt was incredibly thin, perhaps more than my own dress. But I could feel it. Exactly where I knew I had put it, somewhere inside of her chest behind her heart. Inside of her heart. Anywhere it would fit so that it could not be lost or mistaken or forgotten.

I reached to pull some of the braids from her face. How could this girl be such a terror? I longed for her to tell me how she felt—to see if it had been how I had felt. How I still felt, actually. The anger and frustration she had displayed were signs all along that she had been losing her way.

"Sonnet..." I looked up into Kezia's mask, her hands folded in front of her politely while she looked down on us. "I'm sorry for what has happened here."

"Me too. And I'm sorry I didn't...well, I don't know how I brought that essence forward," I confessed to her. "But they have it now. Naya and Warren.. They won't hurt anyone again. I promise you that."

She nodded once, not explicitly stating whether or not she believed me. Instead she said, "You did something incredible. When that light burst out of you, the living world could see it."

My heart buckled in surprise. Any calmness I had felt suddenly turned to a shaky uneasiness, that contradicting feeling that you were being scolded and praised all at once. "I don't think I could do it again."

"Good," she concluded. I watched the formal hardness return to her face, that deviant lioness who I imagined wished she could carry a throne around just to sit on in front of the others. "This realm may be another page of the world, but it should remain a separate page."

Her metaphor made me incline my head toward Edythe. "Speaking of which...I think Edythe might be able to help you find journals to read. She can even turn the pages for you."

The lioness ruler turned her eyes to Edythe, assessing the oddity of the violet gown and the petiteness of the Taker's face as she met her gaze.

"Don't let the dress and smallness trick you," I warned. "She's a spitfire."

"Is that so? Miss I-don't-grovel?"

Despite myself, I laughed. Leander broke into a grin, nodding his head in thanks. Not even the panther could deny I had been right in my suspicions: Kezia liked to read, and she was desperate to read something she hadn't read a thousand times over. I would have to remember to have Edythe visit the Hall of Inquiry, too, just to clean up the mess I had made when I had accidentally knocked over their books. The idea of scattered journals and old bread laying on a marble floor covered by a mirrored ceiling just didn't sit right with me. Yes, it would have to be dealt with.

I got back to my feet and watched as Leander pressed two fingers to Naya's wrist, tracing small circles on the back of her dark skin. "Did you know her?" I asked him, my eyes narrowing slightly.

"What?" Leander started, then peeled his hand away from hers. "No, of course not. I've been dead for much longer than she was ever born."

"You seem...gentle with her." To avoid a smart quip, I stepped closer to Kezia.

"She's been through so much. I can feel it," his shoulders tensed suddenly. "I know what it was like to be transfixed, desperate to reconnect with your living family. If it wasn't for Kezia, I would have never gotten out of it."

I felt myself frown, a small knot forming in the back of my throat. Curiosity burned within me. "We might never know why it happens... but what were you like in it?"

"Just empty. Like it was somewhere I had to be but couldn't get away from. Then

Kezia got to me and...before I knew it, honestly, I was looking at my mother who was much older and my nanny had died." Leander cleared his throat, the pale skin there bobbing slightly while he did so.

"We all love our families and our home. Our familiar places," Kezia whispered. "But they're dangerous places. When I got to Leander's estate, his mother was incredibly frail. Whatever nanny he did have was long gone. Time works mysteriously when you're dead. There is no sleeping or time where you dream. It's all at once. And it moves quick. So quickly you wouldn't even believe it."

"Like a blink," I murmured. "But if Naya's unconscious now, then what happened? Maybe something I did was wrong."

Kezia opened her mouth to reply, but it was another voice that finally decided to speak up.

"I've been awake this whole time," Naya coughed. Her eyes fluttered open, a glossy distance in them that made me tremble. They moved to study Leander. "I just wanted to rest in this one's arms for a bit."

CHAPTER TWENTY-ONE

"Naya!"

My voice carried, bringing Edythe, Warren, and Marvell closer. Each of us crowded around her, but she made no move to sit up or stand. True to her word, she wanted to rest in Leander's arms. The panther, who had been so gentle and calm before, suddenly took on a smug demeanor.

"What happened?" I asked swiftly. "How do you feel?"

"I...I don't know," she confessed. Edythe and Marvell blocked her line of sight to the dead body that was laying in the street, just beginning to be moved by the rest of the living world. Moved to a cemetery or wherever it was that they would take her. What a blessing and a curse, I thought quietly. Someone to ensure your body did not rot. But no longer having a soul to be able to witness it, from anywhere that souls might go.

I wondered whether or not they would try to hide it from Naya like a terrible secret—or if she even remembered at all.

"Do you remember what happened?" Warren asked, echoing my thoughts.

"What you did was so incredibly—why didn't you tell us?" Edythe blurted, her face twisting into a shade of red. "We could have helped you. We could have been there for you."

"What do you mean 'been there for me'?" Naya gritted her teeth, scrambling out of Leander's lap. She stood to her feet; her eyes looking across us wildly. I thought I saw Marvell shrink slightly beneath her sharp gaze. Leander let go of her, stepping up to stand beside Kezia as though to protect her. "You and Marvell do whatever you guys want. You never *include* me. He saves souls and you save souls. You don't even have to help them cross because you found a way to *save them.*" Her eyes filled with water, lips trembling.

"Yes, we did. And why is that such a bad thing?" Edythe demanded.

"You don't even get it, do you? How hard it is to listen to you two talk about how you saved someone. How you were able to manipulate the living world and prevent their death. That isn't fair to me and you know it. You know *why*," she hissed, the muscles in her throat constricting as she attempted to keep the tears from spilling.

Kezia, Leander, and I shared a similar expression. We were each confused and partly concerned, if only because we had just witnessed Naya in the form of a ravenous creature ripping phantom limbs apart to feed the desire that controlled her. I was frightened that what I had done to her was not enough to keep that creature at bay. That it would break free and display itself, as quickly and wordlessly as my hand was able to change without me recognizing.

"That's not our fault," Edythe gasped, looking at Marvell in disbelief. Pain etched itself on her features and she reached toward Naya, forcing her to look into her eyes. Naya resisted, pulling herself out of Edythe's tight grasp. "We tried to save you. We did everything we could, but it didn't work. So you started to possess people as a way to get back at us?"

I realized then what had made Naya so deranged, hitting me like a branch that one of my brothers may have whacked me with. Edythe and Marvell had been saving souls at the time of Naya's death. From the look in her eyes and the words she spoke right down to the fact that she was standing in front of us at all, they had not been successful. My heart suddenly gave a twinge of regret and sorrow. I couldn't imagine having the opportunity to have been saved. If arms had been reaching out to catch me and I had missed them entirely, slipping and knocking my head against the rocks anyway despite every best effort. It would have been a flicker of hope, of good fortune, that you needed to watch pass you by without having any say about it. And not having any way to change it. Then to have to witness those very same arms save souls time and time again, pretending that it didn't bother you.

Marvell shook his head, tight wrinkles forming on his forehead. "We wanted to save you just as badly as you wanted to be saved. But it was too late. *We* were too late. Please, Naya. Don't think we haven't regretted it ever since. We are so lucky to know you now, but please don't think we didn't try our best to help you."

"Did you think you could just pawn me off to Warren and I would be happy?" she cried. "I can never be happy here. We're *dead.* How do you....how do you just accept that?"

"Because it's the way it is," Edythe's hands balled into fists. "Nothing will ever change that." Her words reminded me of Naya herself when she had turned away so suddenly back in Vena, determined to make me see that what I suspected in the others was not true. What didn't make sense to me is why Naya would be adamant that she was not a monster, then do something as monstrous as slipping in and out of living bodies.

"Naya...every time you touched a soul or helped a soul cross over...you weren't helping it," I said slowly, hoping to pull her attention off of what Edythe and Marvell had not been able to do for her. "You were being corrupted. Turned into a wraith. Do you remember anything from what has happened?"

Recognition flickered on Naya's face. "No but...I know I've been changing...I just didn't know that it would...that I would—" She cut off, looking into the open space Edythe's absence had created. She saw the tossed mess of brown hair that had come undone from the tight bun at the girl's neck. The sallowness of her skin that signified she was dead, gone from the shell of her body.

"That girl..." she choked. "I was...I stepped into that girl."

"Yes," I murmured slowly, afraid to follow her line of sight. "Why did you do it? After telling me you weren't a monster. Like you weren't something to be afraid of."

"Why?" Edythe cried again, pulling Naya's attention back toward her. "Why were you doing that? You were *possessing* people, Naya. How could you do such a thing?"

"I didn't know it would turn me into something...something like Warren," she sobbed, her chest jerking like it was being tugged. But it was the intensity of her cries, the sudden onset of emotion that tore its way to freedom. If Warren was offended by the comment, he didn't show it, his face a pale compilation of sadness and confusion. "Every time I stepped into their bodies I could feel what it felt like to be alive again. I...I killed her. I can't believe it. Sonnet was right. She was right all along. We're monsters. *I'm* a monster."

Tears escaped her and she folded her arms around her body, her braids getting stuck in the creases of her flesh. Edythe's arms wrapped around her tightly, and Naya allowed herself to be held, turning her head into the crook of Edythe's neck while she cried. Watching them was so intimate and vulnerable I suddenly felt like I was intruding on something I couldn't understand. I considered them both friends now, but they had known each other first. Just as I had felt connected to Warren, there was a connection to the people who had found her.

"I'm so sorry," she whined. "I thought I could do it and nothing would happen. I could finally feel the grass—real grass, not what I imagined it would feel like. I could eat and taste things again. I could feel things again. It's nothing like I remember. It's different now. The sun is warmer. The air is...is beautiful. It's all beautiful."

"Like you can appreciate it more," I whispered, allowing myself to step in toward the two girls as they clutched each other. My hands trembled and I swallowed down the weakness that gripped me. "Like it was something you were missing in death. The essence of life. Naya, it's not your fault. I know this is confusing but...I don't think you're a monster."

Naya's eyes flashed and she looked at me like she was remembering my name or remembering the fact that I existed. Finally she whispered, "I was empty. I know I smiled and laughed and joked but...emptiness was inside of me. The only way I could even remotely feel what I wanted to feel was when I was in someone else's body. Not mine. Not this...this nightmare that I'm in."

"You just wanted to go home," I concluded.

The stealer's face twisted and she reached up to cover it, to shield it from the accusing stares of the rest of us. Leander and Kezia stood silently together, not particularly knowing what to say. I supposed that not even the rulers, the self-proclaimed souls in charge of an entire realm, could find the words that would heal the heart of someone who had a burning desire to feel alive with no way to truly grasp it. Not even when they had long done damage to their souls and their bodies, turning into monsters they could not recognize.

"I'm sorry you had to see me like this," she muttered. I wasn't sure exactly who she was talking to, but something about it felt like it had been meant for me. I wondered if Naya had felt the warm bond brewing between us, each different from the others in ways we couldn't explain. Edythe shushed her, closing her eyes so that she could savor the moment they were in together.

"We need to leave," Kezia said coldly. "We can't linger like this in a city. People are going to start to notice—they'll start to be affected by us. And there is certainly a lot of commotion to draw them here."

Marvell flashed her an irritated glance. "You think we don't know that? Where should we go?"

Warren moved already, dragging his fingers through the air in order to create a portal. I had no idea where he was taking us. Perhaps outside the city or maybe back to Foxcoast. But what I did know was that I had felt the life essence inside both of them, and that was enough for me to know that somehow everything would be okay.

Looking at Naya, I wondered if she even knew or realized what had been placed inside of her. I wondered if it was enough to keep her satisfied. There was nothing I could do—that anyone could do—to make death seem like something that could compare to being alive. Not when being alive was such a blessing, something so beautiful that it was meant to be enjoyed slowly and deeply. Too many of us had forgotten to cherish it and found ourselves mourning what we had lost in death. Despite our ages and the ways we had died, we each seemed to have one thing in common: wishing we could, for just one more moment, breathe with real lungs.

I wasn't sure how long I had been dead. Time had moved too erroneously for me to really follow. I couldn't count how many sunsets and sunrises had passed, certainly not when I had been slipping from continent to continent like jumping on and off a horse. And already I felt the blurry uncertainty of what being alive felt like. Was it the warmth I felt when I touched another soul? Was it the murky sound I heard when Edythe closed a window? Or maybe life was something more universal; the understanding that we would all die eventually, that fact leaning over our heads whether we wanted to face it head on or not.

Maybe the wounds inside of us all would never heal, no matter how tethered to life we felt. I couldn't expect to become a savior and turn everything right with just one blessing of a power that not even I fully understood. But for now, I knew that Naya and Warren would have life inside of them. An essence that would keep them from pining after something greater, forcing them to desperate measures, like possessing bodies or, in Warren's case, refusing to believe that he had ever helped anyone in the afterlife.

Marvell moved to touch Edythe's shoulder. Still holding onto Naya, the three of them slowly disappeared before my eyes. Just before they became an empty space in the places they stood, I watched as Naya's eyes scanned the tall buildings of the city she had desperately tried to get back to. Whatever she felt as her eyes recognized where she was seemed to flicker across her face in a variety of heartbreaking expressions. Grief, anger, defeat. I watched her eyes turn warm and cold again, her cheeks twitching with anger and then swelling with grief.

But with her being held tightly by people who cared about her, I knew she would be supported. I knew we would do everything in our power to ensure she never lost sight of herself again. That she would never turn into that monster, that wraith, and tear into souls.

Before I could ask what had happened and where they had gone, I remembered that each of us were tethered to the place we considered home. They were well on their way back to Foxcoast, where the salty air felt heavy and the skies seemed to be covered by clouds constantly. So I turned to Kezia and Leander, moving so I could take Warren's hand while he waited patiently near his traveling portal.

"You two should come back with us," I insisted, each of them glancing toward each other with caution. "Please. Let us get a chance to know you more. And you can know the others. I know things are tense right now, but I think it's important that they all see what I see."

"And what do you see, sweet one?" Leander mused.

I smiled toward them, a small and pathetic smile but the only thing I could muster given the circumstances. My eyes brushed along Kezia's brown waves, the red tint to them evident even beneath the shade of the buildings. The glittery mask that covered her eyes. The exposed skin and seductive presence that was shrouded in a strong, confident attitude. I then looked to Leander—the tall, attractive soul clad in a sharp black outfit embroidered elegantly with golden threads. His tufted hair, round face, and narrow eyes that pierced mine with mischief.

"Two rulers of the realm who are fair and just," I confessed, echoing their own words. Words they had spoken to me when I had met them, questioning their power over me and their self-proclaimed titles. "And have a duty to introduce themselves properly to their subjects."

Despite themselves, they both smirked. Then they made a show of deciding to hold onto Warren so that they could pass through the portal.

✦ ✦ ✦

Coming back to Foxcoast felt right.

A relief washed over me from the very thought of it. Being tethered to a place was beyond calling it a familiar space, beyond calling it a second home. There was something inside of my phantom being that wanted me there, like the entirety of it had become an integral part of finding my peace. When I had first seen Foxcoast, I had wanted to run away from it and escape it—certain that I didn't have to spend my afterlife with strangers. Certain that what they told me and what they believed to be the truth was something meant to trick me. I could not have imagined I would change my mind and find the thought of spending an eternal afterlife with them all to be a perfect way to spend my days.

My one and true home would always be Enya. Somewhere, I had to remember that I had a family. I had my mother inside of a grave, my brothers growing older each second, and my father. I wished I could tell them all that I had learned. I wished desperately that there was a way I could get back to them, to see them one more time. I might have all of the time left until I turned to stardust, but they didn't. They would likely have a much shorter time. No matter how short their time, I could only hope that they would squeeze every last minute out of it, right until the very end when they were too weak to open their eyes anymore. That death would not come for them the way it had come for my mother and I. Maybe someday I would see them again. Even if it was brief. That would be my hope and my dream.

The moment we stepped through the portal I saw Warren had brought us to the edge of the cliff side. A powerful wind brew from the sea to make the grass look like a fast current. The clouds were characteristically gray, determined to not let any sunshine through to shine light on our new beginning. I could see the bright white of the cottage with its black shutters looming in the distance, the dirt path freshly turned to mud. It was so different from Zarya that I found it suddenly easy to imagine Naya's disappointment. I had always been a soul that loved the wilds—the trees, the grass, the open fields. Foxcoast was becoming like a second home, and in a lot of ways it already was.

Only the four of us stood out on the open plains, the other three likely already inside of the cottage. Before we could move to greet them, Kezia and Leander's expressions made me burst out into a laugh. The former looked thoroughly intrigued by the small space that four of us called home. The latter, however, looked as though he had just been tricked into loitering inside of another tool shed.

"Sorry, it's not made of marble," I scoffed.

Leander rolled his eyes. "Don't act as though our Hall of Inquiry was not the most *marvelous* thing you've ever seen."

"Oh, it certainly was." My shoulders gave a small shrug of indifference. "I don't suppose either of you are in the mood to give up your thrones to reside with us commoners?"

Kezia made a soft clicking noise with her mouth, then turned toward the ocean. "I don't think so. Is it always this gloomy?"

"Yes," Warren said quickly. I pressed my lips together to stop from smiling, amused by his eagerness to tell her anything that might deter her from wanting to ever visit.

"Such a shame. I don't think I can handle it forever," she admitted, then moved to turn toward the cottage, winking at Warren while she brushed past him. Leander moved to follow with a smirk, amused by his companion's tormenting attitude.

"Wait," I called out. The two of them turned toward me expectantly. A sudden nervousness crept into my stomach, but I knew they would be honest with me when I asked. Warren's hand reached out to take mine, squeezing it gently. "I never really found out how both of you died."

Somewhere inside the cottage I was positive Edythe would have felt a chill down her spine from my *bad manners*. Or maybe she was too preoccupied with Naya to even notice such a disturbance. Either way, it was a question that had been silently tearing me apart. I wanted to devour everything I could about the other souls in this realm, starting with the mysterious sparkles that coated Kezia's face like a mask.

As though she knew what I was thinking, she reached up to brush her fingers over the glittery layer on her eyes. She tossed her hair back and grinned devilishly, that wicked grin reaching from cheek to cheek.

"I was poisoned," she said matter-of-factly. "By someone who I trusted very much. And when I died I promised I would do anything I could to keep on going. To wind up somewhere I knew would be safe and where I could watch over things."

Poisoned. I gaped, trying to imagine who could do such a thing to someone. Even more, who could do that to someone they knew and knew well? It made me view Kezia in a different light. A girl who might have been so devastated and determined to hold onto life that she created a space where she would never really die. I wondered if what she believed to be true actually *was*. Could it be possible that she actually created the realm we wandered in?

"Do you really think you created this realm?" I asked hesitantly.

"How else could you explain the ability I have to feel all that goes on in it?" she challenged, always the lioness.

"I think that's what has been given to you." My eyes flickered up to Warren, remembering his explanation of things when I first sat with him on the edge of the cliffs. That someone out there, being or not, gave us our gifts. Maybe even for a purpose.

"I was very sick," Leander offered, pulling me away from challenging his partner.

"In a suit?" Warren wondered, eying the expensive fabric that Leander adorned.

"A burial suit," he corrected with a scoff, gesturing to the gold embroidery of swirls and florals. "My mother and father probably put me inside of it right before I died. To prepare me for burial. I don't mind. It beats living an eternal afterlife in a leather jacket." The thought seemed to truly horrify him.

"So that's it?" I asked. "You died from illness?"

"Not everything has to end in tragedy, sweet one. Some things are just natural." The panther winked, then jerked his head toward the cottage. I wondered if the impatience he showed had something to do with Naya. The way he had touched her skin and held her was so gentle it reminded me of Warren—albeit the uncorrupted, more lavish one.

I couldn't be sure if it was my place to say whether or not having someone like Leander around would make Naya's problems go away. Even though I had given her back an essence of life and something to fulfill the parts of her that had been missing before, the support and love of another could become irreplaceable. But it would be a slow start, something I suspected that not even the creator of the universe could force together if it wasn't meant to be.

While I watched them go I had the feeling that Kezia and Leander might only be rulers in theory and not in practice. I could—and would—forgive them for what they wanted me to do to my friends. I had enough understanding to put myself in their shoes and see their desire to keep the living world protected. The monster Naya had turned into was nothing any of us expected. The act of possession was so wrong, so deeply disturbing, that I hoped I never had to witness it again in my existence. I didn't want to spend the rest of my days harboring a grudge against the two; not when they had kindly taken me in and allowed me the truth that the stealers did not know.

The lioness and the panther took their time toward the white cottage before they disappeared into the side of it, not even bothering to go through the door. I stayed behind with Warren, turning to face him.

"Do you think everything will be okay?" I asked, reaching up to press a palm to his chest. Checking to see if I could still feel the heartbeat that I felt there, wrapped around the small bit of life that I had put inside of him.

"I think so..." Warren began quietly. "But will we ever know for sure? Maybe not."

I looked into his eyes, reaching up so I could curl my hands around his neck. The wind rose from beneath the cliffs and swept over us, pulling my dress and my hair. The thin fabric of my gown danced around my knees and I shivered from the new exposure and the new feeling. The usually tidy hair on Warren broke free from its confines and stuck up slightly, pushing back against the breeze with strength of its own.

"Is this how it's going to be forever?" I mused. "I mean, nothing to really lose except ourselves. We'll never die. We'll never go hungry or die from thirst. Never get too old or too weak. Too feeble."

"We keep questioning. Keep taking it day by day and night by night. But we have nothing to fear. We know now that what we were doing before was not what we were meant to do," he admitted.

"That's what I mean. How do we know what we're meant to do? What if we're not meant to be here at all?"

Warren pulled me close and hugged me, turning so that we faced outward to the ocean. I watched the waves moving back and forth, the high winds causing the water to look erratic. "We can torture ourselves with questions forever," he murmured close to my ear. "Or we can accept that we may never have all the answers. We will live with the excitement of not knowing what comes next. Just as we did in life."

I paused. "That's very...lively of you to say."

"It's the life you put inside of me, Sonnet. I can see now that this is not the end. We exist here and now, together until we're nothing more than stardust."

We were both silent, ignoring the fact that the others inside of the cottage were either watching or wondering what was taking us so long. Their prying eyes would not bother me in the slightest. Not when I had worked hard to come to terms with the way my new world worked, with the monsters I had begun to love and the rulers I had forgiven. I never expected to become a heroine, or be bestowed with a mysterious power that required me to be choked and suffocated to use.

Perhaps I would never find out why Naya could possess bodies. Why that seemed to be her specialty and her burden all at once. Why Edythe could reach through the realm and right into the living world, paired perfectly with her proper nature that would never do anything malicious with it. Why Marvell was able to sense when a death was near and predict, with his careful and calculative mind, how that death would be executed. Moreover, I would never understand how Kezia could have truly created the realm. If she even did at all. How Leander and she managed to avoid corrupting themselves all this time, stowed away inside of their clock tower where they watched humans toss their coins one after another into a dark pit that their city stole.

The beauty was that I did not have answers to these questions. For every question that lingered inside of my phantom mind, the universe kept its secret answer hidden away from me. I would always dream and suspect and be left to wonder. That was my burden and that was my gift.

Warren's too. For I knew nobody in the world could terrify me like he could. The sight of the king of nightmares would haunt me every time I blinked or found myself daydreaming. A horrifying reminder of the consequence that came with forgetting just how precious and blissful being alive was. Warren had lost himself in a quest for his own redemption—the worse he became, the more intense his desire to absorb the other souls became. His craving was insatiable, so much so that he could hardly contain himself at the sight of the newly dead. Their calls would haunt him. And me, too. I could still hear the faint wails in the back of my mind, pressing against my skull. Willing me to answer them, to go to them and become something I didn't want to be.

Naya had lost herself the moment she discovered she could step into the living world again. She could pretend to be alive, but the cold truth was she never would be again. She had crossed a threshold she would never be able to return back to. Now that I had placed life inside of her, a reminder to satisfy the craving she felt to feel alive again, I could only hope that she would find the beauty of life in other ways. Like the beauty of having close friends. The beauty of having someone simply hold you.

None of us would grow old and wither away. None of us would marry or have families. Each of us had our lives taken before they should have been. Before we were ready. Sometimes by the hands of others, like a man striking down Warren or a dear friend slipping poison to Kezia. Sometimes it was without control, like getting sick. And sometimes it was an unfortunate case of bad luck, like slipping in a river on a rock that was determined to be a fatality. No matter how we died, we each had to remember what is was like to be alive.

It wouldn't be easy. It would be an effort every day to find purpose and meaning. Being dead was by no means what I had envisioned for myself. I would trade a million days inside of the realm for a single day to be alive again. But I would fight for myself, and for others, in order to keep us from forgetting what it truly meant to be living.

"I can feel you thinking," Warren whispered. "What's on your mind?"

"When you first pulled me from the river—what did you think?"

"Other than 'she's crazy'?" he scoffed. "Well, if I'm being honest, I thought you were beautiful."

I squirmed around in his arms to look at his face. "Beautiful? You thought that my shrieking was beautiful?"

"No," Warren laughed. "I thought your fight to stay alive was beautiful."

My own laughter matched his, then died down into a quiet admission. "I never intended to be beautiful. And I never meant to turn your world upside down. All I ever wanted was to understand who you all were and...what I am."

"I don't blame you for any of it. I'm glad now that I know the truth. I really was a monster. So thank you for...recognizing that. And not turning away."

"I did turn away," I reached up to brush his cheek. "I just found something inside of the monster that I knew was worth caring about. So I turned back."

His eyes glistened slightly and he leaned to press his forehead against mine. I breathed deeply, feeling every part of my phantom body as I remembered it should feel. The goosebumps that appeared on my legs. The feel of my hair as it whipped around my cheek and cut into the edges of my eyes. The warmth of skin beneath my palm and the slight fluttering of small birds inside of my ribcage, my hummingbird heart. Even my brain was quiet while I stayed pressed closely together with the soul I had found in this realm and the one I had saved.

Around us the wind pushed against us and the sea clawed against the bottoms of the cliffs. The clouds overhead moved quickly, bringing in a new layer of raindrops that began to speckle our faces. My feet sank into the cold ground, and I took a deep breath, filling my phantom lungs with the heavy air and the salty breeze. In the corner of my eye I could see a hint of the sunshine breaking through the clouds.

And then I pressed my lips to his and wrapped my arms around the king of all my nightmares.

EPILOGUE

"Are you sure you're ready for this?" I asked.

Dusk settled down and brought in a thick haze of orange glow through the windows. The wooden floors and walls were shadowed by the flicker of flame nestled inside of a lamp that rested on the edge of the bedside. Inside that bed a man lay, his body frail and skinny. It had been weathered by age and experience, yet no family of his own surrounded him. I could hear the light flutter of steps that told me someone was walking through the halls and the main rooms of the house, but nobody would be coming in to check on him. And if they did, they surely wouldn't like what they found.

Together, Warren and I linked arms as we watched. The sound of a wailing soul had pierced my ears and, for the first time in a long time, I allowed myself to be willingly drawn toward it. Warren took my hand in his, ready to face what we had been so adamant to avoid the past several months. Or maybe it was years. Time moved far too confusingly for me to keep track. The sun went up and down like nothing—it was no longer important to keep tabs on it.

The muscles inside of my left hand ached, wanting desperately to touch the man's soul that now lingered on the bed near its body. It looked elsewhere, captivated between realms and lost without knowing where to go. A horrible wail came from its mouth, chilling me down to my core. This was the wail that was familiar to us. The one we heard again and again, echoing through the realm and disturbing us in our peace at Foxcoast.

But now we answered it. I pushed down my feelings of longing, stealing a glance at Warren. His soul was quivering slightly, but he seemed at peace, watching with curious eyes like I did. I reached up to press a palm to his heart, feeling the life essence that beat there around his heart. The piece of hope there that fulfilled him and made him feel like he didn't need to consume from other souls.

"Yes," he replied swiftly. I squeezed him gently and nodded.

Together we waited. Waited until the sun fell completely and the room was cast in a different glow, the flame inside of the lamp dancing to amuse us. Waited until it seemed like there was nothing we were going to witness—nothing that might serve as an answer to the complexity and uncertainty of the realm and the world we lived in.

Nothing until the man stopped wailing. My eyes snapped toward him, my breathing catching slightly. This was it! This was what we needed to see. This was what Warren and I had talked about—perhaps even naively thought might happen. I could feel Warren's anticipation match my own. He quivered slightly, both anxious and fearful.

The man's eyes closed, a perfect mirror to his physical body on the bed. Then, very slightly, his lips tugged at the corners in the smallest smile I had ever seen. A smile of peace and belonging. His head tilted back as though he were going to fall—instead, just as his body sprang backward, his soul dissolved in the air. In a single blink the man's soul disappeared, falling backward into the arms of something else that swept him elsewhere.

Every word I had ever spoken evaded me. The man had gone somewhere else. He not only died, but passed through the realm and went beyond. I turned toward Warren, my mouth agape. Surprise and fear flickered inside of his blue eyes, searching mine for some sort of comprehension.

"He's gone," I choked, turning back toward the body in the bed. "Did you see that? He's just...gone. So quickly too—"

"He's moved on. Somewhere better," Warren declared, wrapping his arms around me tightly.

"But his soul...Warren, his soul isn't here anymore. He went somewhere else. That means there's other places, maybe somewhere my family might be... my mom—" The words came out in a rush. I nearly vomited them all over the floor, my pulse pounding inside of my neck.

His warm hands captured my face and he smiled, pressing his lips to mine in order to keep me quiet. I kept my eyes open, dazed.

"Where do you—?" I began, wondering what his thoughts were. Wondering what we could make of this. There was an afterlife, different than this one. It existed. It *had* to.

"Stardust," he declared, smiling again. I paused, then felt my lips pull into a smile alongside his.

Stardust, my mind echoed.

ABOUT THE AUTHOR

TAYLOR BALASAVAGE graduated from Wilkes University with a B.A. in English and a minor in creative writing. She has worked professionally as a writer, editorial assistant, and project manager. Ever since she was five years old, she wanted to be an author, telling stories and connecting to the world in a meaningful way. She currently lives in Pennsylvania with her husband.

For more information, visit www.taylorbalasavage.com.

9 781946 024954